THE L
KEVIN R

NIGHT TO DAWN

Night to Dawn Magazine & Books
P. O. Box 643
Abington, PA 19001
www.bloodredshadow.com
ISBN: 978-1-937769-36-9
Copyright by Kevin R. Doyle
First edition 2015

Illustrator: Teresa Tunaley
Editor: Barbara Custer

To Kim K. It's been quite a while, hasn't it? Here's hoping life has done you right.

Prologue

He was new to this city, but it seemed pretty much like the other three he'd lived in during his short life. Of course, he couldn't know about the nicer sections, if any existed, any more than he knew anything about the better parts of those other cities. As he stood on a street corner and shivered in the late night cold, he accepted things as they were, not even pondering whether fate had consigned him to only see the bad parts of wherever he lived.

They called this particular neighborhood the Zone. Storefronts with, at this time of night, steel shutters locked down; a bar at each end of the block with neon signs, half of them unlit; and furtive, shadowy people looking out from alleyways, no doubt wondering just what they could and couldn't do in the presence of a small boy, looking no more than twelve, who possessed the eyes of someone far older and wiser.

Twelve was probably the right age, more likely than not, and since last winter he'd been thinking of himself as twelve, so before too long he'd have to change it up. Then again, with the shortness of his stature and scrawniness of his limbs, he could pass himself off as twelve for another year or two with no one the wiser.

Not that anyone would know or care.

Across the corner, a large shape stumbled out of a bar, weaving a bit before heading off to the north. A second or two later, a woman, wearing a jacket far too light for the weather, came running out after him. She only made it a yard or two before stumbling on the pavement and going down on both knees. Instead of getting up again, she knelt there and cried, screaming after the man as she pounded the pavement with her fists.

A couple of teenagers, lounging in a doorway a few steps down from the bar, laughed at her.

Yeah, the kid thought, *just like the lower section of the other cities I lived in.*

Victims everywhere.

And where you find victims, predators can't be too far behind.

For a minute, he thought the two teens were going to do something to the woman. Maybe beat her up a bit or drag her off somewhere into the shadows. Instead, they just laughed, then turned and went back to their drinking and smoking.

After a while, realizing that no one was going to pay any attention to her, or not care much at all even if they did, she staggered to her feet and headed back into the bar.

"'Ho," one of the teens called out, which didn't even cause her to turn around.

A biting cold wind came skirling down the street, and the kid hunched his shoulders and clasped his arms across his chest. The outerwear he wore wasn't much. A bedraggled, old-time ski vest, polyester-filled and dark blue, it zipped all the way up to his chin but didn't have any sleeves. The lady at the homeless shelter had lent it to him, offering him gloves and a stocking cap at the same time.

That was on his first night there, but at the time he'd figured on staying for a while, and so he had turned down the gloves and cap, thanking the woman for the ski vest.

Unfortunately, a couple of goons, slouching in a corner and eyeing him a little too closely, had activated his personal radar, causing him to change his plans, and he'd taken off early the next morning, considering the full dinner and night on a warm cot as better than he'd had in months, and headed out onto the streets again.

A car came squealing around the corner, someone leaning out and throwing an empty bottle in the kid's direction. He ducked, glass shattering on the wall behind him, and the car continued on its way, drunken curses floating on the night.

The kid stood still for a moment, face reddening and fists clenching. But he knew it wasn't anything personal. The morons hadn't been attacking him, just anyone small and defenseless who they happened to come upon.

He'd spent his whole life small and defenseless.

He cinched the zipper of the ski vest a little bit tighter, jerking the collar upright so that it would partially cover his ears, and headed off down the street.

He had no clue where he was heading, or when he would eat or sleep next, but he'd been on his own for years now and had come to learn the way of the streets. He figured nothing could come up that he hadn't encountered before, and he managed to stuff way deep down into an obscure corner of his mind the longing memories of the warmth and comfort the shelter had offered the night before.

He was a survivor, always had been, and as he wandered down the nearly-deserted street, in the early morning hours of the Zone, he had no doubt that he would continue to survive.

And that was the last that anyone ever saw of him.

Part I: The Pack

Chapter One

When one of the younger paramedics joked that they ought to test the dead man for rabies, none of those standing around the body felt much like laughing. The jokester's partner, a hard-faced brunette in her late twenties, shot the kid a look that clearly said, *shut the hell up, you stupid ass*, while most of the other people in the small circle just ignored the idiot.

One of the cops thought, but didn't say out loud, that the kid may have had a point. The entire bunch of them — three paramedics, four uniformed officers, and a person from the ME's office — formed a loose boundary around a lump that only vaguely resembled a human being sprawled out on the pavement.

If they looked close, but not too close because of all the blood splattered on the sidewalk, they could make out what had once formed a torso, plus a couple of stumps that may have been hips. One shoulder remained, but no matter how hard they looked they couldn't find the arm that went with it. Or the other arm. Just enough of the head remained to reveal that the deceased had been a man, and, judging by the few strands of greasy, grayish hair that remained, probably an old man.

Then again, by some remote stretch they could all be looking down at the remains of an old woman. At the moment, because of the condition of the body, it was just too damned hard to tell.

One of the uniforms, an eighteen-year vet named Gonzales, considered that maybe the paramedic's joke wasn't that far off.

Because it sure looked as if the old man, or whatever, had been gnawed on, chewed up and then spit out.

"What do you think?" Gonzales's partner, a tiny little thing barely a year out of the academy, asked him. "A wild dog?"

"Maybe," he said, beginning to turn away, "but it's awful hard to imagine a single dog doing that much damage to someone."

"Maybe a pit bull?" his partner asked. She, too, had turned and was following him as he made his way to their patrol car.

Gonzales chuckled, though without much mirth.

"You're still awfully green, Pammy. You see what looks like a wild dog attack and you automatically think pit bull. Why?"

"Well, they've got the reputation ..."

"And that's all it is, a rep." He snuggled himself down in the driver's side of the patrol car and reached for the radio mike. "Got to learn to deal with individuals, kid. Not types. Hell, I've got a neighbor who has a pit that's as gentle and loving as you can imagine. Plays with his two-year-old on the living room floor like you couldn't believe. Other hand, seen some Chihuahuas that could damned near take a chunk out of an arm or leg."

"Get out of here," the younger cop said, "a Chihuahua?"

"Well," her partner keyed the mike and began calling back to headquarters, "maybe I'm exagerratin' just a bit, but we'll leave that for the plains to decide."

Pam turned from the squad car and headed back over to the cluster standing around the corpse. A year ago, just starting out, she would have wondered why they needed to call the detectives when the elderly victim had clearly died from an animal attack. But she knew now that in any kind of death at least one detective had to appear, for formality's sake if nothing else.

The others had all relaxed by now, knowing that they could do nothing until plainclothes appeared on the scene. With nothing else to do, Pam stared down at the body, trying to imagine what could have happened to the old guy.

A minute later, she felt the presence of her partner by her side.

"Plains are on the way," Gonzalez told her. "Said for us to keep everyone clear until they got here. Like I couldn't have figured that out on my own."

"I've never seen anything like this," Pam said, her gaze still fixed on the form on the ground.

"Still think it was a dog?" her partner asked.

She looked up at Gonzalez.

"What else could it have been? It doesn't take the ME over there to know that this guy's been all chewed up. And I've never heard of coyotes in the city. So what else?"

"What I'm getting at is it may not have been a single animal."

"Come again? Are you thinking of a pack or something?"

"Well," Gonzales said, "just looking at it ..." He waved his arm in the direction of the mess on the pavement.

"That's insane, Enrico. Who the hell ever heard of a pack of dogs attacking people in the middle of a city?"

"You ever hear of one dog doing anything that even remotely looks like that?"

Pam had to admit that the whole thing was a new one to her. Like most people, especially those who'd spent any amount of time in the slums of a major metropolis, she'd heard the urban legends about rats snatching babies from their cribs, alligators roaming through the sewers and organ harvesters stalking the singles scene. But something like this ...

"What about rats?" she asked the older cop, fearful he would laugh in her face.

But Gonzales surprised her. Instead of laughing, he turned his gaze upwards and rubbed the back of his neck.

"I thought of that myself for a moment there. It's not the most farfetched of possibilities."

"No?"

"Not at all. Once, I saw what was left of an old wino eaten by rats, back when I'd been on the force not much longer than you have. But that was a guy who'd crawled under the porch of a house, probably trying to escape the weather. It was the middle of winter, and from what I heard later, the ME couldn't really determine if it was the rats or the temperature that had done the poor bastard in. Besides, long ago as it's been, from what I remember, that body didn't look anything like this."

"No, huh?"

"Not really, no. When we pulled that feller out, it looked more like he'd been nibbled on till he was worn down to practically nothing."

Pam pointed towards the corpse, still with everyone standing around waiting for the important people to show up.

"That's not a bunch of nibbles," she said.

"No kidding. Actually, it looks more like ..."

"Lemme go, goddammit!"

The two cops whirled around to see who had shouted behind them. They saw a scraggly, emaciated old man, wearing an old-fashioned jean jacket, dark corduroys and black cotton gloves without fingers. About twenty feet away, another pair of uniforms had pinioned the elderly man, doing their best to keep him immobile while not hurting him.

It was turning into quite a struggle because the fellow, his eyes wild and staring, seemed in the grasp of a manic frenzy. And in fact, as Gonzales turned his way the oldster managed to break free of the two cops, both in their twenties and built like linebackers, and headed straight across the pavement towards Gonzales and Pam.

Both uniforms, the veteran and his rookie partner, set themselves, their feet shoulder-width apart, one foot slightly ahead of the other, and their mass centered. Pam, still learning how to survive on the beat, held her hands at hip level, half

8

clenched. Gonzales had his baton out and up at chest level.

If that crazy-looking son of a bitch got to them, no matter how old and feeble he looked, Gonzalez was going to put his ass down, fast and hard.

Turned out not to be necessary because, just a few yards shy of the two of them, the crazy old dude came to a screeching halt, his eyes fixated at some point beyond the two officers. Turning, simultaneously with Pam, Gonzalez followed the old dude's gaze, right to the welter of chewed-up body parts on the pavement.

"Roy?" the old guy said to no one in particular. "Is that Roy?"

Gonzalez relaxed somewhat but kept his baton out and visible as he walked over to the now-subdued oldster.

"Hey, buddy. You know who that is?"

The veteran cop had caught himself before using the word "was." No reason to heighten the poor guy's anxiety.

The vagrant nodded his head, still not looking away from the remains.

"Think so," he said without looking at the cop. "Think it's Roy. He split off from us last night to go find some food. We told him to stay close, what with all the stories floating around lately, but he hadn't found hardly anything to eat in the last few days and said his stomach felt like ... "

He took another step towards the form on the ground, and Gonzalez walked along with him.

"What's your name, buddy?" the cop asked.

"Uhm," the guy seemed to have trouble keeping his focus. "Jim. That's it. Jim. Most folks call me Jimbo, though."

Standing next to him, Gonzalez was hard put to peg the man's age. Between the lines in his face and the gray in his hair, the cop figured him at around sixty-five or so but knew damned well he could be off twenty years in either direction.

Living on the streets for any appreciable time aged a person in an odd way. Gonzalez had always concluded that a year on the streets equaled about six years of physical deterioration, but after a certain point the decline seemed to stop, as if all that could be drained out of a body had been, and he'd seen some geezers could pass for their sixties who'd actually been closer to the eighty mark.

Pam took a step back, allowing her partner to do his thing.

"You know Roy's last name?" Gonzalez asked the vagrant.

"Say, uh, say what?"

He seemed confused. No doubt, Gonzalez considered, still hung over from whatever had gotten him to sleep the night before.

"Roy's last name. You know it?"

"No, sir. All's I ever knew him by is Roy. Been around here for almost as long as I have, but now it looks like they got him, too."

Gonzalez glanced at Pam, who gave him a confused look, then lifted his gaze somewhere beyond the ambulance, still standing with its doors swung open.

"Looks like our part's about over, kiddo. The suits have arrived."

Pam looked behind her to see the sedan drive up, two obvious detectives climbing out.

Initially, the two detectives looked almost identical. Both male, in their late thirties, and clean-shaven.

Beyond that, though, the similarities stopped. One of them, a guy named Gleason whom Gonzalez had met once or twice, had sandy blond hair and towered over the other one, a red-haired man whom Gonzalez didn't know.

Both men wore the plainest of plain clothes. Jeans, sneakers, and casual jackets. Gleason looked to be sporting about a three-day beard.

Gonzales glanced down at his own uniform, spotless that morning but already showing the wear and tear of the worst beat in town, and wondered where the old days had gone. The days when detectives wore jackets and ties and at least attempted to look professional.

Then again, considering the part of town they stood in, maybe their choice of attire was more practical than anything else.

"What's up, 'Rico?" Gleason asked as the two men approached the scene.

Gleason slouched and stifled a yawn while his partner's eyes darted all over the place and his right hand constantly rubbed his hip.

"Got one guy dead, Ed. Not exactly sure if you're dealing with a murder or not, but it's something way out of the usual."

"Some kind of exposure or something?" the second guy, who looked really uncomfortable in this neighborhood, asked.

Gonzales looked his question at Gleason.

"This is Tim O'Brien. Just transferred over."

Gonzales nodded at the second detective.

"Exposure. Not even close. But we're pretty sure it's something not quite natural. Or at least, not natural in terms of your ordinary street death. But, hey, take a look for yourselves."

The two plains glanced at each other; then Gleason knelt down and got a good look at the corpse. O'Brien stood around trying to appear cool, but Gonzalez noticed that he ended up looking everywhere except at the chewed up body.

He got it then, remembering a departmental memo about a month or so back. Something about someone who had transferred in from headquarters. The guy had been working financial crimes for some years, but when Teddy Stewart had managed to get himself gunned down a few months back, a hole had opened up in homicide.

Filled, Gonzales figured, by the man standing in front of him.

Considering the greenish pall to the new fellow's face, this was probably his first brush with the gritty side of the city.

Gleason stood back up and, although he hadn't touched anything, rubbed his hands together, like wiping away some kind of stain.

"That's rough," he said, nodding to his partner before turning back to Gonzalez. "So tell me, how much of our work have you managed to do for us so far?"

Gonzales grinned, did a half turn and swept his hand in the direction of a klatch of people standing off to the side.

"More than you may have wanted us to," he said.

****

"First thing this morning," the witness said. To the two plainclothes cops, he seemed like a kid. Actually, by his own admission, Tony Rollins had turned twenty-one the week before and had been the assistant manager of the deli for the last six months.

"First thing this morning," Gleason said, "was when you did what?"

"Emptied the garbage."

"Don't you usually do that when you close up at night?"

"Usually. But last night was the end of the month, so the boss and I spent a couple hours squaring up the profit/loss statements before heading out."

The kid stopped talking then. He shifted back and forth, had trouble meeting their eyes, and kept his hands clenched in his pockets.

Gleason probably would have suspected him of knowing more than he was saying, had he not seen other innocent people react in a similar manner upon encountering violent death. At least Gleason's partner, thank God, was beginning to look a bit more normal.

"In other words," O'Brien jumped in, "you left the clean-up until this morning."

"Right." The youngster nodded a bit too vigorously. "And when I was emptying the trash, I came around the side of the bin and saw ..."

The young man motioned towards the end of the alley, where the technical people were still at it, doing all their measuring, photographing, and what not.

"Pretty shocking, wasn't it?"

"Yes, sir. I never ... well, outside of a funeral home, I'd never seen a person's body before. Especially one that had been so ... so ..."

"It's okay," said Gleason as he made a final notation in a small spiral notebook and jammed it into his jacket pocket. "You left everything alone, right? Didn't go too close?"

"Oh, hell no."

"And called it in right away?"

"Yes, sir."

"Then you did good."

The youngster nodded, looking somewhat relieved, though it was clear that he wouldn't be sleeping well for a few nights.

"Do you think ..." This one seemed to have a real issue with finishing sentences. "Do you think I'll be called to testify?"

"Testify?"

"Yes, sir. If you catch the guy who ..."

The two cops glanced at each other, then looked back to their witness.

"I think you've missed something here, son. That old fellow wasn't murdered."

"He wasn't? But what about all the ..."

"Relax, kid. He obviously ran afoul of a wild dog that tore into him."

Tony looked at them for a second, a panoply of emotions crossing that young face, disbelief first and foremost.

"Are you sure about that, sir? I mean, I grew up on a farm, and I've never seen any dog attack that looked like that."

Gleason's partner reached over and patted the kid on the shoulder.

"Don't worry about it, son. And don't worry about having to testify against some murdering psycho. We don't get them often here in the city, but every now and then a stray animal makes its way in somehow and does a number like this. Just because you never saw anything like it before doesn't mean ..."

"No, sir. I don't think you followed me. I used to hunt all the time back home. With my dad and my brothers. And what I mean is I've never seen a single dog, or even a coyote, attack that looked that way."

The detectives again glanced at each other.

"Come again?" Gleason asked.

The kid took a breath, obviously feeling a bit unsure of himself.

"What I meant was, whatever animal attacked that old man, it wasn't only one. I'd lay money he was attacked by a pack."

Chapter Two

Dr. Lewis Preston stood outside the double swing doors, wishing he had a drink in his hand. Preferably a Martini, heavy on the vodka. Having arrived at the morgue a half an hour ago, Dr. Preston hadn't yet had a chance to see what lay on the other side of that door, but in his few short minutes on site, he'd heard enough scuttlebutt in the halls to hazard a pretty good guess what awaited him.

Looking down at his gloved hands, he felt gratified, and not a little surprised to detect not a single sign of tremor. Good enough. Now if he could just keep his stomach from feeling as if it were full of battery acid.

"Sixty more days," the doctor muttered to himself. "Why couldn't all this have just waited sixty more days?"

Sighing, Preston brushed a stray lock of his graying hair into place and, trying to blot out the reality of what awaited him by filling his mind with images of the sailboat he would take possession of in exactly sixty-one days, walked through the double-swing doors into the morgue's examination room.

****

If anything, it looked worse than he'd expected.

Preston had often felt uneasy at the stark contrast between the sterile, metallic furnishings of the exam room and the incredibly brutalized bodies that ended up on those tables. In his time, Preston had performed post mortems on victims of domestic violence, sexual abuse victims, innocent passersby caught in the crossfire of gang fights, and even the occasional mysterious death where he'd never managed to determine the cause.

Not long after the start of his career, he'd begun to actually look forward to the occasional old geezer who had keeled over from no obvious cause. Although tragic in their own way, at least those bodies had never been brutalized by anything more than, in most cases, their owners' bad health habits. But as the years moved on, and Preston began creeping into geezerhood himself, the PM's assigned to him became less and less the peaceful variety and more and more of the violent nature.

Yet only once before, despite his nearly thirty years of working in the coroner's office of a major metropolitan area, had Dr. Lewis Preston seen anything like this.

From what he'd heard around the building, it had taken a near-Herculean effort for the paramedics on scene to get the entire body into the bag for transport to the morgue. And looking down at the remains splayed across the table's gleaming surface, Preston could understand.

Jesus, what a mess.

He could easily make out the mangled form as that of a human being, more specifically an elderly, frail man. But he managed to do so only because of his decades of experience.

Sighing, Preston set about his work.

Some thirty minutes later, having taken his initial measurements and preparing to make the first exploratory probe into the body itself, he looked up to see a couple of plainclothes detectives approaching the doors. Raising one red-speckled hand, he ushered them in.

The two men entered through the doors, almost instantly looking a bit sickly themselves, the shorter one more so than his partner.

Preston knew one of them. The taller one, Gleason. But his red-headed partner, while looking somewhat familiar, Preston didn't recognize . He guessed that he'd seen the man in the corridors of the department. In the old days, Preston had made it a point to know almost everyone in the department. Now, he only met the newer ones in the course of direct contact with his work.

"A dog attack, right doc?" the shorter cop asked.

Preston, not immediately bothering to answer him, leaned closer over the remains.

A few minutes later, when he did speak, he did so without looking up.

"I know that would make your job easier, gentlemen, to just write it off as a dog attack, but I'm not so sure."

"What else could it be? Those are bite marks, right?"

"They appear to be."

"Sure as hell isn't rats. With a baby left unattended, maybe. But not a full grown man. Even if the old guy fell asleep out there in the alley, could rats do that much damage?"

"They could, possibly. I've seen it once or twice in the past. Get enough of them and have them ravenous, or maddened, enough, and it's possible. But it would help if you would remain quiet and let me work."

The two detectives, in unison, took about three steps back and planted themselves against the wall. They waited silently for nearly half an hour as the coroner poked, prodded, scalpled, and incisioned all over the old man's body. At the end of that time, he moved over to a small cart and began stripping off his surgical garments.

"Well, doc?"

"He seems to have been partially eaten," Preston said.

"We kind of figured that," Gleason said. "But was he eaten before or after?"

Sighing, Preston straightened up and turned to face the men.

"You mean before or after he died? There's some evidence that he may have suffered from exposure, but you said that the body wasn't discovered until this morning?"

"That's what the witness said."

"Then I've got some tests to do before I can tell you for sure."

"What's your guess, though? Did he die because of or before the attack?"

"I really don't want to say yet, gentlemen. It's far too early to determine. Judging by the state of some of his organs, this man should have been dead long ago. While I see no immediate evidence of heart attack or stroke, there are a hundred other things in his environment that could have contributed. I'm simply going to need more time."

"What about those bites?"

"What about them?"

Gleason sighed in obvious exasperation.

"What kind of animal made the bites? Dog or rat?"

"I doubt that it was rats, even without the size of the marks."

"How come?" the shorter cop asked.

"Because unless he was soused to his eyelids he would have woken up at some point when they started tearing into him."

"That's a point."

"But even without that, while I'm not an odontologist, I'm fairly certain that those marks weren't made by rats."

"So it's dogs then," said Gleason, "same as some of the witnesses thought."

"Maybe," Dr. Preston said, "but maybe not."

"What else?"

"Well, with the body so torn up it's hard to make precise measurements and angles. As far as that goes, this could have been done by some kind of instrument."

"Like what?"

"I'm telling you I don't know yet. But I remember a case, oh, ten or so years ago, where a man took his wife out in the country and used some kind of garden implement, I can't remember what kind, to make it look like she'd been mauled by an animal. As I recall, took the ME on that one several days to determine the marks weren't bites but merely gouges from whatever he used."

"Wait a minute." Gleason narrowed his gaze. "Are you saying this could actually be a homicide here? That someone wanted to make it look like a dog attack? All that trouble over a street bum? That doesn't make any sense, sir."

Preston gave forth his own sigh now.

"I'm not saying that at all, detective. All I'm saying is that I need more time. Now why don't you two back off and give it to me."

****

But after the two cops had left, Preston didn't return to his work. Instead, leaving the cadaver open on its tray, he stripped off gloves, smock, and the spectacles he used for close-up work and headed to his office. One of his desk drawers held a fifth of bourbon, but with a bit of willpower he could have held off for a while.

The person waiting in his office, however, couldn't be held off.

Preston walked in, nodded to his visitor and, without a word, sat down behind his desk. He reached into his desk and pulled out the fifth and two glasses. Holding one glass up, he cocked his head at the man sitting across from him.

"No thanks."

"Suit yourself." Preston poured out a little more than one finger, leaned back in his chair and took a drink.

"God, that helps," he said a moment later. "You can't imagine what I just went through."

"I think I can," his visitor said, "at least to some degree."

"Did you consult with your men already?"

"No. They came right from the field to your exam room, then headed back out again. It'll still be another several hours before they have time to write up their reports. Then I have to figure out how to get a look at them."

The coroner grimaced.

"Sounds like you're making this too hard, Leo. After all, in your position all you have to do is ..."

"We're still trying to keep this as quiet as possible, Pres. If our count's right, your body tonight is number three. And so far we've kept it out of the news."

"As I'm well aware," the ME said, grimacing at the thought. "But I'm still not sure exactly how I feel about that."

"So I'm calling in favors," Leo said, ignoring the doctor's obvious bait, "such as having you do the PM on all three. But if I flat out ask for the initial paperwork on a brand new case, the boys and girls under me will start to talk."

"Don't you think they're talking already? After all, what I was just going over downstairs isn't exactly your average case of smash and grab."

His visitor sighed.

"I know, and believe me I realize we've got a limited shelf life on this. But until we know exactly what is cutting up residents down in the Zone, I'm going to keep it on the QT as much as possible."

Preston finished off the rest of his drink and thought, not for the first time in the last few weeks, that he was glad he wasn't standing in the other man's shoes. However, his own burden wasn't a heck of a lot lighter, for he knew something that he hadn't yet found a way to tell his visitor. He'd been waiting for a few days for the right time to spring the information, and the discovery of a new body had just mucked things up all the more.

Because anyone with one eye could tell that "cutting" wasn't the right word to use.

Not even close.

More like "chewing."

Chapter Three

There were dive bars and there were dive bars. And this one, beyond any doubt, exemplified the latter.

Jared Woodson hunkered down lower in his booth and slid his glass under the table, pouring its contents onto the floor. He'd done so three times in the last hour, and by his second drink had had to sit with his feet up and propped against the opposite seat. He worried a little that his posture would make someone suspicious, or that as the waitress came by she would notice the expanding puddle on the floor, but Sonny's was so dimly-lit that it wasn't that much of a concern.

All the damned smoke, of course, added to the natural gloom of the place.

Most people who drove by the decrepit old pit, situated on the far south side of town, probably wondered how the bar managed to get away with advertising open smoking on its premises. After all, just three years ago the city had followed the trend sweeping the country and outlawed smoking in any place open to the public.

But as the establishment's patrons no doubt knew, and as the owner himself was fully aware, through a weird fluke in the jurisdictional lines the little strip mall where Sonny's sat, while seemingly part of the city, actually lay about a hundred feet outside the lines, placing it under the county's jurisdiction.

And the county didn't have a smoking ban.

So Sonny's, which had opened a bare two and a half years ago by taking over the space formerly occupied by a small donut shop, had become an immediate hit with the percentage of the population that wanted a cig or two with their beer, pool game, or cheeseburger.

And the fact that it lay outside of the city lines occasionally attracted patrons with less – recreational – pursuits on their minds.

Jared had been working on his current story for nearly a month now, and had been running into more and more resistance from the various city employees he was trying to pump as sources. A rookie reporter would have gotten frustrated by this point, but closing in on forty years of age Jared had enough experience under his belt to surmise that the nervousness, agitation, and downright hostility coming his way from a cross section of the city workforce meant that he was getting close to something.

While he wasn't quite sure what that something was, he knew darned good and well that Paul Allen was at the heart of it.

Allen, a portly man hovering around sixty years old, had arrived in town a little over two years before, hailing from the sunny climes of southern Arizona. He had come to town for a job, more specifically *the* job – chief of police. A lifer in law enforcement, Allen arrived with all sorts of rumors trailing him. A few discreet calls down south, made by a handful of the newspeople in town, had drawn a picture of a Joe Arpaio wannabe who had spent the last six months searching for new employment, all in a dodge to evade a forced retirement.

No one would ever allow themselves to be pinned down on the record as to exactly what the lawman had done to precipitate his hasty departure, but most of the whispers involved some sort of financial chicanery.

All of which left Paul Allen, a newcomer to the area entering a politically-sensitive job, with a fair-sized target on his back, at least as far as the local media were concerned.

Jared Woodson, with his numerous years in television news making him one of the veterans of the local scene, had had his eye on Allen for a long time.

Which culminated in him sitting in the smoke-filled bar, slouching low in his booth, and trying not to get his feet wet.

Sometimes, the glamor and excitement of the job damned near killed him.

No doubt about it, Jared thought as he looked around the room. The owner of Sonny's had hit on a goldmine of an idea. Even at three o'clock on a weekday afternoon, the place was so packed that the background noise formed a constant loud buzz. And Jared, currently on his third attempt at quitting smoking, found the haze that hung over the place damned near irresistible.

The only drawback to the whole scene, he thought as he pulled out his cell phone and checked the time, *is that neither of the two people I'm interested in have shown up.* While he'd taken care to make sure no one, including his news director, had known of his destination, he wondered if his constant poking and prodding of the last month or so had managed to spook the folks involved.

He'd put in more time, including quite a bit of his free time on the weekends, on this than on any story recently, and no city was big enough to mask that kind of intense activity.

But he figured that wearing a bulky jacket, Red Sox ball cap and, since he hadn't been on the air in a couple of days, three-day growth of beard made him look enough like one of Sonny's regulars to not stand out, provided that the waitress occasionally stopping by his table didn't slip in the puddle of beer seeping out from under his table.

Jared wondered, not for the first time, if he wasn't being far too melodramatic. So far he had nothing but a bunch of fog and smoke. Whispers about secret meetings, of the chief skulking around in places he didn't usually frequent, of something going down that Jared's usual contacts down at City Hall didn't want to talk about.

It all seemed to add up to something, even if so far he didn't have the foggiest idea what.

The outer door of Sonny's opened, shafts of late afternoon sun highlighting the clouds of smoke that swirled around the room, and the man of the hour himself walked through the door.

Jared sat back straight in his booth.

Allen looked formidable, for sure. Even across the expanse of the gloomy bar. A bit over six feet tall, he had an ex-football frame only now, well into his fifties, beginning to go to pot.

For a moment, Jared worried that the chief would spot him out, but as crowded as Sonny's was, that seemed a remote possibility.

His cell buzzed.

Dammit. Of all the rotten timing. Not that a man sitting in a bar alone and talking on his phone would raise any sort of suspicion, but he didn't want his attention diverted by even a fraction.

Especially now.

He watched as Allen made his way through the bar, swiveling his head back and forth.

His cell buzzed again, and again. Jared ignored it.

When he had first come across hints of this meeting, it had puzzled him quite a bit. It seemed rather anachronistic to hold a shady meeting in a smoke-filled bar. Then again, if you were going to be talking one-on-one about pulling some shenanigans, face to face would be the best way to go. Sonny's regulars, primarily the bluest of blue collar types, wouldn't recognize anyone from the local power structure outside of the mayor, and maybe not even him.

So yeah, all things considered the meeting here in the middle of the day began to make some sort of sense.

Now, if only he could just pick up on what the hell the whole thing was about.

****

It had begun about three weeks before. Nothing substantial, just shadowy little hints from a variety of places about something going on, something not quite right, with the still new police chief.

After hearing the vague rumors from three different sources, each one slightly more concrete than the previous, Jared had confronted Barb Redland, his news director, about the possibility of doing a story.

"I don't know," Barb said from behind her desk, which at eleven in the morning already had three half-filled yogurt cups spread across it. "It doesn't sound like you have anything substantial yet."

"Main word there is 'yet,'" Jared replied. "The only reason I don't have anything solid is because I haven't started digging. It's not like Terry Henderson down at the PD is going to trot in here and dump a package on my desk."

Barb sighed and leaned back in her chair, staring up at the ceiling. She wore a russet and green silk blouse that did a nice job, as far as Jared was concerned, of complementing her reddish hair.

"You've got a stack of current assignments already on your desk."

He shrugged.

"It's been a slow month so far, and nothing on my plate can't be handled by some of the younger kids. This could be a big one for us, boss."

"And I thought of giving you something else. There's something supposedly going on down in the Zone, rumors of a new gang starting up. Some kind of weird initiation rites or something."

Jared shrugged once more.

"There's always a new street gang on the horizon. How's one more going to be any different?"

"You have any way of knowing if any of the other local outlets have wind of this big tip of yours?"

Jared nearly snorted but realized at the last instant that it wouldn't sound very diplomatic.

"Are you kidding? If I put out even the faintest of feelers, someone else snatches it up and there goes our exclusivity. Hell, can't you just imagine what KTTX would do if they got wind of this?"

"I really can't imagine it, Jared, mainly because you haven't given me any specifics yet. Just what do you think is this big deal that's brewing somewhere among our august city's back alleys?"

So he laid it out for her, at least as much as he'd gathered so far. With tons of qualifiers and lots of contingent possibilities, he told his boss what he thought he had a line on.

After he'd done so, Barb picked up a pad and paper and began making notes about how best to divvy up his stack of current stories among the other staff members.

And he was off and running.

****

As Allen swerved to the left to sit down at a table on the opposite side of the room, Jared's cell buzzed once again.

He almost didn't notice it, though, in his surprise at who the top cop was meeting with.

His phone sounded a second time and, without taking his eyes off the two people at the far table, he took it from his pocket and brought it to his ear.

"Yeah?" he said, without bothering to check who was calling.

"Any luck yet?"

"It's kind of interesting, boss. I don't know for sure who I was expecting, but I sure wasn't prepared for who showed up."

"Meaning?"

"Meaning I'm crouched here in a booth staring across a smoke-filled room at the chief himself."

"So? Didn't you expect him to be there? Wasn't that the whole point?"

"It was."

"So is this a lead or not?"

"Not sure, boss. Allen showed up, but I think the woman he's meeting ..."

"Woman?" the ND nearly shouted.

"Right. A woman. And I'm not sure, but I think she's one of the secretaries down at the county courthouse."

He could almost hear Barb's brain whirling.

"You telling me that Allen's meeting up with a courthouse secretary?"

"Right."

"So it's probably just the two of them screwing around?"

"Maybe," Jared said. "Then again, she could be a contact, a go-between of some kind, and they're trying to make it look like a hook up."

"Meaning in this kind of setting nobody's going to pay attention to what looks like a casual fling?"

"Right. Especially considering the woman in question."

"How so?" Jared's boss asked.

"Well, let's just say this. She's not what you'd call ugly, but she's also not going to have too many guys tripping over their tongues."

A few moments of silence ticked by. A couple of dudes who just had to be truck drivers moved across Jared's field of vision, and when they passed on, Allen and the woman were leaning in closer to each other and holding hands.

Meanwhile, Barb had been considering his last comment.

"If I recall correctly," she said, sarcasm oozing from the phone, "Allen's not exactly a tall hunk of stud, right?"

Jared grinned and wondered, not for the first time, if precocious little Barbara had once been raised on a steady diet of old Cary Grant movies filled with tough-talking, no-nonsense broads.

She sure seemed to do her best to live up to that image.

"You recall correctly," he said. "Not that that makes things definite either way."

"You're saying maybe the lady has hidden talents?" Barb asked.

"Yeah. Or maybe ol' Paul just really likes her."

To which the news director snorted.

"Get what you can here and now," she replied, "but we may have to put this one on the backburner, especially if it's nothing more than a physical fling."

He turned a bit towards the booth's wall.

"Dammit, Barb. We had a deal. You said ..."

"We may have something a bit juicier for you to go after. Get back here as soon as you can."

"Back to the shop?" Jared's original plan had been to go straight home after leaving Sonny's. He wanted to tidy things up a bit before picking up the kids. But for the last few minutes he'd found himself leaning towards following the woman at Allen's table when she left. Try to get a bearing on what role, if any, she played in the police chief's business. If it really was just a case of two consenting adults messing around, he should be able to determine that pretty quickly.

More than that, if he ended up punching in extra time tonight, it would make the third time this month that he'd stood up his boys.

"Can it wait till tomorrow?" he asked.

"Why? You got something better to do?"

While they'd been talking, Jared had done his best to keep his eye on Allen and the woman. No easy task, seeing as how the after work crowd was starting to pour in. He found it difficult to divide his mind between the twin tasks of trying to talk his boss out of giving him more work and figuring out just what was going on over on the other side of the room.

"I was supposed to take the kids tonight," he said. "Maggie's got some shindig to go to, so I'm taking them a few days early. If I have to tell her to hold off, you have any idea the sort of hell I'll catch?"

"Maybe you should take my suggestion of a few months back and get someone on standby willing to sit them. Even in a normal week, there's no rhyme or reason to a reporter's schedule."

"Maybe so. So what's this other job you've got for me?"

"It's a death," his news director said.

"A murder?"

"Not as far as we know. Just a death, though kind of out of the ordinary. Happened last night down in the Zone. We've been hearing rumors about the goings on down there, remember? I'd like you to ..."

"Wait a minute, Barb."

The atmosphere around the subjects of his surveillance seemed to have changed somewhat. Up to now, they'd been fairly restrained in their body language toward each other, but in the last few seconds that had all gone out the window. The girl had slammed herself back in her chair, putting as many inches as she could between herself and the chief. Allen's face had taken on a rather nasty scowl, and though he couldn't hear any of their conversation from across the crowded bar, Jared could tell that their words had become rather heated.

Even through all the smoke and activity between them, he could see the woman shake her head in a vehement "no."

"Come on, boss," he continued. "You really want me to go check out some old wino who keeled over from exposure?"

"The operative word in your statement there was 'boss.' How about we remember that for a while?"

"If you say so," Jared acquiesced, puzzled because Barb Redland rarely pulled out that particular card with her staff. "But what's so special about somebody dying down in the Zone? It must happen at least a couple of times a week, if not a day. And that's just the ones we hear about."

"True," she said, "but it seems to be going on a little more frequently lately."

"Is this that gang stuff you were talking about before? You think some gangbangers are going around offing old guys?"

"I don't think anything yet," Redland said. "And the cops sure as hell aren't talking. That's why we need to check it out."

"Okay," he said, disengaging the call at the same instant that the woman stood up and, just like in the movies, threw the remains of her drink straight into Allen's face.

Damn, Jared thought. *Maybe it was just a dalliance after all.*

That sure seemed like the action of a woman scorned.

Chapter Four

Karen Bannister pulled the black watch cap down tighter on her head, hoping to cover as much of her blonde hair as possible. She cinched the zipper of her windbreaker even higher as she melted back into the doorway.

The weather was about right for a light jacket, but far too warm for a knit cap. But a lot of people in the Zone knew Karen by sight, and while a few of them liked or at least tolerated her, others wouldn't hesitate to cause trouble if they spotted her. As she did her best to merge with the bricks making up the begrimed doorway, she could only imagine what her father would say if he were to see her now.

No doubt, another variation of the lecture she used to hear from him at least once a month, and twice during the holidays.

But at the moment, she couldn't waste time thinking about her dear old dad.

She had a kid to find.

As evening came on with the street lights, at least the working ones, beginning to flicker on, the youth population of the street, never robust, dropped all the way to nil. Even so, Karen didn't intend to head back to the shelter until she had some inkling of whatever the hell had happened to Ricky.

A man, by his staggering no doubt drunk, lurched around the corner and headed in her direction. Karen remained still, hoping either that he wouldn't see her or that he would and just keep on passing. While she had the necessary skills, drilled into her at her father's insistence, to defend herself, she was currently footsore, having been on the streets nearly all day, and worried enough about one of her charges that the last thing she wanted to do was waste time and energy in an altercation.

If it came to it, she might break one of her personal rules and just give the man what he wanted. Karen knew that, contrary to the popular stereotype, most street males who attacked women were after money, not rape. She had something around twenty dollars in her pocket. You never wanted to hang around this part of town well-heeled, and by the looks of the guy as he came closer, stoop-shouldered, long, thinning hair whipping around his face and shoes literally held together by duct tape, twenty dollars would seem like a fortune to him.

As the man came abreast, he glanced in the direction of her doorway, cast his eye over her for a minute, then moved on. As he passed, Karen let out the air she'd been holding in.

When he swung around the next corner, she decided to move on out and get on with her job. Ricky, he'd never told them his last name, had vanished from the shelter sometime in the night, despite the fact that everyone entering or leaving had to sign the register. Somehow or other the kid had slipped out, not surprising since, if they could believe him, he'd been wandering around the state on his own for the last two years.

He'd told them he was sixteen, but Karen and Diane Parsons, the shelter's administrator, figured him for thirteen at the most. Even so, as per policy they hadn't asked any questions of the lanky kid with the greasy red hair and mass of freckles on his face. He showed up wearing dirty Reeboks, jeans cut off to just below the knee, and a Boston Celtics tank top with a faded jean jacket, his wardrobe mixed and matched from whatever he'd come across during his time on the street.

He'd had no bags of any kind, not even a backpack and, as the dentist who stopped in at the shelter once a week discovered that morning, three molars nearly rotted away.

They'd managed to do at least a temporary patchwork on his teeth, get some food into him, and equip him with an old-fashioned blue ski vest. They'd intended to do more for the kid, of course, but before the night staff could blink he was gone, with no one the wiser.

As Karen moved out of the doorway and headed down the street, she swiveled her head in every direction. What she saw, the collection of vagrants huddling down in alleys for the night; two small groups of gangstas squaring off on opposite street corners; one or two far too obvious hookers shuffling down the street; and numerous darkened, gloomy windows looking down on the whole thing, would have been, at the least, discomforting to the average person. At the most, they would have run for the nearest exit.

Even so, mixed in with the usual population of the Zone she saw the average number and type of wayfarers. Almost uniformly male, like most visitors, they evenly divided into two main groups: the teenagers and college kids out for a night of adventure, looking to get lucky with anything they could, and the more sedate, middle-aged, though no less dangerous if some poor girl crossed them, executive types.

Passing by a fortyish-looking man in a gray wool suit, Karen felt like reaching out and slapping some sense into him. Instead, when he gave her a look that seemed almost preparatory to a proposition, she sent a withering glare his way that managed to send him scurrying off.

A few women could be seen around, mostly small groups of thrill-seekers who, when examined closely, looked individually as if they would rather be home safe and secure.

Karen, not for the first time since working for the shelter, wondered why the hell ordinary citizens considered it "edgy" to come to this patch of urban wasteland.

But she, despite her dad's fervent objections, had prowled this scene for the better part of three years, and felt as safe as one could reasonably expect.

Besides, dammit, she wanted to find that kid.

She was going on the assumption, no doubt at least half wishful thinking, that Ricky hadn't strayed far from the general area of the shelter, located just outside the environs of the Zone. He was a street kid, after all, and street kids knew all there was to know about protective coloration.

After all, if they didn't learn real quick how to blend in, they didn't survive very long.

And they tended to keep to the areas where they did blend in.

Under ordinary circumstances, the staff at the Municipal Benevolent Shelter wouldn't concern themselves with one wayward resident. People, both individuals and families, came and went all the time, no questions asked and relatively few answered. It was a common complaint of the bean counters down at City Hall that the staff gave only cursory lip service to numbers and accountability. But a fairly common tenet of charity work among the indigent and homeless stated that too much inquisitiveness would drive people away, thus self-defeating the whole purpose of the shelter.

Still, this was a different case. Ricky, if that was indeed the kid's name, had seemed so grateful that it seemed beyond credence that he would have taken off unless he had a good reason. So, upon arriving for her shift that afternoon and finding out what had happened, Karen had done herself up in her "street" clothes and headed out into the Zone.

It was getting on in hours, by now, and she considered giving up and packing it in. If Ricky didn't show up by the morning, the odds of their ever seeing him again would start to seriously diminish.

She passed by an alley and, noting a huddled form about halfway down, paused for a closer look. She knew with her first glance that the shape was too big to be Ricky, but before she could move on it detached from itself, split into two, and while one of the shapes seemed to press itself into the wall, the other made a motion which could have been turning towards her.

"What the hell you looking at, bitch," a man's voice, hoarse from cigarettes or booze, or both, snarled at her.

Karen didn't flinch; instead, she calmly turned and continued on her way. Without waiting to look any closer, she could guess that the other form, the one pressed into the wall, was female (most likely) and that she had interrupted a business transaction.

And while she'd had her share of near misses over the years, she'd toughened up enough that she felt only a faint fluttering of the heart at the nastiness in the man's voice.

Oh Dad, she thought, *if you'd heard how that guy talked to your little girl you'd probably beat him within an inch, without stopping to realize, or even consider, that his aggressiveness didn't bother me at all.*

She remembered, with a slight pang, the way he'd acted when she was in high school, interrogating each new boyfriend who came along. Damned near acting like he wanted to bring out the clichéd rubber hose.

That thought led to another memory, the first time she'd wanted to stay out until midnight with a boy, and the storm and fury that had bubbled just beneath the old man's surface.

Now here she stood, not quite a decade and a half later, strolling the sidewalks of the city's absolute worst patch of real estate and momentarily interrupting a transaction between a john and his temporary woman.

Had Dad seen how calmly I strode away, Karen wondered, *would he be impressed at my bravery or baffled at my naiveté?*

All of these assorted thoughts, through a straight line causal chain, led her to thinking about David, causing that slight clutch in the chest and tightening of the shoulders that always came when he crossed her mind.

Hell with it, Karen told herself as she stopped, moving far enough to the side of two young men whispering to each other. As she passed, at a distance where they wouldn't see her as a threat, Karen saw money change hands, followed a minute later by some sort of cylindrical items in a glassine bag.

One of them looked her way, but this was a far different, and more dangerous, proposition than the two coupling in the alleyway, so Karen turned her back and began walking more rapidly. Not out of fear but to make it clear she didn't care about their business.

Don't push it, the night whispered to her. *Time to go home.*

Ricky would just have to make it on his own for at least one more night.

And, possibly, for the rest of his life.

Chapter Five

Jared always considered this the loneliest time in the daily cycle of the newsroom. Shortly before five and six o'clock, central time, people were always scurrying back and forth snapping at each other their requests, demands, or pleas to get the broadcast up and running. Then came a lull, between seven and nine, as the various anchors and producers went out for dinner or tended to business at their desks (the reporters usually still out in the field that early in the evening). Then, in the minutes and quarter hours leading up to the ten o'clock broadcast, the whole mad dance began all over again.

Now, shortly after midnight, it wouldn't take much for him to imagine himself the only person in the place. The studio lights had long since gone dark, and he could see only a few isolated desk lamps lit as a few of the younger, rawer reporters or producers performed last minute tasks before they headed home to grab a few hours of sleep before coming back, around five in the morning, to start it all over again.

Jared walked past the various cubicles, able to feel like the sole being on the entire floor. The feeling relaxed him, allowing him to at least begin to unwind from the tension of staking out Sonny's bar.

After Allen and his companion had left, Jared had flipped a mental coin and decided to follow the woman. That decision commenced a nearly seven-hour meander of the city, stopping at an assortment of grocery stores, dry cleaners, and flower shops. Had Woodson not seen her coming out of each establishment with purchase in hand, he would almost have imagined her as some sort of bagwoman, either dropping off or collecting payments from various merchants.

Instead, she presented herself as merely a city clerical worker who didn't have time in the day to do her errands, probably because she spent a lot of time shlepping around after the chief of police.

The lady in question eventually went home, or at least he assumed it hers, to a small apartment complex on the city's west side. Small enough that, from the parking lot, the reporter could see what apartment she ended up in. It then took him just a small amount of walking around to determine the numerical designation of her place.

First thing tomorrow, he intended to use the various resources available to him, both legit and not so legit, to pin down the woman's name, if for no other reason than to confirm that the whole thing was as innocent, more or less, as he figured it was.

And if it was only an illicit affair, with no political overtones or undertones, he was prepared to let the whole thing drop right there.

For now, however, he just wanted to sit at his desk for a few minutes, close his eyes, and relax half of his brain while the other half found a way to make up for this botched night. He'd been a reporter when he and Maggie had first married, so she'd known the score. But he'd lost track of the number of times since the divorce that work had come between him and his sons. Sooner or later it was bound to catch up with him, and he was a little worried about facing Eric and Ryan, once again, with nothing but an excuse.

But as Jared turned the corner of his cubicle and stood over his desk, he saw that any sort of rest wasn't going to come his way for some time.

Barb could have just sent the image to his phone. But he had a feeling that she had wanted him to see it full size instead of on the relatively tiny screen of his phone.

He figured she wanted him to get the full impact of the visual, and had to admit that she'd succeeded.

Flat on his desk lay a blown-up photo, nearly twelve by sixteen. Even at the enhanced size, it took Woodson several seconds of peering to determine that the person in the photo was, in fact, male.

The body was so torn up that the form barely looked human.

A note was posted to the photo, clearly written in Barb's neat, slightly loopy style of penmanship.

Placed in the exact center of the picture, right in the middle of the welter of red spreading out in all directions from that lonely shape on the pavement, the note contained a single question:

"Enough to whet your interest?"

Chapter Six

This late at night, the Municipal Benevolent Shelter could be a downright scary place. Depending on the inhabitants at any given time, you could have a handful of druggies coming down off their high, one or two predators lying under their blankets and planning a way to score a quick one, or an actual downright asylum case kneeling in a corner and screaming about the coming Apocalypse.

Lately, though, they'd had a lot of nights like tonight, when things seemed so quiet and peaceful that you could almost nod off at your desk.

Almost, but not quite.

You never knew when all hell would break loose.

****

Susan was on duty tonight and, as the shelter's resident bookkeeper, sat hunched over her desk, illuminated by a single 60-watt bulb, poring over the income and outgo figures for last month. She looked up long enough to give Karen a quizzical look as she came in the door.

"Any luck?"

Karen shook her head and walked right up against Susan's desk, the better to allow the two to whisper.

"How is it tonight?" she asked.

"Quiet, so far. But there's a couple of women who came in right as we were locking up, looked kind of desperate and needy. We had a few empty cots, so I went ahead and assigned them to them. But before he left, I had Mark position the beds far away from the rest of the crowd."

"You for sure they're hinky?"

"Not really. Just a feeling. Even so, especially with the stories going around, I figured it best to keep them separated and look in on them every twenty minutes or so."

"Stories?" Karen asked.

Susan leaned back in her chair and stared at Karen.

"You didn't hear while you were out there?"

"Hear what?"

"As they trickled in tonight, we began hearing stuff. Whispers. Half sentences. You know. The kind of partial stuff you pick up while you're dishing out the soup and making up the cots for the night."

"I left early this afternoon," Karen said. "Headed out around three, so hardly any of the usuals had shown up yet. What kind of stuff?"

"Supposedly, another homeless guy went missing a day or so ago. One of the older ones again. Only he didn't stay missing for very long. They found him late last night. More like this morning. Some of them were talking about he'd been cut nearly to shreds. Heard half a dozen versions, each more gruesome than the last, by the time we went lights out."

Karen glanced over her shoulder at the dormitory area and saw nothing but a sea of huddled forms under blankets, only the occasional ripple of cloth as someone tossed in their sleep signaling any life at all.

She sometimes thought, when she stayed here during the dead of night, that the various pieces of human flotsam that made their way into the shelter went into some sort of limbo with lights out, entered a state of almost hibernation until the morning sun began inching its way through the front windows.

Of course, Karen only held this view on the nights when nothing happened. On those other nights, the ones with non-stop commotion, hardly anyone got any sleep at all.

It had almost seemed, as some of them had discussed while sitting at their desks, that over the last several weeks the street people had been more grateful than usual for a port in the storm, as if seeking shelter had become even more crucial than in past times.

Which made Karen and her coworkers wonder if maybe, just maybe, the various rumors of people missing off the streets, snatched away in the middle of the night, were more than fanciful imaginings.

****

"So you don't know any more than that?" she asked Susan.

"Nope. And for all I know it's been blown way out of proportion. But as I was getting ready to come in here, I had the news on the TV. And I think they did say something about finding a body down in the Zone. You didn't hear or see anything while you were out there?"

"Not a thing. At least, nothing to do with any sort of killing. Probably just some drug thing that went wrong."

"But if you want something really creepy, go up and stand just outside the dormitory."

Wondering what her coworker meant, Karen walked to the edge of the corner around which the first room of cots was laid out. Peeking around the corner, the room, lit only by a few soft dark blue lights positioned in the corners, seemed peaceful enough. But as she stood there watching, Karen got an inkling of what had spooked Susan.

"It's awfully quiet," she said when she returned to the front, administrative section of the Shelter.

"Been like that all night," Susan said. "Even when they first began trickling in. Including the families. All of them almost silent and huddling close to each other. Even saw a few that I'd guess were total strangers walking side by side, almost touching. During the meal time, hardly anyone spoke, barely heard a knife clink against a plate. And right after dinner, boom. On the cots, under the blankets, and eyes closed. Then just like this all night."

"Meaning what?" Karen asked, though she could already guess where Susan was heading.

"Meaning, I think they're spooked. And spooked good."

"No matter what it is, they probably know more than we do," Karen said.

"Maybe," Susan said, though her tone remained doubtful. "Then again, if there is something going on, maybe you could get the lowdown for us."

Karen tensed, knowing exactly where Susan was going.

"It wouldn't take much." Susan looked away for an instant, as if realizing that she'd overstepped. "At the most a phone call, a couple minutes."

Her voice ending in a mild quaver, she sat tensed, as if fearing Karen's reaction.

"I can't see that doing any good," Karen said after several moments' pause. "When I was a kid, he wouldn't talk much about work, and it wouldn't be any different now."

"But you're not a kid anymore," Susan said.

"True, but I'm also barely his daughter anymore. If there's something going on that threatens our people, we're going to have to figure it out on our own. If the cops show up nosing around, I'll cooperate, of course. But that's as far as I'm willing to go."

Susan looked like she wanted to say more, but a close look at Karen's visage and posture changed her mind.

After a minute or so, the two of them relaxed, leaned back in their chairs, sipped their coffee and listed to the silence of the sleeping shelter.

Chapter Seven

The next night, Karen once again walked the streets of the Zone.

She'd helped out around the shelter until around ten in the morning, then gone home for some long-overdue breakfast and sleep, finally crawling out of a short, fitful slumber around three in the afternoon.

Living with an excess of caution, a trait no doubt picked up from her dad, Karen, unlike many in her generation, maintained a home phone along with her cell. Staggering into the kitchen, she noticed the answering machine on her phone giving about three blinks at a time. She paused and stared at the machine, watching through several cycles as the silent box gave forth those three repeated blinks.

But because anyone who would call her on the landline would be someone she didn't feel like speaking to, at least at the moment, she continued past the phone and proceeded to make herself some coffee.

As she showered, brushed her teeth, and got dressed, Karen made a point of avoiding looking in the mirror. With her erratic schedule of the last few days, she had pretty much figured that she looked like something a whole passel of cats had dragged in from the rain.

Still, a bedraggled appearance would serve her out on the streets. Despite the fact that many residents of the Zone knew her, or at least knew of her and her work at the shelter, the less she looked like an upper-middle class, educated woman, the better.

Now, if she could only have some success in finding a single runaway.

****

"Don't think so, miss," the old black man said from his stoop. He looked up, his expression conveying nothing while she questioned him.

"About this tall," Karen said, holding up her hand. "Red hair and freckles. Real bright freckles."

The old man laughed, though in about as gentle a tone as possible.

"Miss," he said. "You think you have to repeat yourself? I heard you clear as could be the first time. And believe me, if I had seen a kid like you described, he would have stood out from here clear to Parkers Street. But I ain't seen him, and that's that."

Karen nodded, thanked the man for his time, and moved on. Nearly four hours of strolling the pavement and not a whole hell of a lot to show for it. Other than sore feet, a spot of tension in her shoulder blade, and a growling stomach, she'd come up with exactly nada.

She must have questioned nearly fifty people, all with the same empty result. At the moment, she didn't know what else she could do, except give it up and head home. She'd made it as far as Kessler Avenue, which came close to marking the eastern edge of the Zone, and at the moment she couldn't think of where else to go or what else to do.

"Hey," the oldster called when she'd gotten about ten steps away, "why's this one kid so important to you anyway?"

Karen turned back to him, paused for a moment when she realized she didn't have a good answer, and at that moment from around the next corner on her left, came a woman's scream.

Most of the street denizens, though not all, looked up when they heard the screech. The majority glanced in the direction from which the sound had come for only a second or two, then turned back to whatever they'd been doing. Only three old men, wearing faded woolen coats far too heavy for the fall weather and huddled around a bottle of cheap vodka they passed back and forth, continued looking towards the alley in question from where the scream came.

An instant later, though, the picture changed as a middle-aged woman, stumbling in an ultra-tight skirt and ridiculous stiletto heels, lurched out of the alley.

"In here!" she shrieked to no one in particular. "For God's sake, in here!"

With her appearance, a few more of the street people began to stir themselves, but Karen wasn't waiting. She started running flat out towards the woman.

As she got to the mouth of the alley, two men, wearing cast-off suit jackets, joined her. She didn't know the two, one short and rather pale while the other stood somewhat over six feet and looked like he had some Native American blood in him.

The woman who'd screamed, upon seeing that other people had arrived, began hobbling away as fast as she could. Karen thought of grabbing her, but before she could one of the men, the tall, Indian-looking one, touched her arm.

"Let her go, miss. Lizzie don't take too well to strangers, and if you approach her she may pull a knife on you. Let her go, and stay right here while Billy and I check it out."

The man, along with his buddy, made their way into the alley, tattered jackets flapping around them.

A moment later, the one called Billy came back out and looked at Karen.

"You'd better steer clear, lady," he said, his eyes a little foggy with whatever booze he'd recently drank. "It's a pretty godawful sight in there."

Karen pushed past the man and headed into the alley.

She saw the taller one about halfway down the alley, in front of a Dumpster overflowing with green garbage bags, crouching over a pile of – something.

As she got closer, the instinctive lurch of nausea in her stomach told her what the thing was.

The tall man waved her away, but Karen kept coming forward. She fixated first, through all the weltered and bloody flesh, on the thatch of reddish hair.

"Oh, God," she whispered, her stomach clenching at the possibility of Ricky splayed on the pavement. But as she came a few steps closer Karen realized that the body, or what was left of it, looked too large to be a young boy.

But not by much.

"Lady," the tall guy said, at this point kneeling next to the corpse. "You really don't want to be anywhere around this."

But years working in a vagrancy shelter, combined with any qualities she may have inherited from her father, left Karen feeling tough enough to handle most anything.

Or so she thought. But as she came within a few feet of the body, keeping her head enough not to get too close to mess up anything for the police, her right foot shifted slightly out from under her, and Karen looked down to see a smear of blood on the pavement.

Then the man stood and backed off, taking care to keep out of any patches or pools of blood, and as he moved away the body on the ground came into Karen's view.

That clench in her stomach became more pronounced, and she had a hard time getting her breath.

"What the hell could have done that?" she asked, standing side by side with the stranger, vaguely aware of a crowd gathering behind them.

"Don't know," the man said, "but whatever it is, I'm glad it got hold of Annie instead of me."

"Annie?"

"Sure." He gestured. "That's old Annie lying there. Don't know her last name, even though I've known her for what must be years."

"Would anyone around here know her full name?"

The tall man looked down at her and grinned.

"Hell, miss. As pickled as she usually was, I doubt most days even Annie knew her full name."

Another one of them, Karen thought. *Another of the so many nameless, faceless people who populated this part of town.* It didn't do her any good to remind herself that it wasn't just this community, that any city of any size had a similar population. All that mattered to her were the ones in her town.

And one of them, though thankfully not the still-missing Ricky, now looked as if she had been chewed up and spit out by a pack of wild animals.

"You reckon we ought to tell someone," the tall stranger asked her, "or just let things be? It's not like she's the first that this's happened to."

"If we leave it alone ..."

"Right," he finished for her, "by morning the rats will have finished her off."

"Would your friend have wanted that?"

"Friend?" He laughed, a hoarse, barking type of laugh. "Hell, I barely knew the bitch."

Karen had found herself warming to the homeless man, but that last word reminded her of just how dangerous this sub society could be.

"And besides," he continued, "there's nothing left to salvage from her clothing, bloody as it all is. So I guess we might as well let someone know."

Sighing, Karen pulled out her cell phone and punched in three numbers.

She could only hope she'd find some way to keep Dad from finding out about this.

Chapter Eight

"Bannister, Karen Bannister."

She almost held her breath, wondering if either of the two officers would recognize the name. The older one, a black guy in his early thirties, raised an eyebrow, but the freckle-faced white cop--Karen's life seemed invaded by gingers—didn't even look up from his inspection of the pavement.

Karen figured that the gyrating strobe effect of all those flashing red and blue lights, along with a couple of yellow ones from the ambulance blinkers, probably gave her a haggard, drugged-out appearance.

All the other people scurrying around the scene didn't help her nerves any.

"Okay," said the younger cop, "why don't you go and stay over ..."

"Hold it, Frank," the older one put in, "don't you know who she is?"

Dammit, Karen thought.

"Sure, I do. She's a witness to whatever this ..."

"More than that, buddy. Unfortunately, she's a hell of a lot more than that."

He nodded to Karen, then headed off to consult with one of the paramedics. The red-headed cop glanced at her, looking puzzled, then moved off to do his own thing.

Knowing police procedure as she did, Karen figured they weren't done with her, so she walked over and leaned against a wall about fifty feet from the mouth of the alley and just outside of the yellow crime scene tape, and waited. She half turned away from the scurrying back and forth of the various official workers, while working to untangle the tight knot in her stomach.

Going on towards midnight, this stretch of pavement looked darker than most places in the city because half of the street lights were broken, probably not even glanced at by someone in the Municipal Bureau for quite some time.

The condition of the street lights, along with the continual flickering, jabbing and stabbing of the various official blinkers, served to highlight, in a harsh and jagged way, all the people moving hither and yon in the performance of their duties.

Behind all of that, serving as an almost deliberate backdrop, gathered the residents of the Zone.

Karen wouldn't even begin to guess their numbers, though the congested nature of their grouping made it look like more than what actually stood there. Whereas most of them would ordinarily have shied away from any proximity to officialdom, scurrying away like frightened animals whenever they saw any sort of uniform, they now stood silent, almost vigil-like, representing nothing more nor less than a single, homogenous organism.

One of their own had been killed, in an unbelievably violent manner. And while Karen's one quick look at "Annie's" corpse had been enough to make her imagine that some sort of wild animal, or animals, had somehow found their way into the inner city, the exact cause probably didn't matter to most of them.

One of their own had been killed, two if you added in that other killing that had spooked the Shelter's residents the night before and even more if all the whispers floating around had any substance. For a moment Karen wondered if the two were connected in some way, or rather just served as isolated reminders of the dangers of living in this part of the city.

50

Regardless, whether isolated or part of some larger pattern, the street people stood there watching, and they no doubt intended to keep watch until there was nothing left to see.

Plus, they probably believed in the myth of safety in numbers.

A new car, an unmarked one, pulled onto the scene, blue and red lights flashing from the dashboard.

Great, Karen thought, here come the plainclothes.

She leaned further into the wall, as she watched the detectives climb out of their car and walk over to the two uniforms. Karen didn't recognize them, but one looked familiar, as if she'd seen him at some point in the past.

The four cops chatted back and forth for a while, then one of the plainclothes split off from the group to walk into the alley.

He came out a couple of minutes later and walked past the other three, still deep in conversation. The detective then wandered over to the ambulance and talked a bit with the paramedics.

At the same time, Karen noticed the older uniform pointing her way while saying something to the second detective.

Here it comes.

That officer, an average-looking guy wearing a black overcoat, broke from the other two and came her way.

As he approached, in the erratic lighting of the area, Karen saw that this one, too, had pale skin and freckles splattered across his face.

What the hell's this? An epidemic all of a sudden?

She realized that she had her hands clenched so tight her nails were about to draw blood and tried to force herself to relax.

Even though she really wanted to break into a run and get the hell out of there.

"Miss Bannister," the detective called out when he was within a few feet of her.

Sighing, she moved away from the wall.

"Yes," she said.

"Thanks for waiting around. I understand that you were a witness to – whatever this was?"

Speaking in a fairly objective tone, the guy looked straight at her. His expression showed neither precipitate fawning nor barely-concealed hostility, the two reactions she would have most expected.

Maybe this wouldn't be so bad after all.

"Not really a witness," she replied. "At least not to the actual act. I only came upon the scene after the attacker had left."

Grimacing inside, Karen wanted to kick herself for using jargon such as "came upon the scene." Supposing the plain-clothesman had up to now been oblivious as to his witness's identity, that little slip of the tongue should have caught his attention. But, either unknowing or a good actor, he didn't show any reaction.

"Attacker?" he asked.

"Excuse me?"

"You said attacker. Why did you use that word?"

"Well," Karen fumbled and felt her cheeks turning red. *Dammit, when am I going to get over my hang-up about dealing with cops?* "I didn't really think about it. Obviously, something tore into that poor woman."

"Did you see anybody fleeing the scene?" the detective asked.

"No, but I was focused more on seeing if she was still alive."

"See anything at all running away?"

Finally, Karen thought. *It's getting out in the open.*

"You mean like an animal of some kind?"

"Well ..."

"No," she said. "I didn't see or hear anything. Not so much as a shape or shadow. But for what it's worth, I'm kind of thinking the same thing."

"You ever do much hunting, Miss Bannister?"

"Not since I was a kid," Karen said, "and even then only once or twice."

"So did you happen to notice that ...?"

At that moment, the cop's cell phone buzzed. He held up his hand in apology, pulled the phone from his pocket and, half turning away from Karen, began speaking into it. About ten seconds into the conversation, he glanced back at Karen, an indefinable expression on his face.

"Yes, sir," he said before ending the call. Putting the phone back into his jacket pocket, he turned fully to Karen, wearing a whole new expression, one composed of equal parts confusion and annoyance.

"Would you mind coming with me, Miss Bannister? Your father wants to talk to you."

****

By her reckoning, it had been close to six months since Karen had visited her dad's office. Not through any animosity or discomfort, to be sure. Merely because her schedule had been jammed as of late.

At least, that's what she kept telling herself.

The detective, who on the ride over had identified himself as Tim O'Brien, escorted her in the front of the building, past a flurry of uniforms moving hither and yon, to the elevators, and then up to the sixth floor.

Coming right off the elevator and turning to the left, Karen and her escort made their way to the old, varnished wood door over which hung a placard.

"Detective Division – Administrative."

And here we go, Karen thought as she opened the door and, moving ahead of Detective O'Brien, headed towards the office at the back.

He managed to catch up with her as she opened the door adorned with a small brass nameplate: "Captain Leo Bannister, Chief of Detectives."

Chapter Nine

"Hello, honey," said the tall, gray-haired man sitting behind the desk.

He stood up and came around the desk, holding his arms out to Karen. As always, every time she'd seen her father over the last year or so, she found herself choking up.

At the same time, Karen noticed the slight signal her father sent to Detective O'Brien. Through the roaring in her ears, she heard the door close behind O'Brien as he left the room.

"Sweetie," Captain Bannister said as he wrapped his arms around his daughter, "how have you been?"

For an instant there, only an instant, Karen wanted nothing more than to collapse into his arms and cry herself to sleep, as she'd done as a very young child when a nightmare would wake her up in the middle of the night. Or like the time, the day after her twelfth birthday, when her dad came home from the hospital where her mom had been staying, took one look at his little girl, and shook his head. Karen had known then that her mother had passed away, and just like tonight she'd run into her dad's arms.

But she wasn't a little girl anymore, and dammit it had been almost a year since David's death, so at exactly what point did she intend to get her act together?

"I'm okay, Dad," she said, easing herself from his hug. "It was pretty ugly, but I'm alright."

Captain Bannister, eschewing the desk, took his daughter by the elbow and guided her over to a dark leather couch sitting in a corner of the room. As the two of them sat down, Karen finally managed to look her father in the eye.

"Tell me what happened," he said.

So she went through the same story as she had with the two uniforms, taking care to get every detail as exact as she could remember. Upon finishing, she leaned back into the couch cushion, confused by her father's frowning countenance.

"What did it look like?" he finally asked her.

"Look like?"

"Well, you mentioned you thought it was an animal that attacked that woman. Any idea what type?"

"Thought, sure. But I didn't actually see anything. By the time we got into the alley, whatever did it was long gone."

"But did you get any sort of impression at all of what it could have been?"

"Well," Karen said, "something fairly big I'd guess. I'm sure it wasn't a cat or dog. Unless ..."

"Unless a pretty big dog?" her dad prodded.

"Well, sure. But even at that it didn't seem like –" Karen paused, her brain starting to kick into gear, and leaned further back.

"Dad," she said, "why are you interested in a simple street killing? Isn't that a little low priority for the C of D's?"

Bannister sighed, stood up and walked over to his desk. Bending down, he picked up a folder.

"Never could fool you for long," he said. "Ever since you were a little kid, I couldn't pull anything over on you."

He came back over to the couch and looked down at Karen.

"I know you've had a bit of a shock tonight. But can you take one more?"

Mutely, she nodded her head, while feeling, in some odd way, that her world was about to be turned upside down.

"Take a look at this."

Her father opened up the folder and handed it to her.

At first, Karen didn't see what the big deal was although she wondered how he had so quickly gotten photos, nice glossy ones, of the old woman's body, lying in the alley torn to pieces.

Then she looked a little closer and felt her stomach begin to tighten.

"This ... this looks like earlier tonight. But it's ..."

"That's right." Captain Bannister sank down on the couch and placed his hand on Karen's knee. "It's not from tonight. It's another one. From a few nights ago."

"But it looks just like ..." Again, her words trailed off as she tried to absorb what she was looking at.

Captain Bannister reached over and took the folder from her, folding it closed.

"Here's where we are, honey. We've had two attacks, similar in nature, in the same stretch of town in the past couple of days."

Karen laughed, a hoarse, barking exhalation.

"Stretch of town?" Her voice cracked. "Why don't you come out and say it, Dad? You mean down in the Zone, our fair city's version of Skid Row."

Bannister rubbed his face.

"I know we have ... difficulties ... in communicating, Karen. But please don't use this as an excuse for one of your rants."

Karen opened her mouth to say something in return, then realized the futility of it.

After what had happened to David, she and her father would never see things on equal terms.

"But there's something more," the captain continued. "And that's what I need to talk to you about."

"How'd you know?" Karen asked.

"Excuse me?"

"How did you know I was there? I called it in less than an hour ago, more or less. Barely had time to give name, rank and serial number to the two uniforms before ... oh, I get it."

"Of course they called me," the captain said. "As soon as they got your name, one of the patrolmen got in touch."

"Probably the older one. The young guy didn't seem to be on top of things."

"Well," Bannister shrugged, "he's new."

"So why exactly did you have to see me so soon? I figured at least a couple of hours. I mean, it's not like I was in the middle of a crossfire or anything. I was just one of the first to see her body. So why the rush?"

Bannister got up again, Karen noting that he seemed particularly fidgety tonight, and walked over to stare out of his window.

Karen took a second look at the file folder, complete with its official tag, but with that second glance she noticed something that she hadn't before.

Pictures.

Only pictures. No form of documentation at all.

She kept quiet, waiting for her father, in his own way and time, to get to whatever was bugging him. For a few seconds there, backlighted against the darkened window, he crossed his arms, and Karen thought she saw his entire body tense. Then he relaxed, the slightest fraction, and turned back to his waiting daughter.

"I'd like you to quit your job," he said.

"Quit my job?" She felt the heat beginning to rise again. "For God's sake, why?"

"Okay, maybe 'quit' was too strong of a word. But would it be possible for you to take a leave of absence? Just for a while?"

"Dad, I haven't exactly had the best of nights. I know that our father-daughter moments have been lacking the last year or so, but could you please tell me flat out what's the problem? And why am I here anyway? Shouldn't your goon squad, like that one who dragged me in here, be questioning me about what I saw in the alley?"

The captain turned back from the window, and the look on his face caused Karen's heart to catch. She instantly resented the "goon squad" comment and wanted to take it back. But she didn't know how, and as she herself had said, lately the two of them had found it difficult to talk.

"Yes," Bannister said, "Detective O'Brien will be speaking to you in a few minutes. But please answer my question. Could you take some time off from your work?"

"Not without a good explanation," Karen replied.

"Can't you just for once take what I say on faith?"

Both could see a tightness in the other's expression, showing that they both remembered, once upon a time, when she would have taken anything her father said and never question it. But that was back in the old days, before things went to hell and reality crashed into her life.

Before David and one really bad night.

"Wish I could," she said, "but I need something more than your say-so. I don't know if you're aware of this, Dad, but my work's important to me.

"Besides, far as I can tell, you're holding out on me."

She kept her face motionless, not daring to show how much she knew her words hit him. But dammit, if they were ever going to see each other as equals again, they had to start leveling with each other.

Karen saw her father's face tighten even more.

"This," Karen said, flapping the folder in front of her. "Since when do case folders only have pictures, and particularly graphic ones at that? You said this was from a few days ago? No coroner's report, no incident papers, no witness statements? Come on, Dad. What do you really want?"

Sighing, Captain Bannister pulled out his chair and sat down behind his desk.

"Never could fool you, could I? But if you learned so much from all those years hearing me gripe about work, then you should know that I can't show complete files to a civilian."

"I'm your daughter," Karen replied, leaving unspoken the second half of her thought.

Even if I haven't acted much like one lately.

For a moment the captain's arm twitched, as if he wanted to reach out and pat his little girl on the knee. But he restrained the impulse, as both of them had done so often in the last year.

"You are," he finally said, "and it's because of that that I'm asking you, just this once, to trust me and do as I ask."

"The Shelter isn't that dangerous. Everyone in or out is screened, and most of the time we have volunteer guards around. So how ..."

"You're talking about the Shelter," Bannister said.

"Yes?"

"I'm speaking about your outside activity."

Karen breathed deeply, willing herself calm. She had to fight to continue breathing in a normal manner.

"When you go out on the streets," her dad continued. "I want you to stop that for a while."

Karen glanced over at the photo folder, which had ended up on the coffee table in front of the couch.

"You're saying these are connected," she said.

Her father didn't say anything.

"And if they're connected, that means that it probably wasn't a wild animal that attacked those two people."

The captain continued to stay silent.

Karen tapped her knee a couple of times, giving herself time to marshal her thoughts.

"Are you talking about a serial killer? Or is there some new, high-powered street gang out there, like the rumors say?" she asked.

"Please, baby," her dad said, and for a minute she thought he might actually weep. "Just curtail your time down in the Zone. At least for a while?"

Once, she would have trusted him. Once, she would have listened and heeded his warning. But as she sat there, a veil seemed to come over her vision, and instead of her father she could only see a policeman.

The type of person she could never again trust, for as long as she lived.

Sorry, Dad, she thought. *But I just can't believe anything you say.*

She stood up, smoothed her jacket, which she hadn't yet taken off and looked down at the man who had raised her. Who, especially after her mother's death, had devoted his life to her.

When he wasn't too busy being a cop.

"I have to go now," she said. "I've got a stray kid to find."

And she turned and walked away.

Chapter Ten

Karen arrived at work the next day with eyes red from lack of sleep and stomach growling from hunger. After leaving her father's office the night before, she'd gone straight home. But the events of the night had made it impossible for her to get any sleep.

Despite growing up in the captain's household, and her own experiences on the street, Karen knew that she wasn't any sort of expert. As she'd stared at the photos of the dead man, whose wounds had looked so similar to those on the body she'd seen with her own eyes, she couldn't imagine what sort of weapon had been used on the two. Naturally, some sort of cutting tool, but beyond that she didn't have a clue.

What's more, the utter savagery expressed by those wounds seemed to signal a perpetrator, or perpetrators, even worse than the Guatemalan street gangs that had invaded most of the major cities a few years back.

When it came right down to it, she didn't want to deal with any of this. But in a way she had to. If for no other reason than for the safety of the residents of the shelter.

That morning, when Karen had sat down to a quickly-made breakfast of scrambled eggs and bacon, she'd nearly vomited at the smell of the food.

Lucy Richards, the thirtyish brunette who served as director of the shelter, waved at Karen as she came in. Karen managed to return the gesture, but she felt as if her heart wasn't in anything this morning, and she knew what Lucy and the rest of the staff would assume.

She hung up her coat, then sat down at her desk to do the monthly purchase orders, merely another of her myriad, haphazard duties. The Shelter's business was complicated enough, and their staff and budget small enough, that no one, beyond Lucy, had any defined duties or title. Over time, as staff came and went, everyone just took on the various jobs for which they seemed most equipped. For some reason, Karen had enough of a financial head that she ended up doing the bulk of the numbers chores.

At least, when she wasn't out on the streets, being a total failure at tracking down errant residents.

But the figures kept zooming in and out of focus, and in no time at all the computer screen held nothing but a blur. Looking around to make sure no one was looking, she turned away from the monitor and buried her face in her hands.

It wasn't just the visuals from last night that bothered her. It was seeing her dad again, being so close to him, yet feeling that wall of separation that had stood between them for so many months. Then, hearing him ask her to quit her job, the only thing in her life that still held any meaning, had felt like a gut punch.

His request had made sense, at least from a parental standpoint. But it had also served to remind her that the old man still saw her as some sort of frail creature that needed protecting.

Newsflash, Dad, she thought. *I had someone all lined up to do the protecting job for the rest of our lives, and you know how that one turned out.*

A soft rap on the flimsy wall of her cubicle caused Karen to look up to see Lucy standing there.

"I thought the nights had been getting better for you," her boss remarked.

For an instant, Karen thought of telling the other woman, but figured she'd learn about it soon enough.

"They have been," she said. "But every now and then ..."

Lucy pulled up an old castoff chair and sat down next to the desk.

"To be expected," she said. "After all, it hasn't even quite been a year."

Karen nodded without saying anything. Taking a look at her physical state, Lucy had assumed what Karen had expected her to. And while she didn't have to correct her boss's false impression, a lie of omission still counted as a lie.

"You know," Lucy continued, "that I've held back, and the rest of the staff has as well."

"I know," Karen said, feeling a slight catch in her throat. *Dammit, now was not the time to fall to pieces.* "And I appreciate it; I really do."

"And I hope you're aware, corny as it sounds, that we all really do care what happens to you."

Karen nodded, by this point not trusting herself to look anywhere but at her desktop.

"But honey," Lucy said, "I've been wondering if maybe ... you'd want to start talking to someone."

"You mean like a therapist." Staring down at her clenched fists resting on the desktop.

"Maybe. Or maybe someone in a church or just a ..."

"Lucy." Her voice cracked and Karen took a minute to attempt to suck some moisture into her mouth. "I appreciate your concern. But it's not as bad as you think. Honestly, I'll be okay."

Lucy rolled her chair back just the slightest bit.

"Have you thought about starting to date again?" Lucy asked. "Honey, I'm not one to say yay or nay but ..."

"No, it's ... it's not that. It's just something ... family related."

A hand on the shoulder now, making Karen tense up even more. God, she did not want to crack in front of anyone else. She'd worked too hard over the last eleven plus months, put too much into building up her facade, for it to shatter now.

"Have you been talking to your dad?" Lucy asked.

"In a manner of speaking."

Still holding onto a faint vestige of loyalty, keeping in mind that his request of the night before had been out of concern, possibly even love.

"Well, that's good."

Christ, now Lucy has completely confused the issue. Her heart's in the right place, but right about now I just wish she'd back the hell off.

In the next instant, Lucy gave her the opening she needed.

"Listen, kid. It seems like it's going to be pretty light today. Why don't you say the hell with it and take off?"

"Actually, if you think it'll be okay ..."

"Sure. Middle of the week and all that. We've both been around this racket long enough to know that things don't get really hopping till 'round about Thursday night."

"Okay," Karen said, finally able to look her boss in the eye. "But how about I get these spreadsheets done for you first?"

"Suit yourself." Lucy turned to leave Karen to her work. At the door, she turned back briefly.

"Just make sure you're out of here by noon, latest. That's an order."

"Promise. Hey, Luce?"

"Yeah?"

"Has anyone seen or heard anything out of Ricky since yesterday?"

"Ricky? The little red-headed kid that took off the other day?"

"Yeah. Hide or hair of him?"

"Not as far as I know. But if you want, I can ask around."

"Please. And I promise. Noon tops."

Winking at her employee, Lucy left the office. Only then did Karen manage to focus on the work in front of her.

Chapter Eleven

"So what's your thinking?"

Jared lifted his head up from his computer screen and glanced at his news director. He hadn't heard her come around the corner.

"Who took this film?" he asked.

"Lynda Curtis, our new hire. Claims that video tape isn't her thing, but since she's just starting here ..."

"Yeah, I know."

Even after all these years, Jared could still remember his first six months in the business, in a nondescript town down in Oklahoma, where he'd done almost every task around the newsroom, including fetching coffee and donuts for the late night crew. One weekend, even, it had taken some quick fabricating on his part to get out of serving as the station manager's caddy during a charity golf gig.

Crappy as all those tasks were, none of them had equated to something as gory as this.

"Angle isn't very good," he said.

"The cops were doing their best to keep her back. Same reason the *New Post* didn't get much in the way of pictures."

"Makes me wonder," Jared said.

"You mean, like what's so special or secretive about some old bag lady being killed down in the Zone? Why's that such a hush-hush matter?"

Jared glanced away from Barb and back to the images on his screen.

"Yeah," he said, "like that."

"Well, it is the second one like this in less than a week," she said.

"Maybe." He could hear the lack of conviction in his own voice.

"Yeah?"

"The second found," Jared said. "But scuttlebutt around City Hall says that there's a fair number of street folks who have gone missing lately."

"That right?"

"True." He looked away from her and back down to the computer. "And most of them, way the rumors go, are the old and indigent. Just like these two."

"You're saying there may be a lot more bodies bobbing around somewhere?"

"Maybe," Jared said with a shrug. "But people get it down there all the time. In all sorts of ways. One of my sources said that they're thinking this could be nothing more than some new gang initiation thing."

His boss moved away and plopped herself down into a black leather chair next to his desk. She pulled off one of her shoes and began rubbing her foot.

"Barely even noon," she said, "and I'm already aching. Went out last week and bought what the saleslady assured me were sneakers with the most cushioning soles on the market. But after five hours of running around here I feel like a gangster's about to drop me in the lake."

"They don't do that anymore," Jared said.

"You know what I mean."

Jared sighed, rubbed his face, and turned away from his desk to stare at Barb straight on.

"If it's just a gang thing, the cops would have no reason to keep quiet."

"Unless," Barb said, "it's something new and especially vicious. Something that not even the feds, let alone the locals, can get a handle on."

"There could be that," he replied. "Couple people I talked to today, it sounded like they were describing some kind of horror movie."

"How so?"

"Well," he paused, trying, but failing, to think of an artful way to phrase it. "I heard a couple times the idea that this old lady, and maybe the other man, had been bitten."

"Bitten?"

Jared took a deep breath, then threw it right at her.

"Actually, chewed on."

Barb was pro enough that she didn't faint or get sick at the idea, but she sank back into the chair.

"Pretty much rules out a coincidence, then," she said.

"Unless we have two weirdoes running around with the same – ah – fetish."

"So what do we know for sure?" Barb asked.

He picked up a pen and began twirling it in his fingers.

"Seems pretty obvious, from visual evidence if nothing else, that there's some sort of link between the two incidents."

"One would think."

"And even if the two murders end up being random," he drawled at about half speed so his thoughts could keep up with his speech, "how would they know that yet? Wouldn't they assume the worst?"

"I would think so."

"Which means they're suspecting a connection."

"Be kind of hard," Barb said, "not to think so."

Jared put his pen down and looked back at his boss.

"Think we're going in the same direction, Barb. Either real or imagined, the cops may be thinking one of two ways. Either it's some new kind of vicious street gang ..."

"Not exactly unheard of."

"Or we've got a really nutso serial killer roaming around down there."

Barb stood up and leaned over his desk, tapping her finger on the computer screen, frozen to show a slide of the old lady's body, seemingly torn to ribbons.

"Either way," she said, "if this is how it's starting out, what's it going to look like when it escalates?"

Chapter Twelve

Karen had no intention of going home after leaving the shelter shortly before eleven, but before heading to her intended destination she stopped off first to see David.

She turned into the long, circled gravel driveway, feeling her breath catch as it did every time she entered the grounds. She'd made her weekly visit just a few days before on Monday afternoon, yet even so she experienced her normal reaction as she pulled up into the section of the parking lot marked "Visitors."

Like hell, she thought. *As often as I come here, I'm practically a resident myself.*

She chided herself almost instantly. No doubt the events of last night were responsible for her internal churlishness, but that wasn't much of an excuse. In truth, she considered as she got out of the car and locked her door, she almost felt as if she'd taken a step over some invisible boundary, one that divided the everyday world from one lacking either light or hope, the world she'd inhabited ever since she'd lost her man.

But today the sun was out, and as she bypassed the main building and made her way down a flagstone path, pausing a moment to wave at a gray-haired groundskeeper pruning bushes, she could almost imagine herself taking a late morning stroll through a city park.

At least until turning around a bend in the path and coming upon the first row of headstones.

The grounds, here at one of the most exclusive memorial gardens in the state, were laid out in such a way that from any given point you could only see a dozen or so plots at one time, an arrangement that would force the occasional visitor to stop by the main building for directions.

But Karen had been here so often in the last eleven months that she knew her way by heart, and could probably find it blindfolded.

In no time at all, she knelt down in front of David's plot.

In life, her fiancé had been a chemistry teacher from a middle-class background; neither he nor his family could have afforded a plot on these grounds.

His death had been full of ironies, his final resting place one of the more minor ones.

Karen sat down cross-legged next to his stone and began talking. She didn't follow a particular theme, instead free associating whatever came into her head. She mentioned trouble she'd been having with her car, a maxed-out Visa card which she could not manage to pay down, and the latest goings on at the shelter. She talked for a bit about Ricky, who she still worried about, and remarked on how tense and tired her dad had looked the night before.

Then, eventually, she got around to the matter of the old woman's body.

"It looked like a dog attack to me, hon. Not that I've ever seen someone ravaged by dogs, but considering that part of town, and the fact that the wounds, at least what I saw, looked too small to be rats, I figured it for dogs. But what do I know? From the way Dad acted, I'd have to guess that he has a pretty good idea of who—or what—killed her but for some reason couldn't come out and say so. Nothing much changes, does it?"

She cocked her head to the right, as if listening to his response. A rational young woman, she knew that you couldn't actually talk to the dead and have them talk back, but the man represented by that stone had been her life for nearly five years, and even while realizing the inherent falseness of her actions, she got some peace from making believe that he was there to help her work through her problems.

"Yeah, that's what I thought," she told the stone after a few minutes. "It's probably nothing more than a desire to keep things tamped down for the press. After all, we just had that arson spree what, last year? Can you imagine what the media would do with another serial criminal running loose?"

She paused again, pretending to listen to some comment of his. Then, just as she opened her mouth to reply, an elderly woman came around the bend that sheltered this row of plots from the outside world. Although gray and wrinkled, she walked upright and with the gait of someone at least thirty years younger. When she came within sight of Karen, the old woman nodded, smiled, and walked past her to a grave five spaces to the left of David's.

Only when she stopped in front of the tombstone did Karen notice the small handful of tulips that she held in her hand.

Not wanting to intrude on someone else's time, Karen rose to her feet and, stopping to place her hand briefly on the top of David's stone, turned and headed back to the parking lot.

Even though cut short, the visit had bolstered her a little bit, and now she was ready for the next item on her itinerary.

Chapter Thirteen

After the cemetery, Karen headed home. She spent the afternoon checking her mail and tidying up her place a bit before slipping into a faded, cracked leather jacket.

When she'd dressed for work that morning, she'd put on her usual attire of jeans, sneakers, and tee shirt. It was something that Lucy had pointed out to her on her first day of working at the shelter: do your best to dress down so you don't intimidate the residents, but don't give the condescending impression that you're deliberately trying to fit into their world. Find a happy medium and stick to it.

But now, intending to spend at least one more evening looking for Ricky down in the Zone, she wanted to blend in as much as possible.

And if she didn't find him, the law of diminishing returns said it would be time to give it up and move on.

Her initial attempts had been far from her first forays into the city's poorest area. Generally, her trips to the city's most wretched section formed two distinct patterns.

When she went with other workers from the shelter, they did a normal day's business. Distributing food, handing out small cards with the shelter's phone number on them, and urging any stray, solitary females to come with them and get somewhere safe. But over the last few years, and especially since David's passing, Karen had found herself heading down here more and more on her own, most often looking for a particular former resident she had concerns about.

So Ricky, with his red hair and dark blue ski vest, was far from her first stray. But she did worry about him more than most of the others.

However, by the time she'd parked her car in an all-night lot about ten blocks from the outer edges of the Zone, Karen could admit to herself that she had another, even more ambiguous goal in mind on this night.

She had never trained as an investigator. An MA in social work and years of experience handing out fliers, working soup kitchens, and lobbying in the state capital hardly qualified her for any sort of detective work.

During her college years, Karen and her dad had had more than one dinner table argument about the causes and potential solutions of poverty in general and homelessness in particular. Back then, filled with the zest and textbook idealism of her university classes, Karen had often seen the old man as a stuck-in-the-last-century, right-wing troglodyte.

But that was then, when she was a still-untested youth. Now, after years on the streets, she'd come to believe that many of her father's positions back then had been realistic, rather than clichéd. Over the last few years, whenever the two of them had talked politics, Karen had seen just how similar she and her father saw things.

Up until last year, when David had passed on. That one night had done more to rip asunder Karen and Leo's relationship than any amount of arguing over politics and the poor. She knew, dammit, that what had happened wasn't her father's fault. How could it be? When it came right down to it, you couldn't even blame the poor sap who had pulled the trigger, blasting her boyfriend into the hereafter.

But by proxy the captain had become the symbol of first her grief, then her rage.

And things had never been the same between them, and most likely never would be again.

****

So now here she stood, on the fringe of the Zone, less than twenty-four hours after possibly the second most horrific night of her life. Had anyone asked, she would have told them that she was here on a quest to find a young boy who'd returned to the streets after a brief stint in a homeless shelter.

But there was more to it than that, even if she couldn't adequately verbalize

First, though, she had to deal with the two men staggering her way.

"Hey there," the one on Karen's right called out. A tall, scrawny scarecrow of a figure in an open, flapping black coat that seemed about a size too large for him, he shifted a bit from foot to foot as he advanced. He also held out his hand in a somewhat supplicating gesture.

"Do you think," he continued, "that you could see your way through to spotting me a few bills?"

From experience, Karen figured that his use of the word "me" wasn't accidental. He no doubt wanted her to focus on him as a single person. At the same time his stumbling buddy, an average-looking man with dirty blond hair, an old-fashioned denim jacket and brown corduroys, had swerved somewhat to the left, fading out of Karen's direct line of sight while moving in on her from the side.

Her breath caught in her throat, and she felt ice flowing down her extremities. Worrying about Ricky had preoccupied her so much that she hadn't noticed that this portion of the block lay empty except for her and the two men.

"A few bills?" the one in front of her repeated, his voice firmer than before.

"Sorry," Karen said, working her throat muscles to keep her own tone controlled, "but I don't have that much money on me."

By now, the guy to her side had shifted so far that he stood on the verge of leaving her peripheral vision altogether.

"Aw come on, miss. Surely you can spare just a little."

Karen took an almost imperceptible step back, working to keep both men in her line of sight. Out of the corner of her eye, she caught the slightest flicker of concern cross the face of the second man.

"I'm really sorry," she said, her right hand sliding out of her jacket pocket. "But I really have to be going."

The tall guy in front centered himself and let his hands hang loose, as if expecting her to try to surge past him. Just the move she wanted. Instead Karen did about a ninety degree turn, her left foot positioned flat and heel forward jamming out towards the side man.

She intended to impact on his crotch, but her aim was off and instead she took him on the front thigh, about two inches above the knee cap. Not the blow she wanted, but powerful enough to cause him to gulp and slump to the sidewalk.

The problem, Karen knew, was that he would be up and at her in only a matter of seconds, so she continued her turn, by this point doing a near three-sixty with her right hand, keys gripped and jutting out from the knuckles, striking into the tall guy's neck.

Not his face, as most self-defense instructors would tell women to do. The man's height put his eyes, the only really vulnerable spot on the face, out of Karen's reach. But as she lunged just a bit forward, his neck proved a nice, wide target, and her keys snapped into the area just above his clavicle.

"Urghh!" The bastard stumbled back, hand flying to his neck. Karen hadn't come close to dealing him a killing blow, but judging by the sudden bugging out of his eyes the guy probably felt the complete opposite.

She stopped her circular motion to take a breath, bringing both feet flat on the ground. A mistake, though. And she knew it a fraction of an instant later when the smaller guy, by now recovered, grabbed her from behind, encircling her throat with his forearm and bringing down enough pressure to cut off her wind.

If anything, the adrenaline coursing its way through her system amped itself up even higher as she slid her hand into her jacket pocket, the left one this time, and brought out an old-fashioned, but still serviceable, switchblade.

Karen snapped the blade open and jammed it into her attacker's thigh in nearly the same instant, causing the man to let out his own scream, release his arm from around her neck and stumble backwards, groaning to no end. Unfortunately, he jerked away from her with such force and at such an angle that he took her knife, still embedded in his thigh muscle, with him. She let it go despite her attachment to the blade, a gift from an old boyfriend in college during a time of rumors about a campus rapist.

Figuring her safety more important than an old memento, she whipped back around to see the first man, the taller one, hobbling to his feet. He looked at Karen and, evidently seeing something in her that he didn't want to deal with, turned and ran.

Leaving their "victim" to deal with the aftermath.

Which hit her as soon as both men had fled from sight. Her stomach roiling, Karen leaned against the nearest wall and held her hand to her chest. Her legs shook, but only for a minute, and she managed to calm her breathing down. She noticed that several street people had reappeared, most of them no doubt having vanished when they noticed the two men accosting her, and while a few of them gave her short looks, most ignored her.

Pushing away from the wall, Karen straightened up, and took one last, cleansing breath. Feeling almost human, though her stomach still bothered her, she turned and headed back in the direction of the garage where she'd parked her car.

She hadn't done hardly anything towards locating Ricky, but she figured she'd had enough excitement for one night.

Not long ago, she'd started off filled with energy and righteous indignation; now she wanted only to get home, start a fire, and curl up in a blanket with a cup of hot chocolate.

Unfortunately, the streets held other plans for her.

Chapter Fourteen

Three nights now away from that homeless place, and his stomach had begun giving him fits. He'd managed to scrounge a little food in the last few days, but very little. A couple of cold Pop-Tarts, a bag or two of potato chips, and two candy bars he'd managed to snag when a C-store clerk was busy checking out the boobs on a girl leaning over his counter. Enough to fill the stomach, but nothing in the way of actual nutrition to keep the body moving.

A minute ago, a cop car had come cruising down the street, so Ricky had ducked into a handy alley and melded himself into the shadows, keeping still until the cruiser turned a corner and headed off into the distance.

He started to step out from the alley, but something made him stop, pulled him back.

The kid stood there in the gloom, using his eyes and ears as much as he could, trying to figure out what had caused his hesitation. Something, he didn't for sure know what, had gotten through to some layer of his mind.

The shadowy alley behind him seemed quiet, and the street beyond looked no different than any lane in any slum he'd ever seen.

It was dark now, but not yet the time of night where everything seems stilled. There was still movement on the asphalt: a hooker stood on each corner; nearly every doorway had its own huddled shadow, in some cases two; and a scattered handful of geezers, most of them probably too far gone to even know what city they were in, staggered up and down the sidewalks. It all looked normal.

At least, by Ricky's standards.

So what had caught his attention? What tenuous impression had he picked up on that caused him to stop and wait?

In the next instant, it came to him.

Breathing.

Behind him, he heard numerous short, shallow breaths, the kind of brief sipping sound that happened with someone doing their best to hold their breath but every now and then having to suck in just enough air to keep going.

And he didn't hear one such sound, but several.

With the street seeming the safest of all possible places, Ricky turned so that he faced into the maw of the alley, his back to the outer environment. He peered as hard as he could into the blackness but could see nothing but shifting, shapeless shadows. And now that he faced the interior it seemed as if the breath noises came louder, more pronounced.

Now came the slightest of scraping sounds, probably sneaker soles scuffing against dirty asphalt. Ricky began backing out, easing himself into the comparative light of the street scene. Then, as he felt the dim glow of an overhead light filter down onto him, a low, muttered growling emanated from the alley.

He turned sideways and bolted onto the sidewalk, almost knocking down an old bag lady trundling a shopping cart.

He dodged away from the woman, but managed to slam into the cart, spilling its contents onto the ground. Assorted rags, crumpled up soda cans, newspapers and boxes of half-chewed donuts scurried all over the sidewalk.

The old woman began shrieking, while a couple of drunks slouched on a stoop started cackling in their slurred, drunken manner. Ricky picked himself up, wringing his palms, which he'd scraped raw in breaking his fall. The old woman struggled with her cart, seeking to right it while continuing to screech at him. Then, from somewhere within the confines of her cart the old witch found an unopened can of soup, hefted it up, and let it fly at his head.

Ducking, he gave up his momentary impulse to help clean up from his accident and started hurtling down the street, seeking to get as far away from both the old gal and whatever had been stalking him in that alley.

Where he was heading didn't matter. Ricky just knew that he was getting away from something he didn't even want to try to imagine.

Chapter Fifteen

Home. Not the plushest of places, considering the kind of domiciles that most of her friends had by this point in their lives, but it worked for her.

As Karen entered her apartment she stopped, one foot over the threshold, and listened. She'd picked up the trick from one of her dad's detectives, a woman who'd spent two years working the Rape Squad. That was back in the day, of course.

Back in the days when she and her father had spoken on a regular basis.

Before David.

A single woman, the fortyish brunette had informed her, should never, but never simply walk into her home, especially if arriving there after dark. Instead, if her place didn't come equipped with a security system, she should open the door, pause just inside and count. Only a step in, easily within range of turning and fleeing. That way, if someone was waiting inside for you, the action of opening the door would cause them to set themselves, shifting a bit and gathering their breaths for action, and that slight amount of movement would be enough to signal to an alert person, giving them time to get away to safety.

For Karen it had become a fixed habit upon returning home.

A pause, count to twenty, and nothing she could detect. So she stepped all the way inside, turned on the lights, and closed the door behind her.

And wondered, as she did at least a couple of times a week, if she didn't go through the little pantomime as a way of forestalling, even for a few seconds, the memories.

Maybe it was the nearness of her encounter of the streets, or her distress at losing the kid from the shelter.

Maybe it was seeing her dad the night before. Although neither of them had mentioned his name, David's presence had loomed before them, presenting a nearly-impassable barrier between the two of them.

Or maybe it was just a Wednesday night, a little after ten, and the time had come to once again mourn a dead fiancé.

Whatever the reason, the various pictures, furnishings, and bits and pieces he'd left loomed prominent tonight, almost a physical assault reminding Karen of how much he'd meant to her and what a gaping wound his death had left.

From across the room, she spotted the subdued blinking of her answering machine.

And she could guess who those blinks represented. Whenever he tried to contact her, he always did so at home, never on her cell. Probably figuring that at home it wouldn't be so easy to feign an excuse not to talk.

Sighing, she kicked her shoes off, walked over, and punched the button.

"Hey, baby." As expected, her father's voice floated out of the machine. "I don't think we left it very well last night, know what I mean? It's a little after three now. I'm not sure what time you'll get home, but I've got some reports I have to get ready for the chief tomorrow, so I'll be burning the oil till sometime after midnight. Why don't you give me a call when you get in, okay? We really need to talk, honey. After you left it occurred to me that we haven't really talked since ..."

The machine cut him off at that point, but Karen knew what he'd wanted to say. Ever since the night Karen had sat in that hard, red plastic chair at the hospital, listening to a faceless, nameless uniform explaining what had happened, Karen and her father hadn't had a real, grownup conversation.

Sighing once more, she went into the kitchen and made herself a rum and Coke, then carried the drink back out into the living room.

She hadn't bothered to reset the machine or turn on the lights, and in the gloom that bright red light continued to flash.

****

Such a bright red, not dark but vivid. Much like the color of that horrid chair at the hospital. She'd been sitting there for hours, body slumping as if all of her emotional cords had been severed. Naturally, in the middle of a major hospital, activity had flurried all around her. Civilians and medical personnel bustled up and down the hall; machines beeped; metallic objects clanged; and the elevator pinged as it opened to embark or debark new passengers, all of it whirling around Karen in one monotone, indistinct buzz of sound.

With her eyes cast forever down on the tri-colored tile floor, the caulk between the tiles begrimed from years of hasty cleanings, no doubt done in the few quiet minutes in between always-swirling chaos, Karen became oblivious to the sights of her environment. But she could have, with no effort, pictured the whites, dove grays, and muted blues that hued almost every object in the corridor. Everything soft and sterile, save for the caulk between those floor tiles.

And, of course, that abominable scarlet chair.

From numerous visits doing work for the shelter, Karen knew what everything around her looked like.

None of it mattered, though. The few times that she lifted her gaze from the floor she did so only far enough to focus on the swinging doors at the end of the hall. Before she'd arrived, they'd taken David through those doors. At that door, as she'd attempted in a fit of momentary insanity to force her way through, a uniformed cop had met her and, his fingers digging into her elbow to force acquiescence, guided her halfway down the hall to the red plastic chair.

By the time they reached the chair, her mind had begun to slowly work again, and Karen knew that she had to keep quiet and out of the way until the doctors could do their work.

Because somewhere on the other side of those swinging doors, her fiancé lay fighting for his life, three bullets in his chest.

****

Eleven months prior, and to this day she could barely stand to hear her father's voice, even as a recording. Her reaction, both to police in general and good ol' Leo in particular, was about as irrational as they came. Karen knew that, and she understood that time was supposed to heal and all that yuck, all of which didn't change anything.

For better or worse (a catch in her throat at that inappropriate choice of thoughts), that was how she felt about it.

Hungry, exhausted, and still nerve-wracked from her encounter earlier in the night, Karen punched the button that deleted the message.

Chapter Sixteen

Ed Gleason hung up the phone, wondering for about the tenth time this month why a man with his seniority had to man the night shift. Rationally, he knew the answer. Standard departmental policy had all the detectives doing a rotating system of shifts. On paper they were supposed to follow the system to the letter. In practice, between illnesses, family events, and in the case of at least one Robbery detective, just plain laziness and incompetence, the actual schedule would look like a patchwork quilt that the dog had chewed apart if someone printed it out as a spreadsheet.

So for the last few weeks Gleason had had the honor of manning the homicide desk between the hours of three and midnight. Not by himself, of course. A city of this size usually had a contingent of around ten men assigned to homicides. The problem was, from Gleason's point of view, that the H squad had to do at least a cursory rundown of *any* suspicious deaths in the metro area.

Like these weirdo attacks that seemed to have sprung up out of nowhere.

A sharp "clack" caught his ear, and Gleason looked up to see Tim O'Brien, his nominal partner for the moment, crossing the narrow dividing rail that separated the H area from the rest of the detectives' floor. Tim had slammed the gate a little harder than necessary, and one look at his face told Gleason why.

"Another false alarm?" he asked his partner.

O'Brien grimaced, then slumped his shoulders a bit.

"Third one this month," he said as he plunked himself down at his desk.

"Damn, guy. If you're this tuned up now, what are you going to be like when the kid actually pops?"

"Damned if I know," O'Brien said as he began glancing through the various slips of phone messages arrayed on his desk. "All I know is that, in our golden years, when I need to be swiped and swabbed, I hope Crystal appreciates the hell she's put me through for the last eight months."

Gleason grinned and leaned back in his chair.

"Look on the bright side," he said. "At least you were out of the room when the latest call from Bannister came in."

The younger detective's face tightened.

"He still on our case?" he asked.

"Yup. I've been on the force for nearly fifteen years, eight of them in this very room. You know how many times I've had the C of D's nosing into a case of mine? Let alone telling me how to run the investigation?"

O'Brien, having sorted through all the missives, flipped the entire pile back onto his desk.

"I'm guessing this is the first time?"

"Second time, actually. First was about six years back when some looney took a pop at the mayor."

"But on this animal thing, whatever the hell it is, he's been at us from minute one," O'Brien said.

"Yeah."

Unspoken between the two men was the other night, when Captain Bannister took the rare action of having one of his men transport Bannister's daughter to his office for some sort of secret meeting.

"Even more," said O'Brien, "is him wanting us to keep on it. Hell, it's just a pack of dogs, or rats or something. Why doesn't he get Animal Control on it and let us get back to real work?"

"Maybe because there's some question about the actual facts. And with all the rumors running wild …"

"Oh for God's sake. You really think that there's some new kind of super gang trying to kill off all the bums in the city?"

"Not necessarily. Could just be some schizoid with an oddly-shaped knife out there doing a number on winos."

"The hell it could, Ed. I grew up the same as that clerk we talked to the other night. Been all over this state hunting with my dad and uncles. Those wounds we saw were bite marks. On both victims. I don't care what Doc Whatisname says. He can talk about ritual knives or whatever all he wants. My money says we've got a pack of animals running loose in this town, and for some reason, which I just don't get, the C of D's doesn't want to admit it."

"Or the coroner," Gleason said.

O'Brien's brow furrowed.

"He hasn't gotten back to us with a final report yet?'

"Exactly what I'm saying. I called to check up again while you were out holding Crystal's hand. And he has, and I quote 'nothing definite yet' unquote."

The two men regarded each other, smudges under their eyes proof of their weariness.

Few words could express how the two men felt, but the few that could seemed to say it all.

"Ed," O'Brien asked the older, more experienced man, "what the hell is going on out there?"

Chapter Seventeen

Early in the next evening, crouched at her small desk, Karen looked up to see the two men coming her way. Recognizing them at once, she turned away and continued talking into the phone.

"No," she repeated for the third time. "Two hundred loaves won't cut it. That will barely get us through two weeks. We need at least three hundred loaves on the next shipment."

She listened then, as the person on the other end responded. Out of the corner of her eye she watched as the two detectives came up and stood within a few feet of her desk. From what she'd seen of the city's squad rooms, this partitioned-off area of the shelter that served as everybody's office space, replete with tacky wall calendars, sticky floor, and gunmetal-gray desks requisitioned years ago from some ancient government office, probably made the two men feel right at home.

Turning a bit farther away from them, Karen intended to lessen that feeling as much as possible.

"Look," she finally got her chance, "I understand that you're new down there, and I hope everything's okay with Mike's wife and their newborn, but I simply have to have a more than adequate supply of bread."

She paused again to listen, rolling her eyes at the ceiling and hoping that the two cops were getting bored.

She really didn't want to talk to them again. She'd told them everything she knew two days ago, with that old woman's body lying on the sidewalk not fifty feet away. Between that memory and worrying about Ricky, who still hadn't shown up, Karen had barely been able to keep anything down the last few days.

The near assault last night down in the Zone, which she hadn't bothered to report, hadn't helped matters.

"Because we don't have a fixed population," she raised her voice into the phone. "Some months we use a hundred loaves, others four hundred. And since we can't predict how much we'll need, primarily on weekends, we need to ... what?"

Karen swiveled in her chair and mouthed to the two detectives that she'd be right with them. What had begun as a deliberate attempt to make them wait had now turned into a snare that she couldn't escape.

"That's right. Some days we have a few dozen in here, and sometimes a hundred ... Yes, that does mean that we sometimes have to throw old food out, but it's not as often as you might think ... Okay, then, so you'll be able to scrounge up three hundred? Fine. Thank you very much."

Hanging up the phone, Karen puffed her cheeks in frustration, then motioned the two cops to sit.

With only one chair in front of her desk, and that a rather rickety old lawn chair, the smaller of the two, O'Brien, sat while Gleason remained standing.

"What can I do for you gentlemen?" Karen asked.

"Miss Bannister," Gleason began, "we're sorry to bother you, but we have a few more questions about your experience the other night."

"By experience I assume you mean finding an old woman slashed nearly to shreds?"

The bitchiness of her tone made Karen ashamed. Dammit, would she ever start considering cops as normal people?

"Yes, ma'am, the ... body you found."

"Me and those two men."

"Yes, you and those street fellows. But you're the one we need to talk to."

"Why?"

"Excuse me?" out of O'Brien's mouth.

"Why me? Why not track down the others and re-interview them? The taller one could probably tell you as much as I could. We got to that alley almost at the same time, and he was the first inside."

"Yes, we know. But ..."

"Way I see it," Karen interrupted, "there's two possible reasons, apart from possibly pawning a cup of free coffee, that you would prefer talking to me. One is that you consider a street person an unreliable witness. After all, they're all drunks and stoners, right? Except for the gangbangers?"

"Now hold on ..."

"Or is it that you considered, me being the daughter of a captain and all, that I'd be more inclined to help out? If that's the case, I'm guessing my dad didn't tell you a whole lot about me."

For the last few seconds, she'd watched Gleason keeping one eye on her while casting the other around the shelter space. Half turning, he reached out for a small camp chair folded up next to a desk and unfolded it.

As he did so, for just an instant his jacket flapped open enough that Karen could glimpse his service gun clipped to his belt in its holster. She gritted her teeth, receiving a flash image of David's body ripped apart by bullets from a similar weapon.

A real similar weapon.

The image faded almost as soon as it came, as they often did, but its afterimage lingered on a layer of her vision.

A second later, Gleason had arranged himself next to his partner, who gave him a quizzical look before turning back to Karen.

"Actually, Miss Bannister, we know about your ... feelings ... towards the department. Even so, we wanted to talk to you before we went back down to the Zone."

Karen leaned back in her chair and looked closer at the two men. Somewhere behind them, in the common room, a couple of male voices started yelling, one heavily cursing the other. Karen didn't even bother glancing that way. Disputes, usually verbal but sometimes more aggravated, were common enough in any place housing transients. But they never lasted long. If nothing else, one or two professional bar bouncers were always hanging around to donate their services.

Sure enough, after two or three rapid fire exchanges, the voices quieted down.

"What do you mean by going back to the Zone?" Karen asked.

"Well, naturally we need to gather more information. And we thought it would be helpful to get as much insight as possible from someone familiar with the area."

"But you have cops who patrol, don't you? I met a couple of them the other night, so I know they're out and about, even if you'd hardly know it judging by the crime rates down there." Karen paused, taking a breath to keep her voice from screeching. "So why come to me? And besides, isn't this something for animal control?"

The two detectives glanced at each other, and while Gleason stayed impassive, Karen thought that she would love some time to play poker with O'Brien. Between the tightening of his jaw and the frown lines appearing, she could guess at the emotions running through him.

"Let's just say," again from Gleason, "that we're concerned about some stuff going down there, and that we'd like to have some inside info. Sure, we have officers patrolling, and even a few detectives, our grungier types, who can fade into the scenery down there to some extent."

"But they're still made as cops in no time at all, right?" Karen asked.

"Yeah. Not quite sure how that happens, but ..."

"It happens because you're not dealing with a bunch of idiots, public perception to the contrary."

"Ma'am?"

"Detective," Karen sighed, "could we please just cut the shit? Lately, there's a flock of wild tales rushing through the Zone. I personally haven't decided which one is more realistic, but the mere possibility that a number of people have disappeared off the streets, even if it's people that not many care about, should cause you guys to take some action."

"We're trying to, ma'am, but it's kind of difficult when the folks out there have their own problems, which you don't seem to want to acknowledge."

"I didn't say that they don't have problems, but no matter what form those problems take, most of them have come up with some sort of coping mechanism. Some way to conceptualize how they perceive the world in order to survive. If you're planning on spending any amount of time down there, you've got to understand that. Those people see all, hear all and, in their own unique way, know all. Got it?"

"Yes, we do," Gleason said, "and what you're saying is even more reason we could use your help. What do you say?"

"My help? In what way?"

"Well, we were wondering if you would mind going down there with us for a while. Being sort of a guide as we go about our work?"

From the corner of her eye, Karen saw Lucy motioning towards her.

"Excuse me, gentlemen. I think someone needs me for a moment."

She got up, angling herself through the cramped space that now included her desk and the two seated detectives, and made her way across the common area to where Lucy waited.

"You want me to get rid of them?" her boss said as Karen came abreast of her.

"What?"

"Those two." Lucy cocked her head back towards Karen's desk. "I know how you get around cops, and if they're bothering you ..."

"No," she said, "that's okay. But I may have to take off for a few hours, if that's alright."

Lucy peered at her, giving her an intense once over perfected by years of vagrants wandering into the shelter and looking for trouble. Her instincts, honed by years of dealing with society's lowest, were rarely wrong.

"This have to do with that old woman the other night?"

"I think so," Karen said, "but it's kind of weird. They act like they want my help, but I don't quite see with what."

"They think there's something you can do that they can't on their own?"

Karen shrugged.

"I guess. At least, that's what it looked like. But they seem worried about something else."

"Think your dad knows that they're down here hassling you?"

"They're not hassling me, Lucy." Standing up for the two detectives gave Karen an unsettled feeling. It seemed disrespectful to David's memory. But that was rather nuts. Neither one of the two still sitting, patiently waiting, at her desk had had anything to do with David's killing, so why not stick up for them?

Even so, rational or not, that squirmy feeling was there.

"Okay, kid," Lucy said, "do whatever you think's right. But just remember that we've got a lot of work to do here, and you don't owe those two a damned thing."

"Gotcha."

"Far as that goes, from what I've heard, they could just send out a few experts from the zoo, surround the area with a SWAT team or two, and have it over and done with."

"Search me," Karen said, "but I'll tell you this. I'm willing to do my civic duty, but only for a day or so. Beyond that, they'll have to find another patsy."

Lucy patted her on the shoulder as Karen turned to go back to her desk. The two men had stood up, awaiting her return, but she decided to make them wait a bit longer.

"You need to give me a few minutes," she said, sitting back down. "If I'm going out for a while, there's some phone calls I have to make first."

Gleason and O'Brien looked at each other, and Karen wondered what was going on in those two heads.

"Also," Karen continued, "if I'm going to spend my time helping you guys, I need something in return."

Now the cops exchanged wary glances.

"Such as what?" Gleason asked.

"Your help finding a missing kid."

"Missing kid?" Gleason glanced around the shelter, fairly quiet in the middle of the day. It didn't at all resemble the absolute madhouse that it turned into most nights by around ten or so.

"You mean missing from here?" O'Brien asked.

"That's right," Karen replied.

"Miss Bannister, we're not missing persons. We're ..."

"I know how the police department is organized, Detective." It came out a bit sharper than she'd intended. "And I also know that you can put in a few words, ask for a few favors, to help move something along. Right?"

"We can. As long as it doesn't distract us from our main job."

"Good enough."

But Karen took a few minutes to clear up the loose ends on her desk, unsure if she'd heard the truth yet, of just what the two of them really wanted from her.

Chapter Eighteen

The body lying on the sterile table in front of him was that of a young girl, surely no more than nineteen. Though with the obvious cause of death having wrecked so much damage, his estimate could be off by as much as several years.

The EMT's had brought the body in nearly an hour ago, yet Lewis Preston had barely begun the procedure. He'd managed to complete the basic measurements and note the basal characteristics: gender, hair and eye color, etc.

He'd also made a preliminary note, not that anyone would ever care, that she was not a virgin.

Beyond that, Preston hadn't done much beyond standing beside the table and staring down at her form.

It seemed that lately his job, here in its closing weeks, had become more political than ever. The girl lying on the slab a prime example.

He could think of absolutely no reason to perform an autopsy, except that the family had insisted on it. You didn't need to cut her open to know what had killed her. At a glance, any reasonably experienced high school sophomore would know what had done her in.

From the gray, chalky skin, pocked with scabby sores from where she had clawed herself, to the rotting, blackened stumps of her teeth, Preston had taken one look at her and categorized her as just the latest in the long line of meth cadavers marching their way through the lab day in and day out.

When the order had come down a few hours ago to do a full post mortem on the kid, Preston had called upstairs to protest, knowing as he did so that it wouldn't do any good. Medical examiners at the top of their game had clout and position, while those with one foot out the retirement door were barely acknowledged or noticed.

Sighing, he picked up an instrument and reached up to adjust the flex-mounted overhead light. In doing so, his gaze lifted and he caught sight of the row of refrigerated bunkers, stainless steel like nearly everything else here in his little kingdom, and paused again.

Preston understood where his uneasy feeling stemmed from.

Politics again.

The third bunker from the right, second row from the top, contained the corpse of an old bag lady brought in two nights ago. The second in less than a week, her body had been gnawed on and partially gobbled, same as the old man before her.

And, just like that first death, Dr. Lewis Preston had been ordered to keep it quiet.

Not to keep the death under wraps. They had neither reason nor possibility of that. But he had received the body early in the morning of the previous day, and even before he'd begun entering the basic stats he'd been visited by his old friend, Capt. Leo Bannister.

****

Actually, you couldn't really count them as friends. Working for a major city wasn't like they showed on TV, where the same two or three detectives, lawyers, and ME's kept showing up on each other's cases. Didn't work that way, though over the span of years you tended to get to know some people better than others. Preston knew Bannister on a casual basis. In the old days they'd probably interacted with each other at least a couple of times a month, much less since Bannister had been promoted up to C of D's.

So it had been quite unexpected a few mornings back, technically morning though still quite dark out, when Lewis had looked up from his table and seen Bannister coming through the swinging doors.

The man had not looked all that well.

It had been months since anything had drawn Bannister down to the morgue. As a captain he spent most of his time behind a desk, so his appearance took Preston by surprise. A few weeks away from mandatory retirement, Preston had about ten years on the captain, yet placed side by side Bannister would, if anything, look five years older.

Preston guessed that something more than the normal strain of his job had aged the cop. And no doubt what had happened nearly a year ago to his prospective son-in-law had done its share. Not just a secret shared by city employees, the whole town knew what had taken place in that convenience store. Preston could only assume that the cop's relationship with his daughter had been, at the least, strained by what had happened.

Even so, it had surprised him when Bannister had asked to see the preliminary report, even though he had the right. Even more surprising, though in hindsight it made sense, the captain had asked the medical examiner to keep quiet about the results of the PM.

Bannister had asked, instead of ordering, because he didn't have any direct authority over the coroner's office, but the intent came across all the same.

Twenty minutes into the old man's autopsy, Preston had gotten a glimmering of the truth. For the last few weeks, stories had been floating around the building about wild animal attacks taking place down in the city's slum neighborhoods, along with other tales about old people vanishing off the streets. At first Preston considered the old man's corpse as possibly the first tangible proof of those stories.

After a few hours, he'd halted the proceeding and gone to his office to do some background research. Medical school, along with all the required ancillary courses, was a long way in the past, and as he'd examined, photographed, and measured the wounds, he didn't dare trust his memory.

So he went looking for documentation to back up what seemed an insane hypothesis, and it didn't take him long to find it.

His first reaction, scientific in nature, took the form of a mild exhilaration at how quickly he'd solved a puzzle placed before him. His second, coming mere moments later, was more political.

Simply put, he wondered how much hell would come down on him when he reported his findings.

Hours later, that hell came a calling, in the form of Captain Leo Bannister.

****

Now, days later, Preston dropped the instrument in his hand and walked over to the steel cabinet which contained the body of the old woman, the second homeless person in a matter of days to die from the same sort of wounds. He rolled the sliding table out and looked down at what remained of the old gal.

The results on this one had been almost identical to those of the old man, which had left Preston with an even sicker feeling in the pit of his stomach. The public had a right to know about any dangers in its midst, but if word got out about the results of his findings, God only knew what would happen.

He could only imagine that someone, or possibly several people, high up in the city's hierarchy was putting pressure on Bannister, just as Bannister was pressing down on him.

Staring down at the partially-reassembled mass of torn and shredded tissue, Preston had the unusual thought that, even ten years ago, he would have seen this as a challenge, as something exciting, the kind of case that most forensics people could only dream about. Now, at his current age, it had the opposite effect.

For the last few days, he'd found himself jumping at small, indecipherable noises. Walking to and from his car in the city parking garage, he'd glanced around, often stopping and straining his ears in a nearly paranoid fear that something was following him.

No case, no bloody cadaver, no office politics, had ever affected him this way. And now, staring down at the woman's shredded remains, an old woman they had yet to identify and probably never would, Dr. Lewis Preston felt that new fear once again washing over him, hands shaking and spit drying in his mouth.

It hadn't surprised him, accustomed to the way the higher echelons worked, when Bannister had demanded that the coroner keep secret, even from the detectives investigating the case, the exact cause of death. In his official report on the first case he'd only been allowed to refer to some sort of wild animal attack.

Which, if you thought about it, came close to the truth.

Witnesses at the scene of both deaths had assumed that, if not some loony with a blade, a dog or dogs had done the damage to the two transients, and for now that's what the brass wanted the public, if they heard about these two deaths at all, to believe.

But Dr. Lewis Preston knew the truth, at least part of it, and he wondered just how long he could keep quiet.

Or if he would end up taking his knowledge to the grave.

Chapter Nineteen

Back on Kessler Avenue, this time in the company of two male detectives.

Not that that made Karen feel all that secure.

As it often did in the fall, the dark had come quickly. Just a little past six, the sun was low in the sky. This, combined with a cloudy, dreary day to begin with, produced patches of grayish, partial shadows along the street.

They parked their car within sight of the alleyway where the old woman had died. Karen noticed that they didn't bother to lock the doors.

She must have looked her question.

"Not much point to it in these parts," O'Brien said. "Anyone around here with the energy to jack a car would know exactly how to go about it, locked doors or not."

"But even though no one seems to be paying attention," Karen said, "it's a safe bet that the street's eyes have pegged you as cops."

"Right, and with the GPS installed in all city vehicles, anyone stupid enough or stoned enough to heist the car won't get far."

"So where are we going?" Karen asked.

"Into the alley," Gleason said.

Karen felt a shock hit her. She absolutely did not want to go in there again. "Why?' she asked. "Surely anything to see has already been handled."

"More or less," Gleason said. "Crime scene spent a lot of time in there, going over what they could. But we feel there may be something more."

Karen glanced up at him, then, not wanting to seem like some kind of girly girl, followed the two men into the alley.

Here, what little daylight the street still held was nonexistent, causing goose bumps to parade up and down Karen's arms. Just abreast of the opening, she heard scuttling, shuffling sounds. She tensed. But with the sounds O'Brien pulled out a flashlight, flicked it on, and shone it into the interior.

Just in time to illuminate three teenagers scrambling over the brick wall at the other side.

A brick wall?

Something nagged at Karen, telling her that she'd just noticed something important, but she couldn't quite put her finger on what.

As she stood at the entrance, Gleason and O'Brien, both with flashlights in hand, made their way down the alley. About halfway to the other side, Gleason knelt down and splayed his light over the pavement. Reaching down, he plucked up a small, plastic bag with some sort of tie at the top.

"Explains what those kids were doing here," he said to his partner.

O'Brien nodded and turned to look back at Karen.

"It's okay, Miss Bannister. They're gone."

Karen, heart thudding in her throat, edged her way into the front part of the alley. She looked to both sides, but in the murk saw nothing but stained brick walls and scattered puddles of vomit and urine.

"You're not going after them?" she asked.

"Naw. We're not here to worry about a two-bit drug deal."

Gleason took two steps away from his partner and began shining his light at various points along the pavement.

What the hell's he looking for? Karen wondered.

"Exactly why are we here?" she asked aloud. "The truth, this time. Why are two homicide detectives spending so much time on a simple animal attack? And why drag me down here with you?"

Gleason, ignoring both O'Brien and Karen, had wandered almost all the way to the other end of the alley. He stood in front of that brick wall, at least six feet tall, and roved his light up and down it.

That wall continued to bother Karen. It should mean something to her, should reveal some kind of hidden truth. But what could a simple wall at one end of an alley signify?

"Miss Bannister," O'Brien asked, "before that night, had you ever been in this spot before?"

"No," she snapped, more sharply than she'd intended. "I don't make a habit of hanging out in slum alleys."

As much as she could tell in the murk, O'Brien didn't take any offense at her tone.

"Of course not. What I meant was, you spend quite a bit of time around here doing work for your shelter, correct?"

Karen nodded

"Not so much on this particular street, but yeah, in the general area."

"So you wouldn't know if this particular spot held much ... activity?"

"By activity do you mean drops, like that bunch you just ran off? Or are you speaking about other things? Such as animals?"

"Either. Or both. Anything at all out of the ordinary."

Karen started to snap something back, then turned around and looked again at that back wall. It loomed over the shadows back of the alley, and the small, troublesome thing about it began to jell.

"Detective O'Brien," she said, "there's a lot of stories going around, but most of the street people think a pack of dogs killed that old woman. Right?"

O'Brien turned away, as if not wanting to acknowledge her question.

With the cop turning silent, Karen walked further into the murk, being careful not to trip over the trash strewn about.

She passed Gleason, who had knelt down to inspect the trim of what looked like a low window in the building wall that formed the north side of the alley.

He glanced up at her but, seemingly preoccupied by whatever he was looking at, let her go.

A second later, Karen stood in front of that tall back wall.

And the truth hit her.

Not all of the truth, but some.

Enough to make her wish she were somewhere far away from this alley.

"Mr. Gleason, it was dogs that killed that poor woman, wasn't it?"

"That's our working theory," he said without looking at her.

"And the homeless man, a couple of days before? There's no way it could have been wolves or something, right? Not here in the middle of a city?"

O'Brien was still somewhere up in the middle of the alley, doing God alone knew what. Gleason straightened up from his crouch, the slight cracking of his knees sounding like lightning in the quiet of their surroundings.

"What do you mean, Miss Bannister?"

"Well," she said, without taking her gaze from the wall, "that would be an easy thing for the coroner's people to figure out, right? By comparing bite marks and such?"

"Ed," O'Brien said as he came into view, holding something down by his thigh, "remember what the boss said."

Gleason nodded and turned back to Karen, who could only assume that the "boss" was her father.

"We're pretty sure it was dogs."

"Pretty sure?"

"Well, it's rare, though not unheard of. At first we considered that it could have been a swarm of rats, that would have been somewhat more understandable, but dogs seem more likely."

"More likely?" Karen asked, wondering if her face expressed her incredulousness. "Why are you having to guess? There's been an autopsy on both, right?"

"Of course."

"So what did the coroner say? Surely they can figure it out, can't they?"

The two cops glanced at each other again, indecision seeming to flow between them.

Finally, O'Brien broke a bit.

"Coroner hasn't told us the exact nature of the wounds," he said.

Karen had no doubt that she showed her disbelief.

Standing in that darkened spot with those two men, she knew that more than her natural antipathy of the last year made her distrust what they said. Even without that distrust, brought on by David's death, she could have told they were keeping something from her.

Even more than that, though, was the wall.

"Gleason" she said, speaking to the taller man because he had seemed a bit more open than his partner, "if it was a dog attack, how did it or they get out of the alley?"

With the darkness almost complete now, Karen could feel the man stop motionless, his gaze focused on her.

"What do you mean?"

"Well, those two men and I got here only moments after the woman screamed. We got there right after she was attacked, and she was lying about halfway down the alley here. But of course you know that."

"So what's your point?"

Karen took a breath. Not sure exactly what was going on, she didn't want to antagonize either of them.

"My point is that neither the men nor I saw any dogs, or any other kind of animal, running out of this alley. And although they pretty much milled around and didn't help much, there were a lot of people out there, and none of them saw anything either. So with a high brick wall at the end that they couldn't possibly climb over, where did the animals go?"

Gleason didn't answer her, and she could hear the other cop walking up closer to them.

"Miss Bannister," O'Brien said from right beside her, "it's obvious that they scrambled over the wall somehow. What else could they have done?"

"It's not obvious at all. Look at it. Shine your light on it. No way any four-legged animal could have scrambled over that. So why don't you gentlemen do me a favor and just tell me ..."

She paused mid-sentence and strained her ears.

"Look," O'Brien continued, "it's just that ..."

"Shh!"

Karen held up her hand to shush the detective, even while knowing that he probably couldn't see her in the dark.

"Do you hear that?" she whispered.

"What?" Gleason asked, also in a low tone.

"There," Karen hissed. "That."

From the entrance to the alley came faint sounds. Karen strained even harder, enough that she could make out soft scraping noises, like someone trying to move across the dirty, trash-strewn pavement without being heard.

A second late, she revised that impression.

Not someone, but someones.

A lot of someones.

Then, once her ears had attuned themselves to the scraping, she thought she could also make out, though this may have been her imagination, low guttural noises, like some kind of animal instinctively growling, while at the same time trying not to.

"Guys," she said, "there's someone at ..."

But the cops were already a step ahead of her. Both Gleason and O'Brien had turned around and speared their flashlights towards the open end of the alley. As the beams wavered back and forth, the guttural sounds turned into hissing and snarling. As the lights shone on the figures amassed there, Karen for the first time in her life understood the meaning of blood running cold.

"My God," she said, both to herself and her companions, "they're kids."

Chapter Twenty

Although she couldn't see their faces as they stood in front of her, Karen could only imagine that the sight in front of them didn't surprise the two detectives.

And what a sight.

A band of half a dozen boys, as far as Karen could tell, had ranged itself across the alley opening. Only a couple of them could be considered of even average height, with the majority of them standing between four and five feet tall.

As the flashlight beams swept back and forth, the detectives employing a deliberate pattern to keep as many of the kids in sight as possible, Karen managed to get a closer look, though the distance from where she stood to the alley's mouth obscured quite a few details.

As far as she could tell, they all hovered around the eight to ten-year-old range, give or take a year or two. On the fringes, where the beams didn't shine directly, she thought she spotted a few smaller children, around six or seven years old.

Taking in as much detail as she could, Karen saw that they all wore the mismatched, raggedy outfits common to street people, the same sort of clothing she saw on a daily basis among residents of the shelter.

Most of them had long mops of hair. With their postures hunched, they tensed.

And they didn't like the light one bit.

As the flashlight beams swept back and forth over them, the boys flinched away, shielding their eyes from the glare.

On top of that, as the beams hit them in turn, the snarling and hissing of a minute before began to turn into actual, honest-to-God growls.

As if they were more animal than human.

Karen absorbed all of this in a few flashes of a second. At the same time, in her peripheral vision, she could see Gleason and O'Brien shifting, centering themselves, and she could detect the slight movements as the two detectives drew their weapons.

"Remember what he said," O'Brien told his partner.

"I haven't forgotten. Just hope to hell I can do it."

Karen didn't know what they were talking about, but at the moment she had eyes only for that ragtag collection of kids hovering around the alley's entrance. They were moving back and forth now, ducking and hiding their eyes behind uplifted arms while shifting back and forth. And even within a few seconds Karen could see their movements growing more frantic, more frenzied.

"Hey, you guys," she said to the two cops, arrayed on each side of her, "what the hell's going on here?"

"Quiet," O'Brien snapped, "let's figure a way out of here."

Karen shook her head in befuddlement. *A way out? Three grownups, two of them trained police officers with guns, against a handful of grade school-aged kids?*

Then, from out of nowhere, she had one of those flashbacks that had so haunted her for so long. A year ago, it had been two trained police officers who had fouled up so badly while attempting to stop a robbery in progress.

They'd stopped it alright. Managed to shoot the would-be robber, a strung-out, fourteen year old, dead on the spot. But in the brief exchange of gunfire, bullets crashing back and forth across the compact span of the store, three of those rounds had found their way into David's chest. David who, at her request on the phone a half hour before, had stopped off to grab a tub of ice cream to go with their dinner.

Two trained police officers had brought her life to a screeching halt, shattered it beyond repair.

And now, as she observed the agitated group of kids blocking their way, their growls becoming louder and more insistent, Karen realized that on this night her life rested in the hands of the same type of people who had effectively ended it eleven months before.

At least the night couldn't get any more bizarre than that.

An instant later, she realized her error when someone from the band blocking their way, the taller one who'd stayed in the center of the pack, lifted his head up to the sky and gave forth a long, mournful cry.

Karen felt O'Brien grab her by the arm.

"Get ready, Miss Bannister. We're about to move."

"My God," she said, "does he think he's a wolf or something? Does he ... wait ..."

She turned to O'Brien, barely noticing the harsh pressure on her wrist. No doubt the cop was nearly as frightened as she was.

"Are they the ones that ..."

She got no farther because, to her left, Gleason cried out.

"Get ready, Tim. Here they come."

And with that the pack of kids, none of them probably older than twelve, lurched forward like a single organism.

And they did it fast.

Chapter Twenty-one

From then on, it was all a blur for Karen. She registered shifting bodies, snatches of jaws biting into nearby flesh, padding of feet on the pavement, and growls.

Lots and lots of growls.

The first rush of the band of kids overwhelmed the three adults. Karen felt O'Brien's grip leave her in nearly the same instant as she heard the cop scream out, a shrill, high-pitched screech of a sound.

To her other side, Gleason cursed, and that was the last sound she heard from him. But she did hear plenty of snaps, snarls, and guttural noises. That first rush had thrown Karen to the ground and everything seemed to be happening above her. She tried to roll to the side, get away from it all, but in both directions she rolled into fresh, viscous puddles that she knew, by the metallic odor if nothing else, to be the blood of her two companions.

Then, when the nightmare surely couldn't get any worse, a whole new range of cacophony assaulted her ears.

Gobbling, munching, the tearing of flesh, and Karen knew, even with her eyes clamped shut to keep it all out, that her two protectors were being devoured.

Someone stepped on her head, knocking Karen half unconscious, and as she slipped into some sort of blessed half-aware state, she realized the truth that her father had kept from her.

Dogs weren't responsible for the bloody deaths down here in the Zone.

Not even rats, wolves or any other sort of beast.

Just children.

Part II: The Alpha

Chapter Twenty-two

Upon awakening, Karen lurched upward, but she didn't get far before something forced her back down.

"Don't move, miss. Just lie there for a minute and rest."

Her breathing felt harsh, constrained, and in another second Karen noticed that an oxygen mask straddled her mouth and nose. Panicked, she flared up again, this time consciously, only to be again pressed down.

"I mean it, lady. Stay right there. Don't even think about moving until we check you over."

Feeling helpless, Karen had no choice but to relax back onto whatever she was lying on. The voice, masculine yet rather soft, said something to someone else, but Karen couldn't make out any more than a mumble. With her unfocussed vision, she could only see an indistinct mélange of colors and shapes. A white background, along with a flashing strobe effect in her peripheral vision.

A loosening of pressure on her arm, which in her groggy state she hadn't noticed before, along with the ripping of Velcro told her that someone, probably the owner of the hands, had been taking her blood pressure.

In the next instant, a slight pressure across the back of her head took away the plastic through which she'd been breathing. After a few moments, Karen could see that she rested in an ambulance.

About every ten seconds, a whooping sound from outside signaled more emergency vehicles entering the area.

"Okay," said the man who'd been hovering over her, "why don't you try and sit up now, but take it easy, okay?"

Karen placed her hands palms down at her side and eased herself up. She looked around, trying to take in her entire surroundings, still not exactly sure what was going on.

With only the two of them inside the vehicle, the man crouched in front of her looked like a standard-issue paramedic. Tall, hard to tell how tall with him crouched down, he had the long, blond hair of a surfer and a thick, equally blond beard. His shirt sleeves, rolled up almost to the elbows, showed, even in the uncertain light, deeply-tanned arms.

"Okay," he said, "hold still now."

As he shone a light into Karen's eyes, she cast her mind back, trying to piece together what had happened.

For the moment, she could remember nothing but bits and pieces, but those fragments brought forth a cold, dead feeling along her spine.

The paramedic turned off the penlight and tapped a few keys on a laptop.

"Am I alright?" Karen asked.

"Far as I can tell, but we'll have to take you in to be really checked out. The rest of my crew should be back in a few minutes, and then we can take off."

"Where are we?"

He looked at her.

"Don't you remember?"

The fragments had begun to solidify, enough so that Karen had become more aware of her surroundings.

"Kessler Avenue, right?"

"Just off of it, yeah."

She sat up straighter and looked through the rear windows on the other side of the ambulance. It was still dark outside, and she couldn't make out much other than muffled shapes hurrying back and forth.

Plus that constant strobing of emergency lights.

"Gleason? O'Brien?" she asked.

The paramedic, a patch sewed onto his shirt identified him as Jason, looked puzzled.

But only for a second.

"You mean the two cops? Those detectives?"

"Yes," Karen said, somewhat surprised that she actually felt concern.

"Sorry, miss. But they didn't make it. They're loading them up right now."

Before Karen could think of what to say, the back doors of the ambulance opened.

"How's she doing?" asked a gruff, old-sounding voice. The combination of evening shadows and wildly-colored lights made it difficult for Karen to make out the man's form.

"I think she's okay," Jason said. "But won't know for sure till the docs get a look at her."

"She up to answering a few questions?"

Karen wondered if the man even realized she was conscious.

"It's up to her, but make it quick. We've got to get going."

With the doors open, the hubbub outside sounded even more frantic and confusing. Karen could understand. One uniformed officer gunned down on the streets would have been bad. But two detectives killed at the same time, especially when they'd been ...

The walls came crashing down, and her memory roared back into focus. She began trembling, her insides clenching and roiling.

Her immediate surroundings, the sterile interior of the ambulance, the hunky-looking paramedic, and the questioning form in the doorway faded away, and she could see only the back part of the alley, the group of kids ranged across the mouth, blocking their escape and the torn, ripped bodies of Gleason and O'Brien.

But how the hell had she survived?

A slight shifting of weight within the ambulance brought Karen back to the present, and a balding, heavyweight man in plainclothes squatted over her.

"Miss Bannister? My name's Rogers. Eric Rogers. I'm with Homicide."

Karen nodded, but said nothing.

"We've got a bit of a problem here, ma'am. Two dead cops."

"I know," Karen whispered.

"And a civilian found lying alongside of them, one who's barely scratched."

"I wouldn't call her barely scratched," Jason piped up from behind them. "You can just look at her and tell she's been roughed up quite a bit."

"True," Detective Rogers grunted without turning to look at the younger man. "But the point is that she's alive, while the other two are torn to goddamned shreds. You mind telling me how that happened, miss?"

Karen's brain had been getting clearer and clearer with each passing second, to the point where she could now think in real time. She couldn't answer the man's question because she didn't know. She remembered the attack, remembered seeing Gleason and O'Brien going down, but beyond that lay nothing but fog.

"Well? I'd really like an answer. How did you live when two trained men, with weapons, didn't?"

Karen glanced over at the paramedic, who was trying to look busy while not doing much of anything.

"Detective Rogers," she said, "could we talk privately please?"

The cop glanced back at the younger man and gave a curt toss of his head. The tanned paramedic frowned, then cracked open the back doors and prepared to crawl outside.

"Okay," he said, "but only a few minutes. Then we really have to get her down to Metro to be checked out."

"Fine," the cop growled. "But where's your driver?"

"Up front last I saw. Don't worry, he can't hear anything from there."

The younger man nodded to Karen, gave her a brief smile, and headed outside.

The cop turned back to Karen, not looking happy at all. Karen figured that, with two of his comrades dead, nothing much was going to satisfy him for a while.

And she had a feeling she was about to make things a whole lot worse.

"You know who I am?" she asked the cop.

"Lady, everyone on scene knows who you are. Before they left headquarters, O'Brien and his partner left word as to where they were going and with whom. But don't think that your last name lets you off the ..."

"That's not what I mean," Karen interrupted. "What I'm saying is, you're aware that I came down here at the request of those two, right?"

"Yeah. Supposedly you're some big expert on urban squalor, but why the hell that matters ..."

"Detective," Karen cut in again. "God knows I don't want to be antagonistic, but as upset as you may be, I was attacked tonight and had two men die right in front of me. So if you don't mind, could you drop the attitude?"

She could tell by his expression that Rogers didn't like being spoken to that way by a civilian, captain's daughter or not. No doubt the knowledge of her father's identity was the only thing keeping the man in check. Regardless, her approach seemed to do the trick, and she saw a noticeable lessening in the man's tension.

Now if she could only say the same for herself.

"Alright, lady. Attitude dropping, at least for now. So why don't you tell me just what the hell happened in that alley back there, and I'll let you go off to the hospital."

Karen took a deep breath, giving herself the time to figure out her exact strategy.

"Detective, if I had to, I'd guess that you already have a pretty good idea what killed those two men. Am I right?"

Against the backdrop of the red and blue lights flashing into the ambulance, Karen could see the man's face settle into what she could only call an unhappy resignation.

"And more than that," she continued, "I'd guess that my father sent you down here to perform cleanup on the situation."

"Cleanup?"

"Come on, detective. Are you going to tell me that you don't know exactly what attacked us in that alley? I'm not versed in criminology, at least no more than I picked up around the dinner table as a kid, but even I can't imagine, by any stretch, that the coroner's office didn't realize early on that the marks on both that old man and the lady I stumbled over the other night were caused by human teeth."

"What's your point?" Rogers grumbled, his tone even more subdued.

"My point is that I'll answer any questions you have, but I want to talk to my father first. I want to know if it was on his orders that your two guys brought me down here, with each of them having one weapon apiece, knowing what we were going to face. Now dammit you find my father and tell him I want to know!"

The last few words came out in something of a screech, and Karen could feel herself losing control. Maybe she was more injured than either she or the paramedic had thought, so it was a welcome sign when the doors opened up and Jason popped his head in.

"Everything okay in here?"

Karen and Rogers glared at each other, but no doubt the older man found it hard to feel superior when facing down a possibly-injured woman. Finally, he shrugged and turned to crawl back out.

"I'll pass your message along, Miss Bannister, and be in touch again after you've been checked out."

Karen nodded and watched the cop crouch walk out of the ambulance. Only when he had disappeared into the swirl of activity beyond the open doors did she allow herself to breathe once again.

The young paramedic came all the way back in.

"You okay in here?"

Karen gave him a weak smile and nodded. With the cop's departure, the wave of fatigue that she'd been pushing back against since returning to consciousness flooded over her, and that was all she knew.

Chapter Twenty-three

Jared was taking a chance with this story, and he damned well knew it. But things were getting weird out there, at least according to his police scanner, and after a quick call to Barb he'd decided that it would be better to start at the top.

A couple of quick phone calls had left him with the partial conviction that he would find his quarry at headquarters, and with the clock coming on to almost one in the morning, that's where he went.

The first nervous jangle hit him as soon as he crossed the threshold. While their fair city constituted a major metropolis, meaning that on most days the cops had their hands full around the clock, he sensed a little too much activity going on for this time of night, especially on a week night. Both uniformed cops and plainclothes officers were scuttling all over the place, the whole scene reminding Jared of the last few moments preparatory to a major drug bust.

When he scanned the open first floor, he saw that he wasn't the only media person around. He spotted two other television people, including that cute new hire over at the third-rated station, a couple of guys from the local paper, plus a network correspondent who'd been in town doing a series of specials on the local drug trade.

Again, more than you usually saw in the middle of the night.

Not taking the time to greet any of his rivals, Jared strode across the polished, checkered floor to the Public Information kiosk. He gave his name to the young, uniformed officer manning the desk and stated his desire to see Detective Rivers.

Detective Third Grade Tom Rivers worked vice, and the day shift at that, so the odds of finding him at his desk were long. But the kid at the PI post probably didn't know that, and while ordinarily he'd probably call up to check, he looked a little frazzled right about now.

"Go on up, Mr. Woodson," the kid told him. "But they're kind of busy up there, so he may not have time for you."

Jared flashed him his best television smile.

"I'll give it a chance, anyway, Officer. Thanks."

Spinning to his right, Jared moved to the nearest bank of elevators, timing his move in such a way that he had one cage all to himself.

The detectives' section, as he well knew, resided on the sixth floor.

Without hesitating, he pushed the button for the tenth, the highest floor in the building.

On his way over, he'd decided to start at the top, and that's exactly what he intended to do.

****

Stepping out of the elevator into an empty hallway, Jared made his way to the chief's office. He'd been here several times in the past, the last time a few years back when a small-time gang war had been escalating, and easily remembered the way.

Upon entering the outer office, he first saw the sweet young thing he'd seen meeting up with Chief Allen only a few days before in the smoke-filled environs of Sonny's Bar. Even with her hair done up differently, he had no doubt it was the same woman. The fact that she sat behind the main receptionist's desk filled in the final piece of the puzzle as to her identity.

So much for his possible big scoop. The big man was getting it on with his new secretary. Whoop de doo.

"May I help you?" the young woman asked.

"Don't think so," Jared said, adopting the most confident air he could, "got a meeting with the big man himself."

Before she could say or do anything, Jared swept on past her and made his way to the inner office door. A quick twist of the handle got him inside.

"Who the hell are you?" Chief Allen snapped as Jared closed the door behind himself.

He did a quick scan of the room. Besides the chief, who looked a lot more official and domineering in these surroundings than in a bar in the middle of the afternoon, the room held two other men. They both had that look unique to cops who, while still carrying the badge, hadn't been on the streets for years. It took only a second for Jared to ping on both of them.

Deputy Chief Mark Grayson, a slightly balding, reddish faced man who could stand to lose about twenty pounds.

And the other one, who Jared recognized quicker because he stood lower on the command chain, was the Chief of Detectives, Leo Bannister.

Three of the top cops in the city, squirreled away here in the dead of night.

And yet, according to the scanners, all because of a dog attack?

"I said, who are you?" Allen repeated, beginning to look a little florid.

Jared hadn't expected this high powered of a conference.

"Come on, Chief," he said. "You saying you don't recognize me? I'm ..."

"He's a reporter," Bannister broke in. "Works for Channel 12."

"Oh crap," Allen said, beginning to lose a bit of his color.

"So what's going on, boys? I'm assuming that you're here in response to ..."

"Why we're here is none of your business," Allen interrupted. "And more than that, you're not wanted here."

"So tell you what. Just give me a comment about this rash of deaths going on down in the Zone and I'll be out of here."

Jared had come in without a cameraman or a recorder. He wasn't looking for something to go on the air with yet. He just wanted info.

But he wished now that he had brought some sort of backup with him.

"You need to go, Mr. Woodson," Bannister said. "We're busy, and this is supposed to be a secure office. So unless you and your station are looking for a whole lot of trouble ..."

"Just tell me this, Captain. Why are the police concerning themselves with a wild animal infestation? Wouldn't that be a matter more for Animal Control than for the department?"

"Goddamn you, mister, would you get the hell out of here?"

Bannister's outburst, not to mention a slight shaking of his body, made it clear that the old boy was under intense strain. The looks on the faces of his companions added even more to Jared's suspicions that he had stumbled into the middle of something really bad.

And the stony glares coming his way made it equally clear that he would receive no cooperation from this bunch.

At least not tonight.

These three men were mad at him, sure.

But they were also scared. Terrified, if he was any judge.

But why did Bannister seem the most worried of the three?

As gracefully as he could, realizing that he'd overstepped it, Jared got the hell out of there.

Chapter Twenty-four

He didn't come to see her until the morning.

Karen was still asleep around nine, having been cleared and checked out of the hospital sometime after midnight, when someone began buzzing her front doorbell. Fogged by a helping of sleep aids dispensed to her the night before, to help her get over the shock of her experience, she turned over on her side and burrowed deeper into the pillow. But her visitor wouldn't give up, and after a number of buzzes, which ran into the double digits, she groaned, swung her legs over the side, and staggered to her feet.

She slipped into a threaded and pulled sky blue robe, one she'd had since college, and headed into the living room. The sleep aids hadn't helped as much as she'd hoped. Visions of blood, flashing teeth, and torn flesh had punctuated what little slumber she'd managed to get. So as she made her way into her living room, she knew that she looked far from her best, but at the moment didn't give even the faintest bit of a damn.

When she looked through the peephole and saw her father standing outside, she cared even less.

Still, she had to face him sooner or later, so she undid the deadbolt, threw the chain, and opened the door.

Her dad looked like hell. Overnight, it seemed, he'd grown a whole crop of wrinkles that she'd never noticed. Beyond the wrinkles, his skin and hair looked flat, lifeless. His shoulders slumped as he stood there, and even with her standing right in front of him, his eyes shifted back and forth, unable to meet her gaze.

In the instant of opening the door, all her anger of the previous night, her rage at what she'd considered a betrayal of the highest order, evaporated, and she wanted nothing more than for her daddy to hold her and tell her everything would be all right.

But something deep inside, maybe the memory of Gleason and O'Brien, two strangers giving their lives to protect her, held her in check.

So instead of rushing into his arms, Karen folded her arms across her chest, burrowing as far as she could into the security blanket of her robe.

With her dad standing there looking at her shamefacedly, she figured she'd have to open the conversation, even though she didn't quite know how.

"I expected you at the hospital last night," she finally said.

"I know." Captain Bannister shuffled his feet and glanced around the room before looking directly at her. "I wanted to get away, but there was so damned much to do. The captain in charge of the patrol division sent a uniform down there, and he called into me every half hour. So I knew you were okay, but still ..."

A thought flared into her mind.

"Dad, you've been in charge of the DD for how many years now?"

"More than I care to think about. But what's that got ..."

"Have you ever lost anyone before? I mean directly under your watch?"

A moment passed, possibly a bit more, before he answered.

"Directly under me? No. Obviously, we've had a handful of officers die over the years, but of the detectives in my division, none. Until last night."

Karen, feeling wretched all over again, swung the door open and gestured him in.

****

"You've known all along, haven't you?" she asked.

They faced each other across her small walnut dining table. Her father, taking up her offer, cradled a mug of coffee in his hands. Karen, intending to go back to sleep as soon as he left, had settled for a small glass of orange juice.

"Yes."

He looked so beaten, so utterly brought down, that Karen almost didn't recognize him.

"That those two old people down in the Zone, and probably some of the missing ones as well, were killed by children. You had to know. If nothing else the autopsies ..."

"Of course," he interrupted. "We knew with the first one. The old man. The ME on that case is one of the best. Counting his days to retirement, he's seen practically everything there is to see."

"And he figured it out?"

"Not right away. All he knew at first was that the marks, the punctures and tears on the old guy's body, had to be tooth marks but didn't match either dogs or wolves. Let alone rats."

"Wolves?"

"Had to consider every possibility. It's not unheard of for wolves to enter populated areas."

"Sure." Karen took a sip of her juice. "In timber country, somewhere on the outskirts of the forest. But I've never heard of wolf packs running around an inner city."

"Neither had we. But we were desperate for any sort of rational explanation, no matter how tenuous. Figured we had to get it nailed down quick before all the nutsos started talking about zombies in the street and such."

"So how did ..."

"Like I said, kiddo. Preston's a good man. Thorough. Started checking off every sort of mammalian teeth marks until he could get to the answer."

"Which he did?"

"Yeah. And pretty quickly, too."

Karen shut her eyes for a moment. Even sitting here in her kitchen in the morning, all she had to do was close her eyes and the sights and sounds of the alley the night before washed over her.

She still didn't know for sure how she escaped. An act of mercy, perhaps, on the part of spectators, and Karen was struck once again, as she'd often noticed during her work, that the homeless, the indigent and wasted, the hopeless, seemed to have more empathy for strangers than the average citizen.

Almost like a herd mentality.

"So the doc figured it out early on," her father's statement brought her back to the present. "That that poor old guy was attacked by people."

"Not people, Dad. Kids."

"Well, of course." The captain shrugged. "Youngsters, but what we don't know is ..."

"You're not listening to me. We're not talking young people. Not teenagers or anything like that. We're talking kids. Children."

Her father looked at her for a moment, and Karen couldn't figure out if he was in parent mode or cop mode.

At the moment, the way she felt, it didn't matter much.

"How old?" he finally asked.

Karen shrugged, causing a ripple of pain across her back and shoulders.

"Once they hit us, it wasn't much of anything but a blur. Just a bunch of arms, legs and ... teeth. But I've got a strong impression of the size of them. They were small, Dad, really small. Like no more than ten years old, if that."

Bannister bit back an oath and stood up. He strode over the kitchen window, staring out at not much of anything for a while before turning back to his daughter.

"Did they ..."

Karen waited for him to continue.

"Did they ... bite you, honey?"

Karen stifled a laugh, wondering if the situation was naturally funny or if she was suffering from some latent shock. She had expected something else entirely but found her father's question bizarre to say the least.

Then she looked at him, standing at her window, and noticed how tightly he had his hands clenched behind his back.

"No, Dad, they didn't. I'm sure they would have, but I'm guessing some people showed up and they took off."

Her father's taut, strained shoulders slumped, and he turned back to look at her.

"Dad, just what the hell is all this? Who are they? And why are they doing this?"

Captain Bannister turned back from the window.

"We don't know yet, honey. But we think that you, along with Gleason and O'Brien, were incredibly lucky last night."

For a moment, Karen gasped, not sure that she'd heard her father correctly.

"Lucky?" Her sudden outrage made her voice crack. "You think those two men of yours were lucky? You must be somewhat out of the loop, Dad, if you think anything good happened to those two."

"Baby, please listen to ..."

"No!"

Karen stood up, so forcefully that her thighs cracked into the table edge, causing juice to slosh over the rim of her glass.

But after getting to her feet, she didn't know what to do, so she stood there trembling.

His face had twisted into an almost unrecognizable shape, as if he ached to come over and take her in his arms, cuddle her, and protect her from the nasty world outside. But he stayed rooted in place, so used to leading his own force yet, in the face of his daughter, who'd verged on the edge of panic for the last twelve hours, uncertain how to proceed.

Karen took a deep breath, finding somewhere within herself the power to calm down, if only a little.

"So tell me, Dad. Why are your two dead officers so lucky? They died protecting me. What more could have happened to them?

Captain Bannister placed his hands flat on the table, pressing down on its surface. Karen cringed at the intent way he stared her down.

"They and you could have been eaten," he said.

Chapter Twenty-five

Simon really didn't want to see the old guy this morning. He'd wandered for hours now, trying to think of a way to break the news to the old guy. He had first considered burying the lead, so to speak, and puffing up the fact that they'd snagged two adult males. Even more, not just the ordinary drug-addled, diseased, and hopeless prey that they had been munching on.

No, sir. These two had been young, at least comparatively, and healthy. More than that, they'd possessed, though the pack hadn't known this at the beginning, guns. In Simon's former life, he would have instantly ID'd the men as cops, but now, in his new incarnation, he didn't classify humans by occupation or social status. In his new life, humans fell into only one of two possible categories: predator and prey.

And, he guessed, at some point down the line, potential mates. Something else he'd been meaning to bring up to his leader, just waiting for the right time. Which, he was wise enough to know, wasn't today.

When he gave it some thought, the two men should have fallen into the predator class. After all, cops counted as the enemy, didn't they?

One thing that annoyed Simon, really bothered him, was the whole gun thing. He and his boys should have spotted the men right off, based on smell if nothing else. After all the training they'd received, the countless hours of drills upon drills upon drills, the weakest, youngest member of the pack should have known about the guns from a couple of blocks away. The distinct odor, comprised of gunpowder, oil, and iron, should have served as a damned red flag warning them that these guys fell into the predator class.

Simon stopped outside the basement door, glancing behind and to the side to make sure no one was watching. The paint-peeled building, wood rotted and rat infested, had at one time been home to a rotating roster of drug addicts looking for a place to shoot up, rejects from homeless shelters searching for protection from the elements, and five-dollar whores seeking any flat surface to lay down and spread their legs.

For some time now, no such denizens had infested the place. Instead, all three stories, as far as anyone on the outside could tell, sat empty and abandoned.

As Simon searched the surrounding area, he didn't just use his eyes. He employed all the faculties that had been drilled into him: sight, hearing, and smell. Smell was the trickiest because this neighborhood was, by its nature, home to so much filth, along with the body odor of most of the people who lived in the area, that it took intense concentration to refine and isolate individual odors.

Concentration which he and his boys seemed to have lacked the night before.

Finally convinced that he'd approached unobserved, the kid walked about three yards to the side to a door that hung half off its hinges. He stepped through the open slot between door and frame.

Simon stopped just inside the doorway, again extending his senses, seeking to pick up anything out of the ordinary. Not planned in any way, but this point in his training it had become an instinct.

His senses brought to him the things he'd expected. The soft scurrying of rats in the walls, the faded smells of urine and feces from former transients, and the steady, slight creaking of wood long unpainted and neglected.

130

All normal, all expected.

His faculties also brought news of what awaited him down in the bowels of the building.

He turned to the right, heading down a former service hallway to a solid door at the far end. When he reached the door he paused, hand on the tarnished knob. He still hadn't come up with a good explanation as to why the woman had gotten away, and he did not want to confront the old man without some sort of reason.

At best, he could expect to have his place in the hierarchy lowered. At worst...

It occurred to Simon that he'd been standing outside the door, which led down to the basement, for several seconds. Not a good idea. The man waiting down there might be elderly, ancient in fact, but he was still the sharpest person he had ever met. No doubt he could sense Simon standing there, and the longer he had to wait the angrier he would get.

Squaring his shoulders and taking in a deep breath, Simon threw open the door.

He didn't bother to announce himself. They all should have heard and smelled him coming long ago.

The building's original construction had been so cheap and hasty that the stairs heading down into the basement, the same as those for the upper floors, were made of wood rather than concrete. Over the decades of negligent management and flat-out abandonment, those stairs had become warped, rotted and termite infested, making it impossible for an ordinary person to walk down them without all kinds of sagging, squeaking, and rattling.

Simon glided down them without making a single noise.

The basement interior looked as murky as it always did. Four small square windows let in a few dusty rays of sunlight, barely enough to illuminate more than a few feet beyond the walls.

It didn't matter. Simon's trained eyes allowed him to see shapes and movements almost as clearly as if under direct daylight.

Most of the pack lay on the dirty concrete floor, though a few crouched on their haunches. They all turned to look at him as he stood on the bottom riser, their faces almost blank. As he expected, they showed neither sadness nor joy at his approach. A few of the younger ones, who hadn't had as thorough of training as the others, expressed faint looks of expectation. But most, glancing his way, showed only the expected expressionless facades.

Then, after that brief second of looking the kid's way to acknowledge his presence, a standing dictum in the pack, they turned and looked towards the far corner of the basement.

A low grunt, indistinguishable to normal ears, sounded, and Simon stepped down from the stairway and shuffled in that direction.

He kept his head down, his trapezius muscles hunching up by instinct.

Had the kid looked up, he could have stared directly at the form in the corner. But that would be an unacceptable breach of protocol and, considering the tenuousness of his current position, probably fatal. So instead he moved forward with that hunched posture, shuffling his feet across the dirty concrete, with the hair on his arms, neck, and head, vestigial for most people, on high alert.

Counting his steps, Simon stopped six paces from the back corner. He didn't kneel. He merely stood and waited.

A low, phlegmy cough sounded in front of him. Then, in the next instant, a hoarse, cracked voice sounded.

"Well?"

Despite his obsequious manner, Simon's heart railed against what he perceived as the injustice of the current situation. It wasn't like he hadn't tried, hadn't attempted to score the girl as well as the two men. It was just that...

"Well?" the scratchy voice repeated.

"I'm sorry, sire. You sent me forth on a hunt and I failed."

While an outside observer would have perceived the proceedings as some sort of royal ceremony, as in a way it was, to show any but the most modest deference would quite possibly set the entire pack on him.

As it was, behind him Simon could hear the younger, smaller ones beginning to whimper and whine. He couldn't blame them. The tension in that basement was so thick he felt it almost impossible to breathe.

"You didn't entirely fail," the hoarse voice said. "You dispatched two males."

"Yes, sire. We did."

"But that was all you did. Just kill them."

Simon ducked his head a little lower, this time in genuine shame instead of fear. Behind him, the shifting and scattering of the younger ones served as a reminder that most of the pack had gone hungry the night before. True, a few had foraged for rats and other vermin. One member, he'd heard, had stumbled upon a newborn kitten and brought it back to share with a few others. But for the most part the rich, warm meat that most of the pack required for sustenance had been denied them.

Denied by his failure.

"And you left the female alive," the shadow figure in the corner continued.

Although he knew better than to make excuses, fear prompted Simon to speak.

"It wasn't our fault." Even as the words left his mouth, he knew he should have said "my" instead of "our." If he was going to break protocol, including everyone else only compounded his shame.

A moment of silence lingered in the corner before the owner of the cracked voice answered.

"Really? How not your fault?"

"A crowd came from around the corner. They spotted us and started raising a ruckus."

Simon realized that he was trembling even more than before. He was exaggerating, practically lying, and if anyone had told the old man the truth, it was all over for him.

It hadn't been a crowd that stumbled upon them.

Not quite.

****

The two males had attempted to put up a fight, but the members of the pack, drilled and hardened on the streets, had moved too quickly for them. The cops had been trained to deal with human opponents, and while that term technically described the pack, the tutelage of the old man had made them more.

Much more.

One of the cops, standing about two steps behind the other, had partially drawn his gun, before Jimmy, one of the larger members, had attacked him from the side and chewed into the wrist of the hand holding the gun. Growling, Jimmy had worked the wrist back and forth, blood spraying and splashing onto his face. But, as was normal with members of the pack, the taste, smell, and feel of the blood had only heightened Jimmy's powers, and in another few seconds two snapping sounds indicated that his teeth had done their job.

Somewhere in all of that, the cop had screamed, but it had only lasted an instant because, while gnawing on the wrist, Jimmy's fists and nails had been at work, alternately punching and slashing at the man until his body, even before the snapping of his wrist bones, had gone into shock.

Because of his relative size, at least relative to the others, Jimmy had taken on the one male alone while the other members, with Simon standing back, had attacked the second. These four, all of them checking in around nine years old, didn't look like much individually.

But that was one of the secrets of the old guy's genius. Alone, most of the pack members wouldn't even be noticed, let alone feared. But together, working as one and especially when the lust for blood had taken hold of them, they were unstoppable.

So the four smaller ones had taken on the other male together, and the cop never had the chance to draw his weapon before falling to the ground, his throat gnawed open and his legs half chewed off.

Which had left the female.

As the seconds ticked by, the fight progressed and Simon circled the scene of action, homing in on the female. In the first flurry of movement, she'd dropped to the ground, half pushed there by one of the cops, no doubt trying to protect her. Simon wasn't even sure if she was conscious as the mayhem swirled around her, but that motion of falling to the ground had saved her, at least temporarily.

The pack members had, for the moment, ignored her in their haste to deal with the more immediate threats. All according to training, and as the growls, screams, and sounds of snapping and crushing bones filled the alley, the kid thought about how pleased the old man would have been could he have witnessed this. The pack would feed well tonight.

It was too bad that their leader would only hear second hand accounts of the magnificence of his acolytes on this night.

And that quickly the two males were dead, sprawled on the pavement, the snuffling, snarling members of the pack crouched around them. The woman lay prone between the two corpses, and the pack members looked towards Simon, low growls escaping their throats as they waited, driven nearly mad by the sight, smell, and taste of blood, for his command.

He approached, sniffing the air, the aroma of hot blood blocking out nearly everything else.

Then the female shifted on the ground, groaned, and the pack members lurched back, three of them growling and one, the little Hispanic who hadn't been given his name yet, whining.

With a short, guttural command Simon caused the others to fall back, and he approached the woman, suspecting she was about to regain consciousness.

His first instinct was to kill her. Kill and then eat. With three full-grown, healthy adults the pack could feast for as long as a few weeks without having to venture out again. The old one would be pleased, and the kid would rise even higher in his estimation.

Then he crouched over the woman, sniffing around her form, and some new instinct sputtered into being. He bared his teeth at her, but some instinct held him back, unsure of his purpose. His fingers twitched as his brain, physically that of an eleven year old boy, tried to discern what had made him pause.

Behind him, he could hear the pack shifting, their uncertainty manifesting itself to his ears.

Simon snarled, tamping down whatever strange urge had stayed his hands and teeth, and crouched lower. His upper lip pulled back, revealing his canine teeth, artificially strengthened and sharpened, and a deep roar issued from his throat.

"Hey, what the hell are you punks doing in there?"

Simon froze, half crouched over his prey, and glanced over his shoulder. The rest of the pack got to their feet, shuffling back and forth, and Simon looked past them to see two people, a man and a woman, typical specimens of this part of town, standing in the lighted opening of the alley.

The woman screamed, and the man began to take a step forward, then hesitated.

"Let's go," Simon hissed to his followers.

"But the meat," whined the little Hispanic one. "We need it."

"We need to survive even more," the kid snarled. "What do you think Old One will say, or do, if some of us get captured?"

"They wouldn't dare!" spat out Jimmy, except for Simon himself the oldest and largest of the group. "They're weak, pathetic. They wouldn't dare attempt to ..."

But already other humans had appeared in the mouth of the alley, most of them males and a few of them large and imposing, even in the half light. The hairs on the back of Simon's neck, the few he had barely into puberty, began to crawl upwards, and the uncertainty of danger caused his upper lip to once again curl back from his teeth.

"We go now," he said, primarily to Jimmy. "If they get together ..."

He left the thought unspoken, having no need to say more. The natural, inherent fear of humans which nearly all animals, no matter their size or ability, possess had gripped the smaller cubs. Even Jimmy looked spooked now.

"Can we at least take home some of the meat?" he whined.

Simon looked again towards the mouth of the alley. There looked like nearly a dozen people massing there. What had happened to the people of his past life, his human life, who would do or say anything rather than get involved?

"No," he said, even as his stomach grumbled at the thought of the treasure they would abandon. "Carrying dead weight would just slow us."

As he spoke, Simon saw that the crowd of street people had grown, and some of them had some sort of clubs, probably boards they'd scavenged from somewhere. His instinctive fear of humans, everything that the old man had drilled into him about them, ratcheted up even further.

"Let's go," he said just as one of the younger, less trained cubs crouched down over the still-unconscious female, teeth bared and jaws extended.

Without speaking, his agitation increasing by the second, Simon launched a kick at the cub, his foot slamming into the rib cage, sending him rolling onto his side and squealing.

"Now," he repeated, turning his back on both the pack and the meat lying at his feet.

He headed off towards the back of the alley, away from the hated humans milling around the front, and his keen ears picked up the faintest sounds of the pack following. The cub he'd kicked whimpered, just the slightest note, and Simon growled out a low warning, not audible within three yards of them.

Certain that they followed, the kid now attuned his senses backwards, to the humans in the front of the alley, and things appeared to have happened as he'd predicted. Not able to see far into the gloom, the few souls brave enough to enter the area had stopped at the three humans lying on the pavement, allowing the pack to get away.

In no time at all they'd be home free.

But with their bellies still empty.

****

"You trained us to stay hidden," Simon said to the old dude.

The shadowy form sighed. He still had not come out into the feeble light of the basement, and the kid knew that he probably wouldn't.

"I did. But I also trained you to hunt. Hunting means returning with food for the pack. How many times now have you scored on your prey yet returned without it?"

Simon hesitated, searching for the best words to use. It had been three times, in fact, and part of the reason he'd been gone for the better part of a day was to figure out his strategy. He sensed, with basic intuition, his place within the hierarchy slipping, the incident the night before only being the most recent, and flagrant, example.

Behind him, the pack tensed, most of them probably crouched on their haunches, awaiting his reply. It was a tricky moment. If he gave the wrong answer, he could find himself ostracized from the pack. At the same time, timid acquiescence might embolden some who wanted his position.

"Three," he finally told the old man. "Three times we've gone out, killed, yet returned with nothing. But I think I know why."

"Really?" The scratchy voice sounded intrigued. "And why would it be?"

Simon took a deep breath. He had to do this just right because his entire future rested on his answer.

"I believe we pushed too quickly. You've trained us well, sire. Guided us and protected us. And you've done that well. So much so that we're almost ready to survive on our own, which I'm sure is your ultimate wish. But we're not quite there yet. We need just a little more time in which to make sure that we're ready. Then we'll be able to ..."

Simon's voice trailed off as a low grumbling came from the corner. He still kept his head dipped, shoulders hunched in that subservient mode, not daring to look his master in the face. Behind him, the pack continued shifting and grumbling. *Almost as if they're waiting,* he thought.

Waiting for the word to expel me.

Or possibly rip me to pieces.

"I chose you as my second," the voice in the shadows croaked. "And you've disappointed me, not once but three times."

Simon stayed silent. When the old fellow wanted to talk, no one else dared speak.

"You have a lot of growing yet to do. Even if you're the best among the pack, you're still only a child."

I know that, Simon thought. *But not any child.* Unlike nearly anyone else his age on the planet, he'd been honed, sharpened into a weapon by that shadowy form squatting in the corner.

Surely that counted for something?

"And as a child, you may not have thought through all the results of what you did. For instance, have you considered the most important question of last night?"

Simon paused, the slightest of moments, to see if the question was rhetorical. When it became clear that the figure in the corner wanted an answer, he spoke slowly.

The rest would no doubt interpret that as a further sign of weakness, but probably better than giving a wrong answer.

"I guess ... we should be concerned about ... the witnesses. It's one of the reasons I wanted to leave so quickly. The first time anyone's seen us, at least that we know about, and I didn't want them to get a good ..."

"That's a point," the old man interrupted, "and not a bad one. But it shouldn't be the main concern. I hear that there wasn't much light, and the most the people in front could see were shapes. So what should be the main concern?"

A growl started deep in Simon's chest, but he managed to smother it. So the old guy had "heard" about the conditions the night before. That meant someone, maybe more than one, in the pack had talked, had attempted to spread poison against him. Not good. But nothing he could deal with right now.

Above all, he wanted to remain second, wanted to keep his now-shaky hold on power.

"The woman," he said, realization flashing in to stave off further embarrassment. "We left the woman alive."

"Almost," hissed the shadowed shape. "*You* left the woman alive. The others merely followed your lead. How much did she see?"

Simon fought hard to suppress the trembling he felt. Nearly twenty-four hours since the failed attack, and only now did the enormity of his mistake present itself. The woman had survived and had been conscious through at least part of it. Could she possibly...

"She's a potential threat to the pack," the leader said, his voice stronger and more forceful than at any point up to now.

"Deal with her."

Chapter Twenty-six

She took several days off work. No problem, as far as her boss was concerned. She had offered a week or two, if necessary, but Karen knew that the one thing she needed was a feeling of normalcy, at least the illusion of living in a world where roving bands of little kids didn't eat people on the streets. After that revelation from her father, the fact that the first two victims had been not just bitten into or gnawed on but partially devoured, Karen knew she would count herself lucky if she had one night without nightmares for the next year or so.

There wasn't much else for the two of them to talk about. Karen couldn't really read her dad's face, and she never found the nerve to ask him if he'd approved Gleason and O'Brien taking her out that night. When he left her house, after a few more awkward minutes, she wondered how much time would pass before they saw each other again.

As if the whole David issue wasn't enough of a wedge, she couldn't shake the feeling that the captain had held something back. Whether out of protecting her or some other motive, she didn't know, but she felt that she hadn't gotten the entire story.

She spent most of the rest of that first day lying in a tub of hot bath water, nursing her aching muscles and staring up at the ceiling trying, with little success, to make her mind a blank.

The ER doctor the night before, after hearing a bit of what she'd gone through, had suggested that she consider counseling somewhere down the line, citing his concerns about PTSD. *Thanks Doc,* she'd thought, *but the idea had already crossed my mind.* If she found it necessary, she knew several good people through the shelter. Whether any of them were qualified to work her through the kind of horrific experience she'd had was another matter.

She spent most of the second day at her kitchen table, staring out the window and wondering exactly when things had gotten so crazy. Through her job, Karen had learned that the world was a rough, rough place. Even without a cop for a parent, her time spent in working the streets had taught her that. Even so, for a long time she'd managed to convince herself that the dirt and terror she saw didn't impact her. In the old days, she'd managed to blind herself to reality.

David's innocence had been one of the things that had drawn her to him. A high-school chemistry teacher, he lived as far removed from the orb of crime and poverty as possible. With him, she had managed to partially wipe away, at least temporarily, her knowledge of that other world.

So yes, Karen's life had, with the exception of the occasional bump, run along a more or less normal track.

Until the day her fiancé had stepped into a convenience store to grab some ice cream, and had ended up being mistakenly gunned down by a cop.

That had caused her to reevaluate everything, and not in a good way.

Then she ended up attacked on the streets by a gang of kids interested, not in money, revenge, or even violence for the sake of violence, but in actually preying on her and her companions.

Or so the captain said

Now, nothing made any sense.

On the third day she made it out of her house. She managed a trip to the grocery store, a long-delayed stop to pick up dry cleaning, and a quick dash to an ATM machine to get some pocket money.

She returned home by noon and, with a storm coming in from the east, decided to curl up on the couch with a glass, or two, of good wine and laze the afternoon away.

But every now and then, as the sky got darker and droplets pelted the windows, she knew the time had come to go back to work, resume her normal life.

Chapter Twenty-seven

Her alarm buzzed right on schedule: 7:30 a. m.

At first, Karen went through the routine of a normal morning. Shower, shaving of legs, breakfast, brushing of teeth. Spent about five minutes selecting what to wear, the first indication that something may still not be quite right. Usually, she had her clothes laid out the night before. A bit pretentious, considering that her normal workday attire consisted of running shoes, blue jeans, and a tee shirt, but she always made a habit of saving a few minutes each morning by laying out her clothes at night.

Almost always.

Hadn't done it the night before, which made her pause for a second. Then she shrugged, opened her drawers, and grabbed the first few things she saw. But she ended up putting those back in favor of another outfit. Then, only two steps out of the bedroom, she turned back and replaced those clothes.

Spent about three minutes sitting on her bed staring at her dresser drawers, figuring out how she wanted to look for the day.

She ended up settling on the combo she'd originally chosen.

Something clearly not right here.

A quick brush and comb over the hair, deciding at the last minute to put it up in a ponytail, something she hadn't worn in years. Like riding a bike, she had her strands pulled back and clipped in place in just a minute.

Rinsed her dishes in the sink, thought of putting them in the dishwasher but for some reason didn't feel as if she had the time to do so. Three days gone from work, a lot of the shelter's paperwork had no doubt piled up on her desk.

At the last minute, she decided she needed another cup of coffee, or at least half a one, pulled a mug from the shelf and filled it up, then stood at the kitchen counter, staring into the swirling liquid.

Something definitely wrong.

Briefly considered if she might be experiencing the PTSD the doc had warned her about, then dismissed that as too fanciful. The night in the alleyway had been a horrifying experience, to be sure. But trauma?

Hell, she'd been unconscious through the last half of it. Something else was bothering her, something she couldn't quite pin down.

Without drinking any, she tossed the just-poured coffee into the sink. Whatever her issues might be, she wouldn't find the answers standing in her kitchen.

Then, just as she set her mind to putting one foot in front of the other and walking out into the world, came a knock at the door.

Karen looked at the clock. Who the hell would be calling on her at eight thirty in the morning? She felt an instant, overwhelming need to run back to her room, jump into bed, and throw the covers over her head, but the urge passed as soon as it came.

She made it to the front door just as whoever it was knocked a second time.

Glancing through the peephole, she saw a slightly-familiar, fortyish man, his hand raised for a third try. No one she knew, at least not off hand, and Karen had no idea what he could want with her.

On the plus side, his knocking had forced her to come up to her door, leaving her inches from stepping out and actually heading to work, something that had seemed so far away a few minutes ago.

For a brief instant, she wondered if her experience of a few nights back had left her with a mild case of agoraphobia.

Shrugging, she went ahead and opened the door.

"Miss Bannister?" the man on her doorstep said.

"Yes?"

"My name's Jared Woodson and I was wondering if..."

"I know you," she interrupted, her hand clenching the knob in case she needed to slam the door on him.

"Well, yes, I get a lot of ..."

"Where's your camera?" Not the only question that came to mind, probably not even the most important, and Karen didn't even try to keep the snotty tone out of her voice.

"Miss Bannister, I know you may see this as an intrusion, but ..."

"Got that right, mister." Karen had to admit to herself that the man was a pro. She'd interrupted every attempt he'd made to say anything, but he didn't show even a flicker of annoyance.

"And since this is an intrusion ..."

He paused, expecting another interruption. When Karen kept quiet, he looked a bit surprised, then went on.

"Since this is an intrusion, I figured I'd make it as low key as possible. I was wondering if I could talk to you about what happened."

"What happened?"

Standing in her doorway, Karen craned her neck. Although she'd seen no signs, she'd wondered during the last several days if her father had had some kind of surveillance on her. It wouldn't be out of character for him to do so, and considering their relationship over the last months, she considered the odds better than even that he wouldn't tell her.

Hard as she looked, though, she couldn't see anything.

"Miss Bannister," the reporter tried again, "it's common knowledge what happened to you last week."

146

"Then why do you want to talk to me? If it's such common knowledge ..."

"Because it's rather interesting that no one on my side of the fence, whether newspaper, TV or anything else, interviewed you after your – experience."

"Maybe they all had a little more consideration than you, Mr. Woodson."

The man sighed and placed his hands in his pockets.

"We both know better than that, ma'am."

For some reason, Karen grimaced at having a man slightly older than her call her "ma'am."

"I did some digging, and practically everyone, including people from my station, took a run at you. But they ran into interference."

Karen paused, unsure of what he meant. Sure, for the last three days she'd walled herself off from the world, but she wouldn't have been that hard to contact. As far as she knew, no one had tried to get ahold of her.

Then it came to her.

"You mean my father?"

"Right. No one's sure what he did or who he threatened, but I know for sure that in the newsroom the word came down loud and clear to leave you alone."

"And yet here you are?"

Woodson grinned, causing lines to crinkle in his face.

"My news director gave me a few days of personal time. Off the books. I decided, out of consideration, to give you some space before coming over."

Karen sighed, wishing that her dad did have a few of his troops positioned somewhere close by.

"What can I do for you, Mr. Woodson?"

"You can tell me about what happened to you."

Something began clicking in Karen's mind, and for the first time in days she felt almost awake.

"What's the official story?"

"You don't know?"

This guy kept his expression a blank, but it was clear that he didn't quite believe her.

"Believe it or not," Karen said, "I haven't seen a single slice of media since that night."

"I can almost believe it. The story is that you and a couple of detectives were down in the Zone and got assaulted by a gang."

Karen almost laughed.

"And what do you think?" she asked Woodson.

"I think you saw something down there. Something a bit more out of the ordinary than a regular street gang. Something that the major players in town, including possibly your father and for sure his chief, don't want people to know about. Right?"

It would be traitorous to her dad to tell this man anything. Then again, for the last year she hadn't felt much loyalty to the department in general and her father in particular. What little loyalty or trust she had held had been wiped away four nights ago in that alleyway.

"Yes, Mr. Woodson, you could say it was something out of the ordinary. And I'm willing to share, but there are two things I need to do first."

"Which are?"

"I need to call my boss and tell her I'm not coming in again today."

"Down at the Municipal Shelter," he said.

That surprised her a bit, though she knew it shouldn't have. She wasn't exactly a private citizen anymore.

"Yes, at the shelter."

"The second thing?"

Karen hesitated, wondering if she should take time to think this over. But she dismissed the idea almost instantly.

"The second," she said, "is that we need to set some ground rules."

Chapter Twenty-eight

"So how much do you remember?" Woodson asked her.

They paused at the mouth of the alley. The crime scene tape, though ragged and frayed in places, still cut it off from the rest of the street. Karen stared into the interior for a minute before answering.

"More than I did four days ago," she said.

"Is this where we run up against ground rule number one?"

Karen's first insistence had been that she didn't want to come right out and say what she'd seen. The reporter had balked at first, but Karen had held firm, explaining that she wanted him to consider things from as objective a viewpoint as possible.

His frown showed that he didn't believe her, but Karen thought she knew what she was doing. Her memories of that night still consisted of nothing but bits, pieces and flashes, and she didn't want to unintentionally take him down a wrong path.

Standing on her doorstep, Woodson had hemmed and hawed all over the place, but he'd given in. But something had seemed off about it, as if he was giving a performance for her benefit, and Karen wondered if there wasn't more to the story than she knew.

The postulation of a few more rules followed; then they were off in his van towards the Zone.

In the daylight, more people were out, mostly younger despite the fact that it was a school day. A few more vagrants, both men and women, slumped on the sidewalks and reclined against walls. Down a couple of blocks, a small convenience store, windows heavily-barred, was doing a brisk business, more likely than not in lottery tickets.

So two middle-class looking people, loitering in front of an alley marked with police tape, drew a few furtive glances, but so far no one had accosted them. With her experience down in this area, Karen wondered why, after all this time, no one had disturbed the crime scene tape.

"So what's their story again?" Karen asked.

"Gang attack. Two detectives and a concerned citizen, looking for a missing person, got jumped by some street thugs, and before they split the two cops were killed."

"How many media people showed up at the scene?"

"You really have been on a news blackout, haven't you?" Woodson asked.

Karen grimaced. "Believe me, Mr. Woodson, if you'd gone through it, you'd want to stay away from the world as well."

He nodded, even though he couldn't possibly have understood. "Quite a few showed up," he said. "All three local stations, plus some people from the paper and a few bloggers. Someone said there was even a radio crew here at one point. After all, it was a ..."

"I know, a big story."

Karen crossed her arms over her chest and stared into the alley. Here in the daytime, it didn't look that formidable.

Mounds of dirt built up in corners, littered with fast food wrappers, liquor bottles and, she suspected, used condoms. The few windows that looked out over the dirt, at least those left intact, almost totally blackened from years of grime.

In short, the crime scene looked just like any inner city alley anywhere in the country. Or the world.

Aside from the yellow police tape, nothing would alert a casual observer that, not one, but two, attacks had taken place here. Karen stepped all the way up to the yellow tape and focused as close as she could on the middle portion of the alley pavement.

Jared Woodson came up alongside her.

"Whatcha looking for?" he asked.

"I was wondering if they cleaned it up."

"Cleaned what up?"

Karen turned to look at him.

"With all the media here, did anyone get any tape? Or pictures?"

"Only of the front section here. Jamie Sanchez, over at Channel 11, managed to snag a few shots of them bringing the bodies out, but they had them completely covered with sheets."

"Of course they did," Karen said. "After all, they were already dead. And it served to cover up the wounds."

He looked at her at that remark, but didn't comment.

"True. But a couple of the shots that Sanchez got showed an awful lot of blood on those sheets."

Karen shivered, thinking, for about the thousandth time, just how close she'd come.

"What about me?" she asked.

"Huh?"

"Were there any pictures or tape of me?"

"No. They had you already rushed out by the time anyone got here. Besides, standard protocol. We wouldn't have done it anyway."

Karen nodded, thankful for small favors.

"Back to my question, though," Woodson said, "cleaned what up?"

"The blood," Karen said, looking both ways up and down the street. "I'm wondering if they managed to clean up the blood."

She reached out, lifted up the yellow tape and headed into the alley.

****

"That's a lot," Woodson said.

Karen looked at him, then knelt down on the pavement.

Two large swirls of hard brownish stains, with numerous lines of varying widths, spoked out from the main splotches. Mixed in with those large swirls, individual drops of differing sizes.

When she didn't say anything, Woodson tried again.

"Any of it yours?" he asked.

Karen shook her head, still looking down at the pavement.

"I only had a few scrapes. They didn't have time to get to me before ..."

"This wasn't a gang hit, was it?"

She shook her head again as she stood up.

"So why all the secrecy? You ready to tell me what happened?" Woodson asked.

"Ground rule," she said. "I want you to get there on your own."

"Right. But you still haven't given me a good reason why."

Karen looked at the man. She'd never seen him in person until this morning, but of course he'd appeared on the local news off and on for the last several years. He was a fixture in local media, the current station he worked at being the second to employ him. As a casual citizen looking in from the outside, Karen had never heard a bad word about him, something rare for a television person these days.

However, she had occasionally heard her father talk about what a pain in the ass Woodson could be, which worked to raise him in her estimation.

Still, she couldn't bring herself to let him in.

"Wait a minute," Woodson said, taking a step back. "I think I get it. The time off work, despite only minor injuries. The hemming and hawing up one side and down the other. You didn't need time to heal up. You weren't hurt that bad. And you didn't need the time because you were depressed or going through shock."

"How can you tell?"

"Because I've covered the streets in this city for a long time, miss. And the way you're looking now, I've seen that look on dozens of people over that time. You're not depressed."

Karen stood silent, waiting for him to blurt it out. She hadn't yet managed to say it to herself, and for some reason she desperately needed to hear it.

"Not hurt," Woodson repeated, "and not depressed. You're scared."

"No," she said, clenching her hands in front of her. "I'm not scared, Mr. Woodson. I'm terrified."

****

Woodson, who by his agreement with Karen hadn't brought any video cameras along, used his cell phone to take pictures of the alley, primarily of those large blood spatters about halfway back.

While he did this, Karen stood by the entrance, leaning against a dirty brick wall and watching the street scene. Any ordinary, suburban-dwelling middle-class person would have been anxious to leave, but she'd worked in this area and similar ones long enough that she could tell the danger was minimal. True, several passersby, some of them rather sketchy, paused and glanced into the alley, but inhabitants of the Zone lived longer by not prying into anyone's business.

"Okay," Woodson, said, coming up behind her, "I've got enough for now. Enough to show my news director at least. Depending on how things go, we can come back later and, crime scene restrictions or not, get some decent tape."

"Okay." Karen shivered, though the day was warm, and crossed her arms.

"Anything coming back to you?" Woodson asked her.

"Just the same bits and pieces. Right about now, I need a drink."

Woodson glanced at his watch. "It's not even noon yet," he said, looking at Karen.

She didn't respond, but he must have seen the tightness she could feel in her face.

"Let's go," he said as he guided her towards the van.

However, they'd only made about ten steps when Karen froze and grasped his elbow. Woodson looked down at her clasp.

"What's wrong?"

"That kid over there." Karen made a slight motion up the street and to the right.

Woodson looked in that direction, not responding for a moment.

"Red jacket?" he asked. "Greasy brown hair?"

"That's the one."

Karen's voice had turned into a hoarse whisper.

The kid in question was leaning against the corner of a run-down apartment building. His hands thrust into his jacket pockets, he seemed to be making too much of an effort to appear inconspicuous. Looking no more than ten or eleven years old, pale skinned and, even from a distance and with the jacket, noticeably underfed, the kid had his head craned back, looking up at the sky.

Yet despite the fact that he looked and dressed exactly like almost every other young person inhabiting the Zone, to Karen he just didn't seem to fit.

"What about him?" Woodson asked her.

"I'm not sure," she said, "he just ... "

Images flashed before her mind. The same blurred montage that had haunted her for four nights, but this time with a difference. Mixed in with the growls, snarls, gnashing teeth and flying blood, she now saw, or thought she saw, this little kid standing off from the others, as if directing the entire action.

But that didn't make sense. The boy lounging against a corner wall was about as far from a gang chief as you could imagine.

"Where do you know him from?" Woodson asked her.

The scenes kept flashing across the screen of her mind, repeating themselves in a continuous loop.

The reporter took her by the arm and steered her into the car. It had tinted windows, and only after the doors were shut and locked did Karen relax.

"So tell me," the reporter said as he started up and pulled into traffic.

Karen clenched her hands together to keep them from trembling.

"He was there," she finally said. "With the others. The ones who ..."

She couldn't think of the right word to say. "Attack" sounded too mild, while "ravaged" seemed impossible in a sane universe.

"There's stories going around," Woodson said as he turned a corner and headed out of the Zone. "Stories about a new type of gang down here. Stories that sound just a tad unbelievable."

Karen turned to look at him. They were at least three blocks away now, and she felt her tension lessening with each block they traversed.

"How unbelievable?" she asked.

The newsman turned to her.

"You tell me," he said.

Karen shivered and leaned back in her seat. She tried closing her eyes, but when she did so all she could see was the alleyway that night, the two cops falling to their knees and the gang of kids descending on them.

"To hell with ground rules," she finally said. "Let's go somewhere where we can sit and talk. Because no matter what you may have heard, the truth is far worse."

Chapter Twenty-nine

He watched them drive away, fighting to control the new anxiety shredding his nerves. It took actual physical effort to keep his face composed so that all the people around wouldn't notice anything. And it took a lot of that effort, because all of his instincts shrieked at him to flee.

Crossing his arms so tight that he thought he might break a rib, Simon realized that he was suffering from a conflict between two of his mentor's teachings.

Ever since he'd come under the old man's influence, the concept of flight in the face of danger, real or potential, had been drilled into him. The old duffer had used an assortment of training techniques, including locking him in rooms with deranged winos, tethering him by his ankles and inviting strangers to strike at him, and throwing him into pools of freezing water in the middle of winter. At the time, Simon had hated the old man and just waited for the chance to lash out and escape.

But as the months, then years, went on, he came to realize that the older fellow had done all of that out of love, working to hone him into as efficient a survival mechanism as possible.

Survival, as the mantra had gone, being the prime necessity.

Yet almost as forcefully as he'd pounded in the concept of survival, Simon's teacher had stressed the necessity of blending in. Only by blending in, he'd taught, could his pupil hope to survive.

Hard lessons, harsh lessons. But he'd learned them so well that, when the time came, Simon's mentor had allowed him to train some of the younger members of the pack. All part of a master plan, the full dimensions of which he'd only recently begun to fully grasp.

It had become obvious to him, if not to the others, that the teacher was preparing for the time when he would no longer be around. After all, someone had to carry on the line, had to preserve the traditions. To that end, it wasn't enough that Simon learned the lessons; the old guy had to know that he could teach as well.

At the same time that all these musings ran through his head, an even more primal force was working on Simon.

He was hungry. So damned hungry.

Since that major screwup, what the old guy referred to as a "fiasco," the pack's movements had been restricted. For the most part, the old man did not allow them to leave the lair. When they did, he forbade them to range farther than a block in any direction.

Because of this, their diet had diminished. Most of the younger ones, the smaller cubs, probably didn't see it as that big of a deal. Rats, various other vermin, and the occasional stray cat or dog more than sufficed. But for the older ones, in the ten to twelve age range, such small portions amounted to near starvation.

Simon forgot his privations as he saw the car pull away and, after waiting a few moments to make sure they didn't come back, moved away from the wall and headed off in the direction he'd been going when he'd first noticed the female from the other night. The part of his mind still human, the section that the animalistic impulses hadn't expunged, wondered at her identity and intentions.

She had come to this area once, in company with two males, and at the time the kid hadn't known or cared what their business was. The three of them presented potential food, pure and simple, and nothing beyond that mattered.

But now she'd returned to the same area from which she'd barely escaped with her life, and she had another man in tow. This moved her from the category of prey into that of, if not predator, at least danger.

The kid couldn't guess as to her motivations, but he did know her actions were out of the ordinary for humans in this area. His only decision now was whether to run back to the lair and consult with his elder, or prove himself by handling the situation on his own.

After all, his human intelligence, youthful as it was, told him that if she returned here once, she may do so again.

The only question was how to handle her when she did.

Chapter Thirty

"Come again?" Barb Redland, Woodson's news director, asked him later that night.

Wanting to keep things as quiet as possible, the two of them had decided to meet in a night club slightly east of the downtown area. While not quite the sort of place where the city's rich and mighty hung out, it rated at least a couple of steps up from Sonny's Bar. And while the venue wasn't unknown to most of the media people in town, it wasn't a common hangout.

So they felt safe in meeting here, though Jared hadn't yet told Barb the reason for all the furtiveness.

His opening statement to her confused things even more.

"I said," Jared repeated, "that I need to take an official leave of absence."

Barb sat back in her booth and stared at him.

"That's what I thought you said. And it doesn't make any more sense the second time around. Besides, if I remember correctly, you're scheduled for your vacation in August."

"I'm not talking a vacation, Barb. I'm talking leave of absence. I have to be gone from work for a while, and I want to be off the payroll while I am."

"This almost sounds as if you have some kind of family problems. But I haven't heard you say anything about problems lately between you and Maggie, or the boys for that matter, and both of your parents passed away some years ago. So what exactly's going on?"

"I can't say. Not just yet."

Barb tapped her fingers on the table.

"I'm not quite following this, buddy, but I think I'm going to decline your request. By my count you're working on two major stories right now, the Allan thing and the thing down in the Zone. What do you want me to do, just turn them over half done to someone else?"

Jared leaned in towards his boss.

"The Allen story is nothing, Barb. Truth be told, the guy's sleeping around with his secretary. End of story. But there's more to those killings in the Zone than most people know."

She sat up straighter now and fixed her gaze on her reporter.

"What are you doing here, Jared? You can't just dangle that out and let it be. Give me something to help me make a decision."

Jared started to reply, but just then their waitress came over to see if they needed anything. Before she half framed the question, he waved her off and, once she'd gotten out of earshot, turned back to his boss.

"Plausible deniability. Hell, I never thought I'd be sounding like a damned congressman, but there it is. I'm going to run the story down, don't worry about that. And if I pull it off, the station will come out smelling like a rose. But if I screw it up ..."

He let the sentence dangle, hoping he'd given her enough.

"What the hell are you talking about here?"

Jared paused, uncertain how to proceed. Sighing, he rubbed his face.

"There's something really bad going down out there, boss. Not just bad in the violent sense, bad as in downright unbelievable. It's not some new type of gangbanger, and it's not a pack of wild dogs or coyotes. And I've got reason to suspect, though not in any way I can prove, that some of the folks in City

Hall know all about it."

His news director took a long pull of her beer before answering, and as she set her mug down he noticed that her hand shook a bit.

"Are you talking about some kind of conspiracy, Jared? Seriously? If I didn't know you better, I'd think you'd gone off the deep end."

"But you do know me. And just now you were shaking. Tell me, boss. Just what kind of stories have you heard about these killings down there?"

"No doubt the same stuff you have. Crazy stuff. Something about a pack of wild animals that's running loose in the city that for some reason they can't track down. Makes you wonder just how inept the cops are."

"Okay, but have you also heard any rumors about people disappearing? There's a couple of bloody killings that everyone knows about, but there's also the possibility that other people, maybe lots of others, have just up and vanished."

"Don't people vanish from that area all the time?"

Jared drummed his fingers a few moments, giving himself time to frame his answer.

"Sure. The run of the mill stuff. Sometimes people just wander away, sometimes they even sober up. And there's always the one off abduction. But this seems to be something different, and it has a lot of folks down there scared."

"And this was before the killings of the last few weeks?"

"Right, and like you said, the word has all been about 'crazy stuff.' But if it was animals, dogs, wolves or whatever, wouldn't they have put Animal Control in charge? Why's it being handled straight out of the cop shop?"

Barb took another drink. Jared had never known his boss to get flat out drunk, but she was looking a little pale about now.

"Are you saying that there's some sort of serial killer down there carving up homeless people?"

"Not ... not exactly."

"I checked your logs from the other day. Did you go ahead and interview the Bannister woman?"

A somewhat grim look crossed his face.

"I went by her house, yeah."

"And?"

Jared placed both palms flat on the table and stared at them.

"She had some stuff to say."

"Want to tell me about it?"

"No way, Barb. Not yet. I need to run it down, and when I do it's probably going to irritate some people, so ..."

"You know who Karen Bannister's father is, right?"

"Of course."

"And so you know what happened to her fiancé last year?"

"What's your point, boss?"

Barb sighed and slid her mug back and forth across the table.

"Sorry. It's been one of those days, even before this little rendezvous."

"So what's your point?"

"My point is that Karen Bannister just may not be thinking very clearly when it comes to anything to do with the police."

"Because her fiancé got caught in a crossfire?"

"And because, rumor has it, she's barely been on speaking terms with her dad ever since. On top of that, so the scuttlebutt goes, doesn't she make a habit of traipsing down into the worst parts of the city?"

"So what?"

"So maybe the lady has a death wish of some kind, and when you tell me about important people getting upset, it makes me wonder if ..."

Jared sat up straighter in the booth.

"Don't worry about it. Bannister may not be the most objective of people, but you know I am. Which is why I'm not willing to let the station be a party to this until I have something solid."

Barb drummed her fingers again, looking at them rather than at the man across from her. After several minutes, she stopped.

'Okay," she said. "You've got your leave, for now. But give me a call the minute you have something we can use, something from you, not from the Bannister woman. If we've got something bad on the loose, and if City Hall is covering it up for some reason, we don't want to tip our hand until we've got the goods."

Jared nodded, doing his best to look in full agreement. He wanted to say more, to give Barb at least some hint of what Karen Bannister had divulged to him that afternoon after they'd left the Zone. But he figured it would be better for her, at least for now, to just imagine a serial killer roaming the bad part of town looking for random victims.

That sounded so much more plausible than what could end up being the truth.

Chapter Thirty-one

They met up the next night at Karen's home. Jared had spent the day running minor errands, all the time wondering how his new ally was spending the time. Wondering if she'd stayed home or gone in to work, he wanted to ask her, but decided it would seem a bit too inquisitive.

An odd position for a reporter to be in.

As he stepped inside, she chained and locked the door behind him.

"Your street looks pretty empty," he said.

Karen frowned.

"What I mean is," he continued, "if what you say you went through is even half true, I'd expect your dad to have guards all around your place."

Karen stepped over to her closet and pulled out a light green jacket.

"Does it matter?" she asked.

"Of course. The last thing I need is to be hauled into court for kidnapping a police official's daughter."

"I wouldn't worry about that, Mr. Woodson. The way things have been between my dad and me lately, he'd probably throw a party if he never saw me again."

"You don't really believe that, do you?"

She paused, shoulders tightening, and an expression that seemed one part sorrow, one part guilt, with something else thrown in, flickered across her features.

"That probably was unfair," she said, "but right at the moment I'd rather not think of it."

"Fair enough," Jared said.

Before coming over he'd spent some time digging around, and had come up with video tape of her that had made the news last year. It had jogged his memory enough that he now recalled following her case for a short while. The night of David Parsons' death and a few days later at the funeral.

She hadn't broken down, at least not in public. Not even a tear, and he remembered thinking at the time that this was one cold woman. But now, seeing her yesterday so jittery yet so decisive, he was beginning to think that his initial assessment had missed the mark.

Not stone cold. Not even cool. Merely someone pretty darned good at compartmentalizing, at keeping the good and bad stuff separated rather than letting it all mix around.

But she seemed to have lost that calculation when it came to familial relationships, and even though he barely knew the woman, he hoped that at some point she could find a way to get that part of her act together.

"So," she said, breaking into his reverie, "my ride or yours?"

****

The problem, as Jared expressed it a while later, was that neither one of them had much of a plan. They both agreed on the overall goal, finding some sort of solid evidence of the existence of a band of cannibal kids that they could present to the public. Jared operated from the need to fulfill his job, the journalist's inherent desire for a scoop. And this would most definitely be one hell of a story. Maybe not Pulitzer material, though that wasn't entirely out of the question. At the least, though, it should propel him out of the local market and into a national gig somewhere.

Karen Bannister's motivation, at least to Jared, appeared far murkier. Even now, in his second day of association with her, he still didn't understand what drove her.

The question of motivation aside, though, the two of them still didn't have a clear idea of how to go about the job.

Not to mention the real danger involved.

"So how do you suggest we proceed here?" he asked Karen, who was driving.

She glanced over at Jared.

"You got any ideas?" she asked.

"A few. But considering that you spend a lot of your working time down there, I figured I'd defer to you."

Karen nodded and turned back to the road.

"We need to seek out anomalies," she said after a few minutes. "Things that seem somehow out of place."

"But you said they were kids."

"Yeah. One or two may have been in their teens, but I'm not sure about that."

"My point is that solitary, wandering kids aren't exactly unusual down here."

As he spoke, Karen coasted to a red light. They were at the extreme fringe of the Zone. In the day, the particular street they'd stopped at wouldn't look all that different from the streets a few blocks north. But at night, when the shadows cast themselves in certain directions and the regular people faded behind closed doors, the tenor of the neighborhood changed.

Not a lot. This was, after all, just the outer edge. But someone who knew their way could spot the shadowed form in a recessed doorway, the two teenagers outside a store exchanging something for money, and the cop cars that drove by a bit quicker than in other parts of town.

Just enough of a difference to notice, and it would be more evident a few blocks farther on.

The light turned green, and Karen drove on.

"I don't know quite how to explain it, Mr. Woodson."

"Jared, please."

"Okay," she said, averting her eyes. "Jared. I'm not quite sure how to explain it, but these weren't regular kids."

"Well, that's kind of obvious."

"No, what I mean is, they didn't move like kids. Didn't sound like them either."

Jared noticed her hunching tighter as, in at least a small way, she took herself back to that night nearly a week ago.

"I thought you didn't remember much about it."

"I don't. Not the way you mean. But I think visiting the alley again last night did something for my memory. Fragments keep flashing at me, enough so that I'm getting a better picture of what we're looking for."

"Okay, so what do you mean, not moving or sounding like kids? How else could they--"

"Like animals," she cut him off, and he heard a new coldness in her voice. "Mr. Woodson, they'll look and sound like animals."

****

They parked in a public garage about three blocks away, then headed out. It was coming on towards twilight, and while Jared considered searching for their quarry at such a time a bit careless, Karen had pointed out that they wouldn't have much luck during the day.

More and more he had the feeling that, whether through actual knowledge or only intuition, she knew a lot more than she was letting on.

First, they stopped once more at the alley where she'd been attacked.

Jared pulled out his cell phone and with a few taps pulled up a map that they'd put together before leaving her place, then expanded it as much as the screen would allow.

He turned the phone so that Karen could see it as well.

A grid of city streets, with two small red dots and one slightly larger dot that waxed and waned in intensity.

"Looking at it this way," he said, "it seems almost obvious."

"Sure does," Karen said, a whole new tension coming over her face.

"In fact," he continued, "so damned obvious that it seems odd the cops haven't tried this as well."

"What makes you think they haven't?" Karen asked.

Jared glanced around. While a few people glanced over at them, he didn't detect any undue interest.

But just because you're paranoid, he thought, *doesn't mean that they aren't out to get you.*

"If the police managed to bust this thing," he wondered out loud. "Would they ever make it public or just sweep it under the rug?"

"I'm sure we'd hear something," Karen said, "be pretty hard to keep it entirely quiet."

"But how much of what they let out conformed to the truth ..."

"That's a whole other matter."

On the phone's screen, the three dots continued to do their thing, two holding steady and the other going in and out in brightness.

The dot that changed brightness marked the location of the alley where Karen and the two detectives were attacked, while the other two marked the sites where the first two victims had been found.

Between them, the three formed a rough triangle.

"We may be completely off here, you know," Jared said, "it's not like either you or I are professional trackers."

As soon as he uttered the words, he grimaced. Karen looked up at him and, for the first time he could remember, smiled.

"Trackers?" she said.

He shrugged.

"So you're starting to affect me. Still, I guess you could say that it's reasonable to assume that somewhere within this triangle we'll find ... what?"

"What we need to find," Karen said, "is kids that don't act like kids."

"You said that before, but what does it mean?"

"Just what I said. They're going to act like animals."

Jared looked at her. The smile hadn't lasted long, and the tension in the shoulders was back.

"As long as we stay in the open, in public view, we should be okay," he said.

"Even down here? You think the folks around here will come to the aid of a couple of interlopers?"

"Not necessarily, though from what I hear some people stopped the attack on you the other night. But if this – gang – or whatever somehow has animalistic instincts, they won't pull anything in open view of others."

Karen closed her eyes, and as Jared watched she shuddered, and he wondered just what she was seeing before she opened her eyes again.

"I hope you're right," she said. "I so hope you're right."

****

They had traversed nearly four blocks, doing their best to blend in, when Karen clutched Jared's arm, hard enough to make him grimace.

"Over there," she said, lifting her hand just a fraction in the subtlest of pointing gestures.

He looked over to the corner adjacent to the one they stood on and at first could see nothing out of the ordinary. At least, what would be considered ordinary for this part of town.

"What?' he said in a register that didn't carry more than a foot or so.

"Those two, over on the corner. In the hoodies."

It took him a minute. The sun had gone all the way down about thirty minutes before, changing the entire complexion of the neighborhood. Both prey and predator were out and about now, and it was easy for one to tell them apart.

The predators prowled the sidewalks, alleyways and building stairwells alone or in pairs, intent on seeking out whatever they needed, wanted, or desired. Whether drugs, sex from any one of numerous possible genders, or merely cheap excitement.

The prey, by contrast, tended to cluster in groups.

A bunch of men in shabby coats huddled around an old barrel that contained a flickering fire, passing back and forth the cheapest bottle one of them had been able to find.

Four or five girls, maybe one of them in her mid-teens and the rest younger, gathered around a street light, knowing that their pimps wanted them out strolling in order to earn their keep, but themselves only intent on surviving until the morning.

Lighted windows in buildings that held what some would call apartments, peering out onto the street scene below before yanking their faces from the curtained windows, lest a stray shot take them out.

Then he saw what Karen had noticed.

Two forms, roughly five feet tall, impossible from this distance to tell if they were male or female. Both dressed in hoodies of some color, though that also couldn't be clearly determined. At first they looked like any other couple of street kids, but Jared had noticed that they stood with their backs to a storefront, leaning into the building and staring straight ahead. They didn't talk to each other. In fact, they barely moved.

Just stood there watching the street.

"You don't recognize them, do you?" he asked Karen. She couldn't possibly, not from this distance.

"No, of course not. It's just that – something about them isn't right."

"How do you mean?"

"I can't say for sure, dammit. I just know I've worked around kids like that for years now. And something about them isn't quite ..."

Jared turned her way.

"What?" he said.

"Nothing."

"What were you going to say?"

"It's nuts, really. But I almost said they weren't ... human."

He took her hand and guided her across the intersection, keeping parallel with the storefront on the other side of the street.

"Let's get a ways on," he said. "See if we can circle around and check them out."

"Jared," she said at his shoulder, "hold on. They're on the move."

****

Neither of them were cops or trained in any way. Yet Jared had been an investigative journalist for a number of years and Karen knew her way around the Zone. It was almost impossible for them not to stand out to the regular denizens of the area, but in this part of town, you survived by not meddling in someone else's business.

They stayed on the other side of the street, walking parallel with the two boys, who seemed to be ambling more than anything. The kids stayed side by side, hoods drawn up over their heads, and almost swerved, ducking and dipping to avoid bumping into other people, all while staying in tandem. It was an odd type of movement, almost the total opposite of the shambling and shuffling young people usually did these days, but other than that, Woodson saw nothing noticeable about the two.

"Are you at all sure about this?" he asked Karen after they'd traversed nearly seven blocks.

"Not really. But there's something about them. They just don't seem to fit in."

"And yet they do. Look how easily they avoid the rest of the sidewalk traffic."

"There's definitely something off about ..."

Jared and Karen slowed down, but didn't stop, as they saw the two kids halt on the other side of the street.

"You've got to be kidding me," Jared said as he noticed that the two had stopped in front of the open mouth of an alley.

"Seems to fit the pattern," Karen said. "This bunch really seems to go in for alleyways."

"If they're part of the same group," Jared said. "We could just be shadowing a couple of nobodies here. Or we may be about to blunder in to somebody else's business."

"I don't think so," Karen said, and a new flatness in her voice caused Jared to look her way.

"What is it?"

"I don't know," she said.

He now saw a slight glaze in her eyes, as if she was searching somewhere other than their immediate surroundings.

"Miss Bannister?"

"Look at the way they move, the way they hold themselves."

By this point the two in question had merged almost entirely into the darkened area, but even so Jared knew what she meant.

"It's hard to put into words," he said, "but I guess you could say that they don't quite move normally."

"Exactly. As they were walking down the sidewalk they almost seemed to swerve through the crowd rather than walk past it. And half the time they seemed to fade into the shadows, almost like an instinct."

"They're wearing dark enough clothes," Jared said. "That alone could account for ..."

A brief, high squeal interrupted him. About twenty people meandering along both sides of the alley opening gave no sign of hearing anything, though that could be from the "see-no-evil" mentality of the streets. And Karen and Jared both knew darned well that they wouldn't have heard the little squeal if they hadn't been concentrating on whatever was going on in that little niche of shadow.

They looked at each other and, as Karen nodded, Jared headed across the street to approach the alley. He didn't have to go to the corner or wait for a light. The Zone, after the sun went down, held a minimum of moving cars. Few people who didn't live here, either in buildings or on the streets, had much of a reason for coming here. And hardly any of the native denizens could afford a car. Hence, minimal traffic, other than by foot.

Not that outsiders didn't wander down to the area, most of them seeking either drugs, whores, or simple thrills. Any given night of the week, the Zone would see at least one gang of high school kids, usually from one of the city's suburbs, heading down to see who or what they could roll, what sorts of stories they could take back to their safe neighborhoods.

Auto traffic in the Zone, at least after the sun went down, usually showed up in the form of middle-class men, though sometimes women, looking for inexpensive hookups, and not just of the traditional male-female type. It was well known that any sort of perversion, whether physical or chemical, could be found in this small, congested area of suffering.

All of this went through Jared's mind as he crossed the street, angling towards that dark opening to see what had caused that squealing sound.

At first, he thought he hadn't been fast enough. Just as he stepped onto the sidewalk he saw a shifting of shadows from the opening and, before he could react, the two young boys stepped out from the alleyway. Not knowing what else to do, Jared kept walking towards them, hoping that the movement would look natural and unthreatening.

For a protracted moment, the two stopped moving, giving him suspicious looks. In the murk he couldn't be sure, but it seemed as if they'd smeared something dark across their faces. One of them lifted his arm up and wiped his sleeve across his mouth.

Rather than ignore them, his natural reaction, Jared turned and gave them a steely, no-nonsense glare. Not the response of a regular person, but more like how a street person would react.

And it worked. The two kids exchanged glares with him for a second, then broke contact and moved off. Woodson watched them go, noticing that even in retreat they employed that smooth, gliding movement to avoid contact with the others on the sidewalk.

What the hell, he wondered, *is it with these two?*

When they turned a corner and disappeared, Jared glanced down the street and saw Karen following them. He gritted his teeth, worried about her getting into danger, but figured that her experience would serve her okay.

Plus, she seemed smart enough to know when to back off.

He wouldn't be separated from her too long, but first he wanted to get a look inside that alley. He reached into his pocket for a small flashlight, which he almost dropped when a streetwalker, black with a brassy blonde wig, bumped into him.

"Watch it, mothafucka," she hissed as she staggered on, barely looking at him. Jared shrugged and, clicking the flashlight on, entered the alleyway.

At first, he didn't see anything beyond the usual grimy brick sides and trash-covered ground. Off to the side, a rusted fire escape canted against one of the brick walls.

Playing his flash back and forth on the ground, Jared only took three sweeps before he found it.

Glancing to the front to make sure no one had noticed him, he knelt down to inspect the mangled hunk of flesh he'd spotted.

It was hard to tell, as badly as they'd chewed it up, but Jared believed he was looking at either the remains of a cat or a small puppy. What remained of the skeleton looked feline, but so much of the flesh had been gnawed away that in the dark he couldn't be sure.

Jared knelt there with his head spinning. Even with everything leading up to this, he had difficulty coming to grips with what lay at his feet, and what that mute testimony portended.

His cell phone buzzed, and so deep was his shock that it took three buzzes before he roused himself to respond.

"Yeah?" His voice sounded flat, wooden.

"Are you okay?" Karen's voice. "They've been on the move for a while and I hadn't seen anything of you."

"I'm okay," he said. "Still ... still in the alley."

"What'd you find?"

"A cat, near as I can tell. Can't be sure because they ... aw, hell Karen those two kids just chewed the hell out of this thing. Damned near makes you sick."

"Is that surprising?" Her voice sounded rock steady, reminding Jared again of just how tough this woman was. "I told you what they did to Gleason and O'Brien. Didn't you believe me?"

"No, I believed you. It's just, when you see it like this, it damned near ..."

"Better catch up with us," she interrupted. "I'm at the corner of Twenty-Seventh and Woodbridge. And I think they're slowing down."

****

He caught up with her about four minutes later, standing next to an actual, honest-to-goodness old-fashioned phone booth. At another time, Jared would have marveled at the object, assuming that pay phones had become extinct. As he got closer, he saw that such may have been the case. The booth glass was intact, but it held neither phone nor phone book.

Jared didn't want to think about the various uses to which both residents and visitor to the area had put the booth.

"Where are they?" he asked Karen as he approached.

She pointed to an old, three-story tenement building on the intersection's northeast corner. The place looked at least a hundred years old, and even in the dark Jared could tell that nearly all the windows had been first boarded up, then had half the boards broken out again.

He didn't see any lights.

"Looks abandoned," he said.

"Right," Karen answered.

"Odd. Rare to find a completely abandoned building in this area. Even the scummiest of places are usually full up."

"In all my time working for the shelter," Karen said, "I've never seen a single structure around here that doesn't have at least some inhabitants, even if it's a bunch of runaway kids squatting."

"So what do you think it means?" he asked.

"I don't know, but you notice it's not just deserted. Look around it."

Jared did so, unsure what she meant, but when a moment later he got it, his breath nearly stopped.

"There's no one anywhere around that entire part of the block," he said.

"Right. It's not just the building that seems empty, there's no one even coming close to it."

Now that he looked at the scene with fresh eyes, it reminded Jared of those old pictures of bombed-out areas of London during the Second World War. The area looked so desolated that he almost expected to see the old tenement turn into fallen down rubble before his eyes.

"What the hell is all this?" Karen asked at his side.

"You've never noticed this before," Jared said, "all the time you've spent down here working?"

"I've got the idea that it's a nocturnal phenomenon."

"Meaning?"

"Meaning that it only stands out like this at night. During the day, when more of the regular folks tend to be out and about, it probably just looks like any rundown building."

"Karen," Jared asked. "Do you know what we're dealing with here?"

When she glanced at him, he wondered if his face looked as troubled as hers did.

"I've got an idea," she said.

176

"Are you sure you haven't talked with your father about ..."

"I told you," she snapped, then paused for a moment,, "that Dad and I don't talk much."

Jared nodded, wondering just how deep those scars went.

"So what's your idea?" he said.

"Testing me?"

Despite the tenseness of the situation, he couldn't help but chuckle.

"Let's just say that I'd rather not blurt it out on my own for fear of sounding foolish."

Karen grimaced, some of the bitterness leaving her face.

"I looked it up the other night," she said, "wanted to make sure I understood the term."

"The term being 'feral children'?" Jared asked.

"Yeah. There's lots of stuff online about it. Have you researched it?"

"I skimmed. But there's a few problems."

Karen nodded.

"We'd have to speak to an anthropologist, I guess, to make sure. But I couldn't find any trace of these exact circumstances."

"By circumstances you mean ..."

Jared cut himself off as, behind them, a low growl sounded. He could tell by the blanching of Karen's face that she'd heard it as well.

And that it no doubt sounded familiar.

He turned, spinning as fast as he could. But he wasn't fast enough. Something crashed into him. Two things, actually. One smashed into his chest and shoulder, while at the same time he felt arms wrapping around his legs. He went down, his head thudding against the sidewalk, as he heard Karen struggling behind him.

He ended up on his back, lights from the street whirling around him. Low, guttural growls sounded as hot saliva dripped onto his face. Instinctively, not seeing anything but blurs of light and darkness, he thrust his forearm upwards.

Just barely in time, it turned out, as something strong yet sharp sliced into his arm and began lacerating his flesh. His legs still pinioned, he worked to focus his vision, and when clarity came he felt a surge of vomit in his throat.

One of the young boys they'd been following crouched over him, but at the moment his face looked like nothing human.

The eyes gleamed, reflecting the lights around. The sinews of the face and neck were stretched taut, taking on the appearance of corded steel. But worst of all, the mouth, sunk into Jared's forearm, worried back and forth. A scream formed in his throat, but the burning in his arm kept him from voicing it as those growls continued to emanate from the child. The child, yes. Looking no more than eleven years old, though with the malnutrition common to the streets he could be somewhat older. Yet at the moment, Jared couldn't interpret this thing gnawing into his arm as a person. His expression and vitality could only be described as animalistic.

Then, as the reporter thought he couldn't become even more horrified, he heard Karen screaming behind him as a new round of ripping began in his left thigh. He began thrashing back and forth, his entire body on fire as he struggled to throw these two creatures off. A grown man, nearly forty and keeping himself in good shape, he should have been able to buck the two off with no problem.

Yet somehow these two children easily overpowered him.

He reached up with his free hand and tried to pry the kid's teeth loose from his arm. He didn't want to hurt either of them, but those small, young jaws were so strong, with such sharp teeth, that he felt on the verge of blacking out from the sheer pain. Nothing, but nothing in his fairly active life had prepared him for the agony he now experienced.

Karen's screaming had stopped, replaced by the sound of feet shuffling away. Spurred on by fear for her safety, Jared changed tactics, curled his free hand into a fist and began hammering on the face above him. He hoped like hell that no possible witnesses had a cell phone because the last thing he wanted was to be hauled up on charges of child abuse.

Actually, the last thing he wanted was to lose either a leg or arm, or both, to the wild animals attacking him.

At first the kid on top didn't seem to take any notice of the newsman's effort, but with his third blow, the first to really connect, another of those sharp, ominous growls, one mixed with something that resembled a whine, escaped from that throat.

What the hell kind of creatures were these? For damned sure, they weren't ordinary children. If he closed his eyes, Jared could almost have imagined his opponents were wolves instead of human beings.

The flow of blood running down both his arm and leg frightened him even more, and he began shaking the captured leg against the ground, desperate for anything to get free. At the same time, a small part of his mind began thinking, and he decided to try an almost-impossible gamble.

"Help!" he screamed, not caring that his voice cracked like a girl's. "Somebody help, get them off me!"

He had no doubt that some people, both indoors and out, heard him, but whether anyone would come to his aid was a whole other matter.

Not waiting for assistance, and with his leg and forearm turning into sheets of fire, he wriggled his shoulder back, got as much free space, only an inch or two, as he could and punched at the face above him again.

He thought he felt a cheekbone crack, or maybe it was a couple of teeth. Either way, he seemed to have scored because the punk on top of him reared back a bit, yelping in pain and loosing his jaws from Jared's arm. Giving him, at least in one of his limbs, a few seconds of relief.

It didn't last, though, because in another second the kid came at him again, seeking another lock on that now-butchered forearm.

Jared pulled the arm into his chest, hoping to keep the kid from securing a grip. Rearing up, he flopped his leg from side to side, again trying to shake the other boy. In a small corner of his mind he realized that, though this battle seemed to have been going on for minutes on end, it actually had only taken a few brief seconds.

As he sat up, the boy at his leg glanced up, a dark savagery in his eyes. He gave forth another of those damned growls, and Jared used his free leg to piston kick the little bastard right in the face.

Before he could even take a breath, the first one rushed at him one more time, jaws snapping and saliva drooling from his mouth. Splayed on the sidewalk, Jared did his best to set himself for the attack, but before he could he sensed a new presence behind him. Half turning, he only got a vague glimpse of the new person before a hard hand, knotted into a fist, reached out and clubbed him in the back of the head.

After that, nothing but darkness.

Chapter Thirty-two

Capt. Leo Bannister slouched at his desk, face steepled in his hands, feeling older and more fatigued than he had in some time. In his entire life, both professional and personal, he remembered feeling this drained only a handful of times.

Once on the night of Karen's birth. It had been a difficult pregnancy, and his wife, Lisa, barely made it through. After enough time had gone by, the doctors had decided to go the C-section route. Not the easiest of procedures, despite what a lot of people thought, Lisa had developed complications, most of which, described in obtuse technical jargon, had gone right over Leo's head. He'd heard something about her blood pressure being wrong, but the rest of it had all been Greek. Concerned about his wife and his new baby, Leo had simply nodded as the doctors talked, then let them go about their business of saving his wife.

Which they had, but not until after nearly twenty-four tortured hours.

Three times in his career, men under his command had been shot on duty, while carrying out his direct orders. While each time the men had survived, those shootings had stressed him out as well.

And then, of course, came the night of David Parsons's death. Bannister had experienced the loneliest year of his life since then, with he and his daughter having, at most, half a dozen conversations.

He hadn't slept much for a few months after because every time he closed his eyes he pictured the accusing looks Karen had shot his way in the hospital that night. The officer involved had been cleared of any wrongdoing, had in fact done the best he could, and Leo had hoped that at some point his and Karen's relationship would have, if not healed, at least started down that path.

It hadn't happened so far, and now came this god-damned business down in the Zone.

What the hell was my little girl thinking?

The phone on his desk buzzed. Leo snatched it up, hoping that Karen was returning any of the several messages he'd left for her.

No such luck.

"Captain?" Det. Sergeant Phil Rosetti's voice, and the man did not sound happy.

"Yes, Sergeant?"

"We, uh, we've got a problem, sir."

Leo steadied his free hand on the desk, pressing into the hard wood surface as a way of keeping himself in check.

"Go on."

"She, uh, she gave us the slip, sir."

Leo pressed his palm even harder into the desk's surface.

"Exactly how did she do that, Sergeant? Did the GPS stop working?"

"No, sir. It worked fine. But it took us to a red Celica in the parking lot of Decker's Mall."

Knowing that Rosetti himself had planted the bug on Karen's car, Leo didn't bother to point out that she didn't drive a red Celica.

"Are you saying there's no way of knowing where my daughter is?"

"Not entirely, sir. Obviously, she gave us the slip deliberately. Still not sure how she got on to us."

"Because she's a cop's daughter. Not to mention has a ton of street smarts. I'll tell you, Rosetti, she may not care much for me or the department, at this moment, but that doesn't mean she forgot everything she learned secondhand over the years."

"Well, Captain, we're working on finding her. We're assuming she's somewhere down in the suspect area, or at least headed that way, so that's where we're concentrating our search."

Bannister pinched the bridge of his nose, attempting to rub away the tension he felt.

"Keep me, informed, Rosetti."

"Yes, sir."

After hanging up the phone, Leo reached into his desk drawer and pulled out two things.

One was a bottle of Jack Daniels. Not bothering with a glass, he uncapped the bottle and took a long swig.

Next, he pulled out a framed picture of Karen and David, set against a country background. It had been a gift from Karen, taken after David proposed. At that time, Leo, despite the usual tensions between fathers and grown daughters, had never felt closer to his little girl.

At this moment, he couldn't remember ever having felt more distant, both emotionally and physically.

Standing up, he walked away from his desk and over to the windows. His office, though not on the top floor, sat high enough up in the municipal building to give him a decent view of the city, especially at night.

Often, when he worked late, he'd take a few minutes to stand here and look out over his city. On most nights, the sight of it, softly glowing with thousands of lights, had a soothing effect for whatever troubled him.

Tonight, he barely noticed the lights. Instead, he saw only the darkness, the shadows.

And he could only think that on this night, the city looked like nothing more than a jungle, full of predators ready to rip the throat from the innocent.

"Where are you, Karen? And what the hell are you up to?"

Chapter Thirty-three

"Hey, buddy, you okay?"

Jared fluttered his eyes. He shook his head once, but the bonging that began made him desist from trying it again. Instead, he lay on the sidewalk, with something hard and angular poking into his side, until he'd gained some semblance of clarity.

The first clear thing he realized was how vulnerable lying here on the sidewalk made him.

The second thing that came to mind was that the person bending over him seemed genuinely concerned.

He was a black man, though old enough to have moonlight white hair. Big, bushy white eyebrows complemented the hair, giving him a grandfatherly appearance. He wore an Army fatigue jacket, once olive green but now so faded that it looked, at least in the streetlight, almost tan.

And he was holding out to Jared a pint liquor flask, the cap unscrewed from it.

This was, after all, the Zone.

"Have a sip if you want," the old man said. "May help you feel better."

Jared grinned at the old guy.

"Couldn't make me feel much worse," he said. He took the proffered flask, sniffed to make sure the liquid inside didn't resemble paint thinner too much, and took a swig.

Only when the liquor hit his nerve centers, firing neurons, did his mind click into gear.

He first thought of his boys, a sudden feeling of remorse that he'd blown them off just to chase a story. Following right on that came concern for how Maggie would handle them if things had gone different, and he hadn't survived the attack.

Then, he thought of Karen.

Placing his hands on the pavement, he began to push himself up, but slipped back to the ground. Groaning, he looked down and saw smears of blood on the pavement under him.

That, plus a wave of dizziness that had passed over him as he'd tried to stand, caused him to look down at his arm.

His shirt sleeve was ripped through, and his forearm resembled one big, bloody gash. But he was alive, and conscious, causing him to feel a bit of relief that the little bastard who'd chewed on him must have somehow missed biting into an artery.

Even so, he'd have to get to a hospital as quickly as he could. "Where's the woman?" he asked the old man. More people had been gathered, probably for some time, watching him, but only his elderly benefactor had bothered to come close enough to help out.

"The blonde woman? That was with you?" the old fellow asked.

"Yes. Did you see where she went?"

"Those kids took her."

Jared's head began swimming.

"Took her where? Did you see?"

He wasn't foolish enough to accuse anyone in this part of town of not interfering. Hell, if he lived in the Zone, he would keep to his own business as much as he could.

As he waited for the man to answer, Jared took a deep breath and managed to get to his knees; but when he tried to stand, he didn't quite have the strength. He stayed on his knees, breathing deep a few more times, before managing to get upright.

He looked at the old man who shrugged his shoulders, either not knowing where they took Karen or not wanting to divulge.

Or possibly not caring.

"I saw where they went," came a voice from the crowd.

Jared turned in that direction and saw the street folks parting way for a young woman, obviously a hooker, who with her pale skin, freckles, and red hair looked out of place in this neighborhood.

"Where?" he asked, and at the tenor of his voice the crowd began to melt away and go back to their usual routines. A few of the older people hung around, but most didn't.

"Over there," she said, pointing to the abandoned edifice that he and Karen had been watching.

"Didn't anyone try to stop them?"

The elderly man who'd offered him a drink a minute before took it on himself to answer that one.

"It was the boys," he said, as if that explained everything.

"Huh?" Jared worked to keep his voice as calm as possible.

"The boys," the oldster repeated, looking at Jared as if he were kind of dense. "No one around here wants to mess with those boys."

The few people who hadn't scattered, including the red-headed hooker, all nodded their heads.

"So how did they keep from taking me?" Jared asked.

A scattering of answers came his way, and the most that Jared could figure out was that during his struggle with his two assailants they had rolled their way out from the shadows and into public view. There seemed to be a partial consensus that a third person had come along and joined the attack, probably the one who had knocked him out.

But although the various street people hadn't joined in the fray, hadn't leapt to his defense, their very presence had scared off his assailants.

Just like animals, Jared thought. Although most wild animals could easily take down a human being, or beings, more often than not even the biggest and baddest would back down in the presence of people.

Not always, but often.

"So they took her into that building?"

"That's right," said the redhead. "At least, they headed in that direction. I lost sight of them somewhere around the other side of the corner."

Jared stood silent for a moment planning his next move. Obviously, besides the fact that he should be in a hospital bed, he didn't possess the skills or knowledge, let alone the courage, to try to rescue her himself. And, despite everything he knew about Karen Bannister, he couldn't think of anything to do other than call in her father.

A task he didn't look forward to in the least.

Chapter Thirty-four

Everything whirled around her.

Coming back to consciousness, Karen had an odd impression of herself as a kid, visiting the local amusement park with her parents. One of the rides, she couldn't remember what they called it, consisted of several individual cars, each set on its own platform, and all of those small platforms resting on a larger platform, set a few inches off the ground. As the ride started up, the single platform would rotate, causing all the cars to swivel back and forth, each in their own direction. This meant that each car on the ride was, at any given time, moving apart from the ride overall.

For an instant, she felt as if she was on that ride now, floating down a dark, narrow corridor.

Ahead of her an overhead light whipped back and forth. But Karen had the presence of mind to realize that the light wasn't swinging; her head was gyrating.

As she moved past the light and saw the dim blur of another one farther down the corridor, Karen realized that she wasn't floating. Only her upper body felt that way. Her legs were dragging or, she understood with a burst of clarity, being dragged.

The swirling sensation continued unabated, and a sudden urge to vomit added to her mental confusion. Acid roiled in her stomach and then, as her legs hit a bump, surged up into her esophagus.

The burning sensation, worse than any heartburn she'd ever experienced back in the days when she and David had made it a point to try exotic cuisines, threatened to overwhelm her before she managed, at great discomfort, to tamp it down.

Only with that immediate danger past did Karen next realize that her arms were suspended above and behind her. The insight came that two people were half carrying, half dragging her.

But to where?

Shaking her head in an unconscious gesture to clear out the murkiness, she searched for the last memory she had, the last tangible experience she could bring forth.

The building, she thought. She and Woodson were standing outside the building a little to the north of the Zone proper. Arrived there by following the two kids after seeing them kill and eat the cat in the alley.

After that, she remembered little of anything.

Her body sagged lower, her abdomen almost touching the ground. Karen swiveled her head to each side to catch a glimpse of her captors.

As she looked to the left, the person on that side looked down at her, and she felt her gorge rising again.

God, he couldn't have been more than ten years old. Wearing grungy blue jeans, a forest green hoodie, and black mittens with the fingers cut off, his greasy black hair hung nearly to his shoulders. Karen figured him for a white boy, but with the grime and muck all over his face it was hard to be sure. When he looked down at her, his mouth opened, which nearly made Karen vomit.

His breath reeked. As he breathed down into her face, Karen smelled dead meat, blood, and general putrefaction. In the dim light of what she could now identify as a building hallway, she couldn't see his dental work, but could only imagine what his teeth must have looked like.

When the kid saw her eyes open, he did the only thing that could add to her fright.

He growled.

His short, guttural utterance, tinged with what sounded to Karen like a warning note, caused his partner carrying her other arm to jerk up short, nearly dropping her as he halted.

For the next few minutes, the two exchanged a series of soft barking sounds and, at one point, a whine, before resuming hauling her down the hallway.

Pure shock causing her mind to clear, Karen figured that she was inside the abandoned edifice she and Woodson had been observing.

But why were they dragging her along like this? To what end?

At the end of the hall the two boys threw open a fire exit door and, hoisting her a little higher so that she could use her feet, began trundling her down the stairs.

Wanting to determine their state of mind, Karen decided to try a little test. She waited until they were in a turn between two flights of stairs, one that had an intact window about six feet from the ground. Even though the old slum building had no power or lights, the full moon canted in such a way that it shone into the stairwell.

Curious to see what they would do, Karen relaxed, sank lower, and let the two support her dead weight.

She got her answer almost immediately.

Barks from both sides. Harsh, demanding tones this time, one lower than the other. Not wanting to put herself in any more danger, if that were even possible, Karen stood up and began supporting herself.

The two kids craned around her to look at each other for a moment, then nodded and, each grasping one of her arms, moved on.

Down one more flight of stairs, and now they were far into the building's basement. The three of them stopped in front of a heavy, iron door. The boy on her right tried the knob, but it was locked, bolted or both. He then raised his hand and, growling even louder than before, enough to make Karen wonder how a young human could produce such a sound, pounded the door with all his might.

An instant later, Karen heard someone opening the bolt. The heavy iron door swung inward.

With a short bark, the boy on her left walked forward again, his companion keeping pace. For a brief, ridiculous instant Karen thought that he had directed the bark towards her, commanding her to move. But that was just too insane.

Almost as insane as the fact that during this entire trek she had not yet heard either of them use an actual human word.

They ushered her through the doorway and into the larger basement area. Windows, more than half of them boarded, made up almost an entire wall. Even so, enough of them remained to allow moonlight into the room, casting about as much illumination as on a cloudy day.

Looking around the large space, Karen realized that she had not yet reached her threshold for terror.

From the construction, it seemed as if the original basement level had held several individual rooms, which had at some point been shoddily turned into one. Exposed beams, remainders of former plasterboard, and plumbing fixtures sprawled all around the floor gave Karen that impression.

The area held no furniture. Instead, she made out blankets and sleeping bags scattered throughout the space and, off in one corner, a couple of park benches.

When she first entered the room, Karen's eyes had taken a couple of minutes to adjust. While her eyes struggled to focus, an odd medley of snorts, shuffling, and grunting started up all around her. Seeing clearly, she understood why.

About thirty or forty people lay, sat, and crouched around the basement floor. Karen couldn't tell the exact number because many of them, indeed most, clung to the shadows, lurking in the corners and under the murkier spots on the walls.

And they shifted about, some on all fours and some standing. Heads moving back and forth, some rubbed against each other. Karen felt them roaming all around, a few moving forward, while most shifted away, constantly working to get as far from her, or so she imagined, as possible.

Blinking, Karen focused as hard as she could. As she got a more accurate representation of the room, her stomach felt empty and sick.

All kids. And all male. Of the assorted people collected there, she guessed that none were older than thirteen or fourteen. Mainly Caucasian, though she spotted some blacks and Hispanics.

It was hard to see the features of most of them because of how they ducked and shied away from her gaze. But she got a clear image of dirty, torn clothing and unkempt hair, along with begrimed features.

Her breath coming hard with fear, Karen flicked her eyes from side to side, trying her best not to look at all those kids massed around her.

In the next instant, she regretted that move.

As her gaze whipped around the basement room, she froze. Her sight fixated on a small area against the far wall, a stray beam of moonlight shining through a broken pane.

Still, motionless, she found she couldn't take her eyes off a frayed, dirty ski vest that, at least from the distance, seemed to be a darker color.

"No," she whispered, despair sweeping over her.

Her few moments of quiescence must have been enough to lull her two captors because, with a twist and forward motion, she managed to break free from them and rush over to that pile of clothing

The old ski vest was small and dark blue, and Karen's stomach clenched as she noticed the dark, brownish stains splattered across it.

"Ricky," she said, to no one in particular.

She moved closer, the mass of kids keeping itself back, and knelt down by the little vest. Had the night's events not numbed her to the core, she knew this sight would have sent her to a point beyond which she couldn't return.

Besides the rust-colored stains, the edges of the garment were shredded, hanging down in jagged strips. The front of the jacket was unzipped, and Karen could see a handful of small sticks residing in the interior.

Oddly-shaped, whitish sticks.

Bones, she thought. *My God, these are his bones. Dammit, he should have stayed in the shelter, where he was safe.*

Two pairs of hands grasped her from behind and yanked her back. The motion served to jolt Karen out of her reverie.

And the next oddity about her surroundings hit her.

The smell. Rancid, like the breath of the boy who had brought her here, but magnified a hundred times. To her mind, rapidly losing its balance, it seemed as if a dozen different types of decay had gathered and coalesced in that room.

Glancing at the floor, she saw scattered all around what probably, in better light, would turn out to be dozens of other tiny skeletons, each one reinforcing what she'd just seen in Ricky's jacket. Small animals and vermin that had either wandered into, or more likely been brought into, this little isolated pocket of hell.

All of this, illuminated by that scattered moonlight worming its way through the windows on one wall, she took in within a few short moments.

In the next heartbeat or two, she became aware of one final feature of the room. The far corner, opposite of the windows, was shrouded in darkness. Yet even that corner didn't hold pure black, but shades of gray that shifted back and forth.

And Karen, almost inured to new shocks, had the feeling that something lurked in that corner. She strained her eyes, searching the recess, but couldn't make out anything more than some sort of vague, hulking shape.

A shove sent her lurching forward.

Toward that corner.

As soon as Karen stopped, she felt another push, enough to give her the message. Not knowing what else to do, she took a breath and continued walking forward.

About seven feet out, a low, threatening growl came from the corner.

Karen froze, and the children ranged across the basement reacted. Some perked up, while others cowered even farther back. A few whimpered in return. Had Karen shut her eyes and listened, she would have sworn that a litter of wild dogs surrounded her even though her brain clearly told her that only human children inhabited the basement with her.

Behind her, one of the two who'd carried her to this place barked, loud and demanding, in response to the sound from the corner. An even lower, but louder growl came in response and Karen felt the two kids back up.

Karen wondered how many more shocks she could take when a new sound came from that mysterious corner.

"Come forward please," said a scratchy, old man's voice, "and let me see you."

Chapter Thirty-five

Lewis Preston leaned back in his black swivel chair and took a small sip of his coffee. He wanted enough in his system to keep him awake but not so much that he became jittery. Even though it had been a quiet night so far, with no new "patients" being brought in, one never knew what the night might hold, so a medical examiner had to keep himself steady.

Then again, at sixty-four he also had to keep himself awake.

He grimaced at the thought that, in a normal world, no way a veteran with his years, and so close to retirement, would hold down the graveyard shift. But between Mortenson's honeymoon, Rachel's father passing away, and a recent hire who yesterday got sick and resigned in the middle of his first autopsy, the ME's office was a bit short-handed at the moment.

When it came right down to it, Preston found he really didn't mind the graveyard shift. If nothing else, it took him back to his first few years with the city, when they assigned him this shift the majority of the time. Back in the days before he'd learned everything he now knew about man's depravity to man, the callousness of the world at large, and the ability of the bureaucracy to twist reality. So it was comforting to sit here, his only companion the ambient noise of florescent lights and body coolers, and reminisce about the simpler times.

The sound of footsteps in the corridor outside made Preston look up. A half a minute later the door swung open to admit a single visitor.

"Well, well," Preston said, "I've seen you down here more this past week than in the last ten years."

"One of those months," Leo Bannister said as he pulled over a chair and sat down in front of Preston's desk.

"If anyone was here to see us, they'd think this was kind of sad," Preston said. "Two old war horses with nothing better to do, hanging out in the morgue in the wee hours."

"Maybe so. Got anything stronger than coffee?"

"I do, but you kind of look as if you've already had some tonight. Whatcha doing here anyway?"

"Waiting on a call."

"A call? Then shouldn't you be at your office?"

"Got my cell. Plus I told the people on night duty to transfer any calls to my office down here."

"Which still leaves the question as to why here?"

Bannister slumped into his seat and half closed his eyes. When he spoke his voice was not quite normal speed.

"I may have screwed things up, Pres."

The coroner took another sip from his cup.

"You talking about what I think you're talking about?"

"Thought I was so smart," Bannister mumbled. "Thought I was being so clever, working to keep things under wraps."

"For the most part," Preston said.

"Right. More or less. Can't keep something like this entirely quiet, but all in all I did pretty well at it."

"Sure, but was it the right thing to do?"

Bannister looked away from his old friend for a moment.

"We had to do something, Pres. I don't want to sound like the sheriff from a 50s drive-in flick, but we couldn't let word get out about what we suspected."

"What we knew," the ME corrected him.

"Fine. What we knew. Rather, partially knew."

"Partially?"

"Look at it this way. All we really know is that there's a group of young people down in the Zone who are going around eating vagrants. Can you imagine the kind of god-damned circus we'd have going on if that got out? And even though I've had people combing that area, we haven't been able to find more than traces of these punks."

"That may be your problem," Preston said.

"Come again?"

"Your attitude. You called them punks. I may be off here, but it sure seems that you're treating them like any other gang."

"What else would they be?"

"Well for one, if they were a standard gang, wouldn't the GTF have had something on them ahead of time? And wouldn't you have run down at least some traces? Besides that, if there were a street gang anywhere in the country that had a penchant, as part of their initiation or whatever, to chew people up, we'd have heard about it by now. I know I'm not the detective, Leo, but you've got to admit I've been at this game for as long as you. Longer actually, since I'm facing the mandatory in a few weeks' time."

"Again, Pres, what's your point?"

The ME picked a folder off his desk and threw it to Leo. Leo caught it, but didn't open it right away.

"What's this?" he asked.

"Print off of some research I did. Had to get hard copies because the old eyes don't take computer screens like they used to. If you want, I can just give it to you on a thumb drive or such."

"Research about what?" Bannister asked.

"Open it up."

Bannister did so, flicking over the first few pages, then slowing down as he began to absorb the gist of the material.

About halfway through, he closed the file and glanced up.

"You can't be serious," he said.

"Have your people come up with any theory that works better?"

"Not yet. But, Jesus, Pres. This is too much."

Preston shrugged his shoulders.

"Take it or leave it. Not my job to do the detecting for you guys. I just thought you may want to see it."

"I've heard of this happening, of course. But ... feral children? When did you think of this?"

"With the second body. When your people brought the first one in, I didn't know what to think. Assumed we were dealing with some kind of cannibal psychosis. Except that the teeth were clearly those of children."

"So what made you think ..."

"Two things, Leo. One, the fact that there were several different teeth represented, plus the size."

"You've mentioned the size before, Pres."

"Of course. Leo, these aren't just young people, they're kids, damned near toddlers. My guess is, of the several samples I acquired, none of them were over ten. Twelve at the very most. So you tell me. If there were a gang that employed eight-year old cannibals, how long could that stay under wraps?"

Bannister tossed the folder back onto the desk.

"So I see your point. At least that far. But how you get from there to the idea of a bunch of mini Tarzans running around the city ..."

"I'll give you that much, Leo. Every recorded instance of a feral child that I could find took place in the wilds, mainly around Africa and India. Occasionally in places like Borneo or Sumatra."

"But you're saying it's happened in the middle of a city? That a child somehow grew up wild right within the middle of civilization? Sorry, Pres. I can't stretch it that far."

"'Fraid you'll have to stretch it even further, buddy. If I'm right, we're not dealing just with one kid who somehow grew up wild in the inner city, but several."

The two old-timers, men who up to a few weeks back thought they had seen and heard it all, locked gazes.

"That doesn't sound possible," Bannister said.

"Not the way I've laid it out. No. Which means that something's missing from the equation."

" Such as?"

"Don't have a clue. But if we find it, you'll find your killers."

A grimace of restrained anguish passed over Bannister's expression.

"You got ulcers now, buddy?" the ME asked. "Or maybe something you haven't told me yet? Just what is this call you're waiting on? And why not at home?"

"I really screwed this one up, Pres. And worst of all, I think they've got my daughter."

Chapter Thirty-six

Hunger gripped him. A ravenous hunger, such as he'd never felt before, consumed Simon. The old one had told him stories about extreme deprivation, but Simon had never experienced it himself. For as long as he could remember, he'd been sheltered and guided by his sire, and while they'd occasionally had lean times, they'd never gone more than a day or so without some sort of sustenance.

This had left Simon, unused to such bowel-clutching want, angry.

For years, he'd done everything the sire had asked of him. Everything demanded of him. As the first to come along, so he'd been told, Simon was the natural one set to take over upon the old guy's death, something he'd been planning on for quite some time.

And now, it had all come crashing down.

Simon had been away from the building, scouting around for some sort of food, and upon returning noticed a small contingent of the pack heading out. In the past, Simon had led all the forays, both large and small, and he wondered now what the young ones were up to.

He couldn't believe that the old one had lost so much faith in him so quickly, and yet here he stood, watching a group of the young ones heading off into the night.

Simon followed after them, intent on knowing their goal.

****

Now, more than hunger fueled his anger. He stood outside of their building, fists clenching and unclenching, trying to control himself. The old man had sent the pack after the woman from the night before, the one who'd managed to escape.

He'd castigated Simon for his failure on that venture, and now here they were taking her into the lair, bringing her right into the heart of their lives. A few nights back, when Simon had stood humiliated before the pack, it had seemed like all their leader had cared about was food and concealment.

And now this.

Simon uttered a low moan, half of anguish and half of rage. He'd served the old man faithfully, done everything asked of him, worked as hard as he could to bring the younger cubs up to par, only to be cast aside after a single failure.

As he stood there, trembling, he could feel the burns of the scars upon his back and the tension in his joints, the remnants of his "training" by his beloved sire. In an instant, all the hurt, pain and humiliation he'd tamped down over the years came surging up.

They brought the woman into the lair.

But Simon would be damned if she would get back out again.

Chapter Thirty-seven

With all the small children, all male she'd noticed, whimpering and whining behind her, Karen didn't see any choice but to obey the voice in the corner. It wasn't black back there, just more shadowy and gloomy than the rest of the basement.

About four feet out from the corner, the voice spoke again.

"Close enough. I just needed you near enough to see. And also to get you some distance from my pack."

Karen froze, peering into the dimness. She couldn't see many details, but she could make out a hunched form, squatting over a pile of blankets or something that looked like cloth. She also got, though she couldn't quite tell where this came from, the impression of extreme age.

Though that may just have been because of the way the voice sounded.

"You got away from us once before," the old man gloated. "Not so lucky the second time, were you?"

Karen took a few deep, calming breaths before answering. She'd had bad times in her life, experienced tragedy, but never had she felt anything near the sort of paralyzing terror that now gripped her.

Not a stupid woman, she knew that the rest of her life could be measured in hours, probably minutes.

"What do you want from me?" she asked.

A minute passed, as if the figure in the corner were contemplating. When it spoke again, the voice held a somewhat wistful tone.

"Things haven't been going well," it said. "I thought I had a good plan, but lately it seems to have come apart."

"Plan?" While the emotion of terror still predominated, she couldn't help a slight bit of curiosity as to the whole situation.

"You were with the two men before, right? The ... policemen."

"Yes," Karen said, wondering at the hesitation. Now that the figure had spoken a couple of full sentences, she noticed it had an odd accent that she couldn't place.

"You know that, if not interrupted, my cubs would have killed you."

"Cubs?" Karen couldn't help but blurt out the word.

"Yes, my cubs. Behind you."

She half turned and looked back at the assorted boys lounging around the basement area. Confused at first, she assumed that the corner phantom meant that all of these were his children. But with most of them hovering around the same age, how could that be?

Did all of this madness have something to do with some bizarre polygamy court?

Beyond that, though she couldn't be sure in the gloom, she thought that she recognized a few of those begrimed, half-hidden faces.

"Okay," she said, drawing out the word to give herself time to think. "Why would they have killed me?"

The figure shifted, and Karen thought she heard a slight creaking, as of bones. With its next words, it made clear that it didn't intend to answer her question.

"The first time you survived was accidental, a happenstance. The second time was deliberate."

A short squealing sounded to Karen's right. Glancing over, she saw a small, tailed shape scuttling out from the side wall. The shape, most likely a rat, only managed to cover about three feet before one of the children, wearing dirty jeans and a stained white tank top, pounced on the animal. With a flashing grin, the boy sank his teeth into the furry body, which for just a second squirmed in his grip until going limp. Chewing as he went, blood running down his cheeks and onto his neck, the boy scuttled back into the shadows. A few of the others cast envious glances his way.

Karen clutched her stomach.

"The little ones are hungry," the scratchy voice said. "I haven't allowed hunting for several days."

Karen stayed silent, not having a clue what to say.

"Since the attack on you and your friends," the voice clarified.

"Okay."

"But when they came upon you tonight, I didn't want you killed."

Karen didn't want to engage in ordinary conversation with the form in the corner. But the surreality of her situation forced her to.

"Why?" she asked.

Somewhere in the basement behind her, she heard a short thud, then a restrained whimper.

"Because I need your help," came from the corner.

"My help? You don't even know me, and I sure as hell don't even know what you are."

A sudden snuffling, then a liquidy-sounding cough interrupted whatever the person in the corner was going to answer. After a minute of phlegmy throat clearing, it continued.

"My cubs know you, have known you for some time. You work down in this part of the city, correct?"

Karen hesitated with her answer, but decided that her interrogator probably did know something about her already. Besides, rule number one in the hostage handbook was to do what you could to personalize yourself with your captor.

"Not all the time," she answered, "but often enough."

"The first time, when we killed the two males, a few of the cubs recognized you from your work around the area. They even hesitated to finish you off, a remnant of their former morality that I hadn't been able to snuff out. Since then, we've managed to piece together a fairly complete picture of you."

"I need to know something," Karen said.

"Yes?"

"Is my friend okay? The one who was with me tonight? Or did your ... cubs ... kill him?"

"They left him alone. Their orders were to capture you, not antagonize you."

Karen felt herself becoming a bit angry, which probably meant she was coming out of her shock. She didn't know if that was a good or bad thing, but at the moment didn't really care much.

"But you wanted to antagonize me last time, when you killed the two I was with. So what's so different about tonight?"

She'd raised her voice, which as far as she could tell didn't bother the being in the corner. However, behind her she heard some of the children rustling and moving about. Even more unsettling, she thought she could hear a few instances of teeth snapping together.

"You may want to lower your voice," the corner being said, "lest they get too agitated. I can't control them as well as I used to."

Deciding to get to the root of the issue, Karen took a deep breath.

"Who are you?" she asked.

The form in the corner had been shifting and squirming, as if trying to find relief from some sort of low-grade, chronic irritation. Now it stopped moving and assumed a total stillness.

"It's not so much a question of who," the voice finally croaked out, "as a what. And I'm not quite sure how to explain what I am."

"But you said you need my help."

"Yes. I believe you can assist us."

"But why would I? By your own admission your – pack here – is a bunch of killers. Forget why. How could I help you?"

"It would take some effort. But I believe ..."

A sharp slam behind her caused Karen to whirl around. On the other side of the basement, the iron door through which she'd been dragged had flung open, so forcefully that it looked as if the knob had cut a divot out of the plasterboard with which it impacted.

A young man stood in the doorway. Not fully grown, but not as young or as small as most of those she'd already seen. He looked to be about thirteen, maybe fourteen, though the gauntness in his cheeks and his wiry form made pegging his age difficult. He had long, greasy black hair that hung to his shoulders, and even accounting for the moonlight illumination he looked unnaturally pale, as if he suffered from anemia or some other blood disorder.

For a brief instant, a ludicrous notion entered her head, making her wonder if she was in the midst of a band of vampires.

But any sort of fantastic nonsense fled in the next instant, when some clouds outside must have parted, allowing even more light than before to enter through the haphazard windows on the other wall.

She could see that the young man who'd just entered was angry, raging in fact. His fists clenched so tightly that they looked like mallets of pure bone. His dark eyes were flashing, practically flaming in his ire.

"Why's this bitch still alive?" he snarled, in a voice louder and deeper than his apparent age would indicate. A voice that, to Karen, sounded somewhat familiar.

"Because," came the old voice from behind her, though somehow not sounding quite so frail and scratchy as before, "I asked that she be brought here."

As the voice continued she heard rustling, the slight shifting of something, giving Karen the feeling that whoever had been lurking in the corner had stood up and moved forward a bit.

"You asked?" the teen at the door roared. He moved forward now, coming closer to the middle of the basement. "Have you gone senile, old man? Do you have any idea what you're doing?"

The children scattered around the room moved restlessly, some of them whimpering, and a few ran over and buried their faces in corners.

Just like a puppy I had as a kid used to do whenever a thunderstorm began.

The argument was still going on.

"How dare you question me?" The corner voice shouted out, now stronger than before. "How dare you question your sire?"

At the change in timbre, Karen turned in an attempt to get her first good look at the mysterious figure.

As he walked out into the dim beams illuminating the room, she felt the final strand of her sanity begin to fray.

Before her stood a wolf.

Part III: The Lair

Chapter Thirty-eight

The paramedics had almost finished treating Jared when another car pulled up. A black Lincoln, it came equipped with flashing blue and red lights in the front grill.

Damn, he thought. *This can't be good.*

Two police cars had already shown up in response to the 911 call that someone, sure as hell not Jared, had made. The sequence had seemed normal at first. An ambulance arrived, then a few minutes later came the first patrol car. While the paramedics, having done an initial patch-up on his injuries, were checking the dilation of his pupils, the lone officer in the first car began asking Jared questions.

Long before any of the official vehicles appeared, a crowd made up of equal parts street people and visitors to the area had shown up. While Jared couldn't deny that a few of the passersby had earlier saved him from his attackers, with the scuzzy looks of most of them, he didn't feel any real sense of security until the officials arrived on the scene.

Despite some grogginess from the attack, he'd retained enough sense to make up the most basic story, keeping Karen's name out of it. But he hadn't thought it necessary to conceal his own name, and as the EMT guys treated some abrasions on his forehead and cheek, the cop went off to his car.

A minute later, another patrol car coasted in and sat idling. Two officers got out of the second car and walked over to confer with the first. After a few minutes of quiet discussion, they walked back over and sat down in their vehicle, as far as Jared could see not doing anything.

But they didn't leave, causing a little tendril of worry in his gut.

"A little shaky, but not too bad," one of the EMT's said as he unwrapped a blood pressure cuff from Jared's arm. "Especially considering how torn up you are. Still, we need to take you in to be thoroughly checked out by an MD."

"Okay," Jared said, "let's go."

The two paramedics glanced at each other for a moment, then one of them went over to talk to one of the uniformed officers. They pitched their voices low enough so that Jared couldn't make out what they were saying. Judging by a couple of brusque head shakes, he didn't think it was the most amiable of conversations.

The paramedic came back over and crouched on the ambulance's bumper.

"Why don't we wait a few minutes," he said.

His partner looked at him, and Jared started to say something in protest, when the black Lincoln with the flashing grill lights pulled up.

Uh huh, Jared thought.

Three men emerged from the Lincoln, two from the front seat and one from the back. Jared assumed that the two front men were detectives or someone higher up in the police hierarchy, but it didn't matter when the third man came into view.

Leo Bannister.

Shit, Jared thought.

Really, he shouldn't have been surprised that the man would show up. No doubt the little tracker Karen had mentioned finding on her car wasn't the only tab the man had on his only child. Jared wondered, though, how much he would field the blame for Karen's disappearance.

He didn't have long to find out.

Bannister came to within about twenty feet of the ambulance and met the first patrolman who had arrived. The two of them spoke in low tones, with Bannister glancing in Jared's direction.

"Okay," the EMT who'd been patching Jared up said, "this is a bit much. I don't care what that cop said. You've been through hell. Let's get you to the hospital and ..."

"We're not going anywhere for a while," Jared said.

"'Scuse me?"

"Trust me on this one. You're not going to be allowed to leave, at least not with me in tow."

The paramedic gave him a puzzled look just as Bannister broke off his conversation with the uniformed officer and turned towards the ambulance.

"Here it comes," Jared muttered under his breath.

"Mr. Woodson," Bannister said as he came alongside the rear of the ambulance, "I'd like a word with you."

"Figured you might."

The captain gave the two paramedics a look developed from years of dealing with suspected criminals, actual criminals, and screw-off subordinates. The two young guys glanced at each other, then put their stuff down and walked away.

They couldn't leave their vehicle unattended, so they got as far as the two cop cars and then hung around, looking confused.

At least, Jared thought, *the captain didn't waste any time.*

"So where's my daughter, mister?"

"I'm fine, sir. Thanks for asking. A little roughed up, but ..."

"I'm not interested in you, fella. I want my kid. Do you know where she is?"

"I have a hunch, but it's only that."

"Well?"

For an answer, Jared pointed off to the side, towards the abandoned building that he and Karen had been watching. When Jared pointed towards the structure, he heard gasps from the crowd.

Looking in the building's direction, Bannister didn't react to the crowd's response.

"You sure that's where she is?" he asked.

"No. Not even close to sure. But that's where we were headed when we were set upon."

A new tightness appeared in the captain's face.

"Was she hurt?"

"I honestly don't know, Captain. But they seemed a lot more interested in putting me down than in hurting her."

"They? They who?"

Woodson had been beaten around not too long before, and he'd had to sit patiently while being checked, patched, and bandaged by a couple of men nearly half his age. Beyond all that, though, he couldn't take his eyes from that building, figuring it at fifty-fifty that Karen was even still alive.

In short, he felt a bad attitude coming on. And while it never made sense to antagonize a police official, especially one like Leo Bannister, the newsman in him had had enough.

"Captain, I'd be willing to bet that you have a pretty damned good idea who's taken her."

A red tinge appeared on Bannister's face, but he kept his voice at a normal volume.

"Mr. Woodson, what were you and Karen doing out here? In this part of town, at this time of night? Tell me, mister, just what the goddamned hell is going on here."

Realizing he'd come off as childish, Jared sighed. This was no time for a *mano a mano* pissing contest. Not with a woman missing.

"Take a seat, Captain," he said, motioning to the other side of the ambulance bumper he still occupied, "and I'll tell you a tale."

Chapter Thirty-nine

Madness.

At first, upon turning around in that moonlit basement, Karen believed that somewhere down the line she had gone completely insane. In flashing bits of moments, her mind replayed everything that had happened during the last week, and she began to doubt whether any of it had actually taken place.

At what point had she lost her mind? The fight on the street, when she'd been snatched away from Woodson? Or at some point during her previous convalescence when she'd struggled to put the pieces together?

Or even farther back? Had she detached from reality at the time of the first attack, when Gleason and O'Brien died while defending her?

For that matter, had the two cops ever existed outside her disordered mental processes?

At some point, maybe, when she'd been searching the streets for Ricky, who'd snuck off from the shelter and whose remains she'd seen here in this hellhole. Did something happen during those two nights she'd been out looking for him that had unhinged her mind?

Hell, why not see just how far she could take it?

Had anything in her life been real since the night a year ago that she'd gotten the call about David? Maybe ever since then, they'd locked her in a room somewhere, force-feeding her medication.

So, yes, as she whirled around to confront the creature that had emerged from its corner hideaway, Karen Bannister was definitely questioning her sanity.

Lurching backwards, she took a closer look at the creature. It wasn't a wolf, as she'd first thought. Not exactly.

But it sure as hell didn't look human.

The creature before her stood about five and a half feet tall. Maybe taller, but it stood with shoulders hunched and back bowed. If it held a cane in one hand, it would have given the impression of an old man crippled over from back problems.

That explanation wouldn't have flown, though, because the thing didn't have hands. At least not exactly.

The appendages at the end of its arms had fur. They looked something like the paws of a dog going through mange. Pinkish skin showed through in places, but elsewhere clumps of wiry, grayish fur covered the flesh. The fingers looked like partial claws due to the long, curved nails that projected outwards.

The rest of the body looked human, except that the arms and legs seemed longer than those of a normal adult, with bony projections at the knees and elbows.

As for the face – God – Karen couldn't describe that face. Essentially human in configuration, it seemed elongated, as if it hadn't developed a snout that nature had intended it to have. Whiskers, a mixture of gray and white, sprouted out all over his chin and jaw.

And the eyes gleamed.

Karen peered closer, attempting to figure out their color. A mixture of reddish-yellow, with numerous other hues mixed in, flickered out from those orbs, making the thing seem angry even though its posture and bearing didn't really support that.

"So now you know," it said to her.

Know? Karen didn't know anything. Except that she was positive she'd lost her mind. But as she turned away from those strange, flaming eyes and looked around her, taking in the basement scene with a new perspective, she felt close to comprehending something.

Close, but not quite.

"I don't understand," she said as she turned back to the thing from the corner. "What are you ..."

"I'll deal with you in a minute, female," the being said as it turned towards the young man who'd barged into the basement.

The two squared off, teenage street kid and creature out of a nightmare, facing each other down across a distance of nearly a dozen feet. Karen moved to the side, realizing that she didn't want to get caught between the two of them, while around her she heard the whimpering and whining of the little kids that the strange being had called its "cubs."

That dim picture forming in her head became a bit clearer, and as she started to grasp the possibility of the tableau before her, she worried anew about her mental stability.

"Why is she alive?" the young man asked again. His voice, though human, came out in a tone resembling nothing less than a dog's bark.

"She's alive," the old figure said, its tone controlled and rather stately, "because I need her alive. And keep in mind that, while you're my second, I'm still the sire."

The younger one fidgeted, his hands curling and uncurling. As Karen watched those hands, its digits genuflecting back and forth, she noticed, even in the moonlight, that the nails were longer even than those of the average homeless kid's, not generally known for their hygiene.

He took a step forward, his shoulders hunching up, as if to protect his neck and head. With a quick flick of his head he tossed his bangs away from his eyes, the motion so animalistic that for an instant Karen couldn't even see the kid as human.

She glanced towards the older figure, who hadn't budged. Yet even motionless, he emanated such an aura of danger that, had the two clashed that instant, Karen would not have wanted to guess as to the outcome.

The two predators were sizing each other up, and it occurred to Karen that in all her time on the streets, all her dealings with the vagrants, the lost and dispossessed, the abused and the abusers, she had never seen an encounter that held such latent savagery.

No, she realized in the next instant. Savagery was not the word. These two facing off with each other, one human and the other of uncertain heritage, weren't savages.

Not quite.

At least not in the dictionary definition.

They were primitives.

Atavists.

Never had Karen seen such a visceral encounter as the one shaping before her.

Then, just like that, it ended. The younger one gave forth a short, peremptory bark, then backed down, hands uncurling and taking about three steps back. His shoulders unhunched, he threw a long, lingering look at Karen, then turned back to the older one.

"Yeah, you're the sire," he said, "but not for long."

He headed across the basement to the door, the smaller kids scampering out of his way as he approached. Several of them, Karen noticed, threw longing, wistful looks his way. As he opened the door, a couple of them edged his way, some of them moving on all fours.

What kind of madhouse, Karen wondered, *have I fallen into?*

As the few younger ones started to follow the departing teen, a low growl from the old figure caused them to halt. They glanced back and forth between the two antagonists, reminding Karen of frightened little puppies, not sure which way to turn.

The door shut behind the teenager, a few whimpers from the younger ones trailing off.

She turned back to the creature from the corner, noticing as she did that he seemed a bit reduced, not quite as formidable as he'd looked a moment ago.

And she couldn't help but wonder if that had anything to do with the fact that some clouds must have massed in the sky, reducing the moonlight coming in through the windows to a faint beam.

"What are you?" she asked from the verge of hysteria.

The strange, elongated face turned her way. Those flaming eyes, now merely flickering, regarded her.

"I'm the last one," it said. "The last natural member of the Brethren."

Chapter Forty

"Are you a werewolf?" Karen cringed at the ridiculousness of the query while unable to avoid voicing it.

The creature before her sighed and shook its head.

"Not really," it said, "at least, not like you mean."

She shuddered, working hard to suppress a giggle.

"Then what are you?"

"The last," it repeated, "of the Brethren."

Around her, all the young children crept forward, as if wanting to hear the conversation but leery of being chastised. It came to her again how they acted so much like a pack of wild animals. The creature in the corner had referred to them more than once as its "cubs." It finally occurred to her that that's what their behavior reminded her of.

A litter of animal cubs.

But these were people, children. How could they possibly ...

"You said that a minute ago," she said. "Brethren. What does that mean? What are you?"

The creature sighed again and slumped even further. Hard to tell in the dimness of the basement, but it seemed defeated, as if time and tide had worn it down.

"I'm not a werewolf," it croaked out, "at least not how you're thinking. But I am a member of a different – species – than you."

"You said the last member," Karen said.

"True. The last natural one of my kind."

Karen turned and looked at the assorted children, who now sat around the basement watching the tableau, mostly silent save for an occasional whimper or sniffle.

They reminded her of *Peter Pan's* Lost Boys.

She was starting to get it.

And she didn't like it one bit.

"Another species," she said, realizing that she was spending an awful lot of time repeating whatever the – thing – in front of her said.

"Yes. One similar to you, though obviously not too much."

"You don't change in the moonlight or anything, do you?" Karen asked.

"Of course not. Come."

He reached out with his cross between a hand and a paw, as if to take her hand. Karen shrank away, the thought of touching him causing her stomach to roil.

"Female!" The voice took on a bitter tone. "If I wanted to hurt you, I'd have already ripped your throat out and gorged on your blood!"

Karen stood, trembling and gasping as her throat closed up.

"Never mind," he said, dropping his arm away from her. "I shouldn't have to resort to fear yet. Just come with me."

Turning his back on her, the sire walked across the basement to the far wall, the one comprised of boarded-up windows. As he did so, some of the kids in the room scurried away from him, while others rubbed themselves against his ankles as he passed.

This is insane, she told herself for the twelfth time. *Those kids are all human.* Apart from their odd mannerisms, they looked normal to her. So what inspired them to have such animalistic tendencies?

As he entered the central part of the room, she got a good look at his clothing for the first time.

A suit and jacket, like a businessman would wear, though worn and patched, as if he'd picked it up in a second-hand store.

Or a Dumpster.

"Come here," he barked, his face set and determined. "Don't even think about resisting. If I have to, I'll set my cubs on you and you'll be dead within seconds. I'd rather not, because things could get out of hand between them. They haven't had a good meal in days."

The reference to their last "good meal" brought to Karen's mind the sight of those gnawed-on bones she'd found in Ricky's jacket.

She couldn't think of anything to do but follow his orders.

At the same time, she found herself praying that Woodson was alive, somehow unhurt, and could get to her with some sort of rescue.

She hadn't come this close to a prayer since the night David died.

As she approached him, the sire positioned himself in the middle of the windowed area, about six feet out from the wall. It was the area of greatest illumination in the entire basement, which wasn't saying much, and she understood now that he wanted her to get a good look at him.

Which left her more confused than before.

In basic outline, he appeared human. Or at least anthropoid. Two legs, two arms, a trunk and a head. Five digits on each "paw" and two eyes and ears. A mouth and nose.

And hair.

Lots and lots of hair.

And it was hair, she saw as she took a step closer. Not fur or anything like that. Fairly straight, though curling in places, under normal conditions it would pass for ordinary human hair.

But he had so much of it, almost covering his entire face, as she'd noted earlier. Not just where the beard grew on an ordinary man, but the cheeks and forehead nearly covered with gray, wiry bristles.

It coated the backs of the hands. Again, in and of itself not unbelievable. Karen had seen men as hirsute before. Then, as he raised his hands up palms outwards, she saw that the hair extended there as well.

What, she wondered, *must the parts of his body covered by clothing look like?*

Since he'd held them up, she examined the hands next and saw that, while at first glance they resembled normal human hands, they had distinct differences. For one, the digits were longer than normal and oddly-shaped, almost cylindrical. The nails that capped each digit were narrower, pointed and nearly black. Not the black of grime and dirt lodged underneath, but a discoloration that seemed part of the nail itself.

While definitely nails, in the dim light they could be mistaken for claws.

"Well?" the creature said.

With his question, Karen glanced from his hands to his face, knowing that she'd been avoiding a too-close inspection of the facial area.

Because that was where he deviated the most from humanity.

While from a distance the face could pass for human, up close it had a definite lupine, or maybe canine, shape. The elongated nose and jaw she'd noticed earlier, but now she could see a pair of noticeably pointed ears. Two rows of teeth protruded from the mouth with an abundance of sharp, canine-looking members.

And yet the thing could talk. How was that possible?

"Well?" he repeated.

"You're not human," Karen said.

"Of course not. But ..."

"But from a distance, in poor lighting, and with a strategic covering of clothing, you could pass for one."

"Very good."

He waited for her to say more.

"So you're not like an actual werewolf," she said, drawing out her speech so her thoughts could keep up.

"No such things exist. Superstition. Pure imagination."

"But you're ..." She paused, not quite sure how to put it into words.

"Yes? Tell me, what am I?"

It clicked then, in her mind, and Karen felt as if she was thinking clearly for the first time in days.

"You're where the stories came from."

The creature nodded, and his features relaxed a bit.

"The Brethren," he said.

"That's what you call yourselves?"

"Called," he corrected. "In the same way some primitive tribes in secluded areas refer to themselves as simply The People or The Folk. As I said earlier, as far as I know I'm the last natural one."

Karen turned from him and looked back over the basement. She saw the kids, most of them huddled together now, as if seeking to share bodily warmth. They looked at her with confused, frightened faces, and Karen thought of all the wayward children who had paraded through the shelter in the years she'd worked there. Those gathered before her could have been more of that batch, more of those lost souls seeking comfort or solace in a world that didn't care for them and never would.

Instead, they'd ended up here.

With the last member of the Brethren.

Last *natural* member, she corrected herself.

She knew the answer then but was unsure whether to feel relieved or frightened at the knowledge.

"What are all of them here for?" she asked as she turned back to the sire.

"Survival," he said, giving her the answer she'd expected.

Of course.

What else could it be?

Chapter Forty-one

"That's right," Captain Bannister said into his cellular. "I need Jameson and his team down here right now. I know he's not in my command. I'll square it with Captain Spears later. For right now, give Jameson the address I relayed to you and tell him I need him in thirty minutes. Forty-five max."

Putting the phone away, he turned and glared at the building that, if the reporter knew what he was talking about, held his daughter. The urge flamed within him to charge through that ramshackle door and pull her out of there, but enough years as a cop had given him the ability to override his emotions.

Barely.

"Thought you all were trying to keep this low key."

Bannister looked over at Woodson.

"Mind your place," he told the reporter.

"Look I'm just saying ..."

"Don't say anything. The only reason you're here is because you may be able to help. That doesn't give you free rein to ..."

"Don't be stupid, Captain. Are you actually going to send a bunch of SWAT types in there without telling them what they're up against?"

"What makes you think they're a SWAT unit?"

"Maybe because I've been a reporter in this area for nearly a dozen years. Don't you think by now I know all the higher-ups in the department? I know who Jameson is as much as you do."

Bannister strode over until he stood only about half a foot from Jared.

"What the hell are you talking about? There's only a couple of runway kids in there. Who formed themselves into some kind of small-time gang. You think our people can't handle something like that?"

"If it's only a few teen runaways, why do you need a full-out squad? Why not just take a couple of uniforms and waltz in there and grab Karen? Hell, you probably don't even need guns. A couple of rookies with night sticks should be able to ..."

Almost too fast to see, Bannister's hand lashed out and connected with Woodson's face. The reporter managed to half roll with it, but even so the blow moved him back a step or two. Seeing the sudden grimace on the man's face, Bannister looked away, staring down instead at his open hand. Seeing the smear of blood there, he looked back up, a tendril of self disgust worming its way through his gut.

The reporter looked like he'd been through several levels of hell. Bloodied, his clothes torn and his arm cut damned near to shreds. Bannister knew that, concern for Karen or no, taking it out on a guy this banged up didn't come close to being kosher.

Ashamed, Bannister looked around. Three patrol cars had accompanied them down here, but the officers assigned to them had stayed in their vehicles, making a big show of their heads being downturned and occupied. And, with three cop cars on the block, the crowd that had initially gathered had faded away into the shadows.

The two paramedics, who'd earlier been patching Woodson up, were another story. They'd come forward a step or two, hands tensing at their sides, and Bannister couldn't really blame them at all.

"Okay, Captain," Woodson said, massaging the side of his face with his relatively-unscathed hand, "you made your point. Maybe I was a little too caustic to a man with a missing kid. But you've got to admit that I've got a legitimate point."

"So make the point," Bannister said, finding it hard to look at the man. "Just knock off the smartass comments."

"My point is that I think you know damned good and well that what's waiting in that building isn't a couple of run-of-the-mill street kids. You and your buddies have done everything you could to keep things hush hush. You know that something damned deadly has been prowling these streets for weeks now, possibly longer. You're not sure just what, but you know it's not anything you've experienced before. Am I right?"

"Okay, so we've got some weird sort of cult. Bunch of Goth kids or something. No biggie. We can handle that."

"No, Captain. You can't. Trust me on this. I've seen them up close. Hell, take a good look at me if you don't believe me. Two of your men were torn to shreds by these things. We both know that it's a bunch of kids, and we both know that they've been cannibalizing people around this area. But beyond that, we don't know much of anything."

"So what do you suggest, Woodson? If you're so damned smart, help me out here."

Jared grinned and wondered if he hadn't taken a step too far.

"I'm not quite sure what I'd suggest. But I do know that if you go in there all out, you'll have a slaughter on your hands, if you're lucky. If you're not lucky, the whole freakin' block may blow up. And how will that work towards your goal of keeping this thing quiet?"

Bannister started to answer, but before he could, the slamming of a door caused both men to look to the side and see a figure coming out from the front door of the deserted corner building.

It was still dark out, and only half the street lights on the block worked, but it didn't take any time at all for both men to recognize the person heading their way.

"My God," Bannister said, and it seemed to Jared that the policeman couldn't decide whether to stay in place or run like hell towards that staggering, fragile figure.

He held his place until she was about fifty feet away, then something broke in the big tough cop, and he hurried over to his daughter's side.

As the two of them came up to Woodson, the uniformed cops got out of their cars and came over. Bannister started giving instructions to the men, and in split seconds they started running off to do his bidding.

At which point, Bannister and his daughter turned to the reporter.

"She doesn't seem to be hurt too bad," the old cop said, a husky catch in his throat. "I don't think we need to use the ambulance, but I want to take her to be checked out all the same."

Karen hadn't said a word yet, and Woodson couldn't define the look she sent his way. It seemed composed of equal parts sorrow and confusion, with a big layer of fear on top. He wanted to ask Karen what had happened to her, but figured this wasn't the time.

After trundling his daughter into the back of his car, Bannister turned back.

"I need you to do me a favor, Woodson. I know you've got a job to do, and while I don't like it, there's not much I can do about it. But I'd like you to keep this under wraps for now, at least until I can talk to Karen and find out what happened."

"She didn't say anything just now?"

"She's barely coherent. I hope it's just shock. Like I said, can't see anything physically wrong, but she sure seems to have gone through some sort of experience in that building."

"Where'd you send the uniforms to?" Jared asked.

Bannister paused, just the briefest of moments.

"Watching the various corners of that building," he said. "I want them to keep an eye on things until reinforcements show up."

"You realize," Jared said, "this all isn't exactly a secret anymore."

"Meaning?"

"C'mon, Captain. You haven't been behind a desk that long. Just because the street seems deserted doesn't mean no one's around. We probably have at least two hundred pairs of eyes on us right now. And these people aren't exactly stupid. They can figure out what your target is."

"Maybe so. But if the locals are as smart as you say, they should be able to figure out that we're doing them a favor here. If that hovel across the street is the source of whatever all this is, don't you think the street already knows it?"

Jared had to concede that the man had a point there.

"I can't order you not to go to air with all this, Woodson. You and I both know that. I am asking that you keep it quiet for as long as you can until I can find out from Karen exactly what we're dealing with."

"And then?"

"Then I'll decide best how to proceed. Or more likely, the chief will decide."

Glancing to the side, Jared saw a massive pair of head-lights coming their way. It only took a few seconds for the lights to show themselves as belonging to a large, military style black van.

"Looks like your reinforcements are here, Captain. You'd better get your kid to the hospital."

Bannister didn't move and didn't take his gaze off the newsman.

Sighing, Woodson dry-rubbed his face.

"Twelve hours, Captain. That's the best I can give you. After that, I'm going to have to run what I have by my station."

Bannister didn't like being given conditions, especially by a civilian, but after a long moment's hesitation he nodded his head, then turned to his car.

As the Lincoln drove off, grill lights flashing, Bannister hugged his girl closer while looking back through the rear view mirror. He saw the command vehicle unloading and heavily-armed, Kevlar-plated cops positioning themselves around the neighborhood, both at ground level and in windows and on rooftops.

As the car turned the corner, the ambulance roared past them, lights flashing silently, no doubt carrying Woodson. Bannister looked down again at his blood-smeared palm and wondered what Karen's mother would have thought had she seen his little display.

At the moment, he couldn't remember ever feeling less like a man.

Chapter Forty-two

Lately she'd spent more than her fair share of time recovering from trauma. Like now, when she lay on a reclined exam chair while a nurse shined a light into her eyes. Karen wondered if she could do anything to prolong the exam for as long as possible.

Better that, she thought, *than face the man standing in the corner of the room.*

The light snapped off as the nurse leaned back and tapped a few notes into her keypad.

"You look okay to me," she said, "but we'll wait for the final okay from the doctor."

"I *am* okay," Karen said, "but I was wondering if you could ..."

"Sorry," the young nurse said, "but I'm needed down the hall. Doctor will be in a moment."

With that she departed, leaving Karen alone with her father.

"So you're okay?" he said, his face showing his skepticism.

"I told you I was okay back when you picked me up," Karen said, "no reason to bring me here."

"Maybe I was being overprotective."

"Nothing wrong with overprotective," she said. "Kind of goes with the whole parenthood thing."

Her dad nodded.

Karen looked at him, still standing in the corner as far from her as possible, and wondered if she and her father could ever have a normal conversation. Every time they got close to each other, the specter of David reared its head before her, reminding her that the man who'd killed her fiancé could, in another twenty or so years, end up in her dad's job.

Illogical to an extent. And definitely unfair. But there it was, and she didn't know how to get past it.

As for what her father saw and thought when he looked at her, she didn't even want to consider.

"So what happened to you?"

"Excuse me?" Karen's heart raced. Ever since leaving the building her brain had been working overtime, but she still hadn't come up with a reasonable plan.

"I said what happened to you," her dad repeated, a bit of impatience creeping into his tone. "Who was in that building?"

Several options presented themselves to Karen, none of them ideal. She could simply tell the old man everything, and hope that he didn't immediately send her off for a psychiatric evaluation.

Or she could stonewall, let him come to his own conclusions, but she feared that such a course would result in him going off on his own, and possibly endangering himself.

She could lie, of course, tell him something to throw him off the track and give herself some breathing room. But that would cause problems down the line, so would she really gain anything?

Then another option presented itself. In a way it seemed the most ridiculous, but it had a small chance, of working out.

"Dad," she said as she steeled herself for a confrontation, "where's Mr. Woodson?"

A pause, no more than a heartbeat or so, as her father took that in.

"Why?" he asked at the end of that pause.

"I need to talk to him. Just him."

The look on her father's face ripped straight into her heart. After her experience in that abandoned building, she wanted nothing more than to run to him and let him enfold her in his arms. If ever a daughter, child or grown, needed her daddy after what she'd gone through, Karen Bannister did.

But if she let anything slip, she'd go back on a promise she'd made to the sire.

At the moment, she couldn't see herself doing that.

"I could hold you, Karen," her father said. "If you force me to, I could hold you as a material witness in the murders of two police officers. And God knows how many other people. We're about to send some men into that building to root out whoever's in there. If you don't talk to me, more cops may die."

She fought to hide her trembling. She had no doubt he was serious.

Still, she had to give the wolf creature time.

And in order to do that, she had to take the first step in mending fences, hard as it would be.

"Dad," she said, "please don't threaten me. What's in that building is nothing ... nothing that your people have ever encountered before. Trust me when I say that, whatever you think is hiding in there is worse, a lot worse, than you even think it is."

"All the more reason to ..."

"Dad, please. Let me see Woodson, let me talk to him. Afterwards, I'll tell you everything. But I've got to see Woodson first."

As she said the words, she felt her heart twisting in her chest. She had no intention of telling her father the truth if she could avoid it. Despite everything, their differing political views, their falling out when she went off to college and got sucked into social work and, most of all, the acrimony of the last year, the one thing Karen had never done was lie to him. Or her mother, when she was alive.

And now she'd told a complete untruth, all to buy time.

Only as the enormity of what she'd done hit her did Karen realize she'd been holding her breath while waiting for his answer.

The tough cop shook his head. A look of such agony that it nearly made her sick crossed his face.

"Two hours, Karen. I'll have Jameson and his guys hold off for two hours. But then you tell me everything. No more secrets."

Knowing she wouldn't get a better deal, Karen nodded her head.

"Okay, Dad. You've got it. Two hours."

The old man nodded his head in resignation and headed out the door.

Karen flopped back on the chair, only now beginning to feel how tense she'd been during that exchange. She hated what she'd done, the way she'd acted. A cop's kid her whole life, she knew just how far out on a limb her father had just gone. If anything happened, to either civilians or cops, during the window he'd given her, the culpability would fall on him.

If she somehow got through the other side of this night, she vowed to do whatever necessary to mend the rift with her father.

Had she had any way to foresee what the rest of the night would bring, she would have rushed down the hall, clasped her old man with her arms, and never let him go.

Instead, she sat and waited for Woodson.

It was all she knew to do at the moment.

Chapter Forty-three

Sgt. Brian Dolson had been a cop for nearly a decade, the last five years at his present rank and for almost eighteen months a member of Lieutenant Jameson's tactical unit. In all that time, while still a young man, he figured he'd gone through almost everything there was to experience. Dope dens, a domestic bombing, and even some nut who, one night during a full moon, had thought he was Dracula and tried to fly off a downtown building. Fortunately the nutso, who had confused the difference between vampires and werewolves, had picked a five-story edifice with one of those fancy, strong awnings over the front door. The awning broke his fall enough so that he lived, though barely. So yeah, Sgt. Dolson figured he'd pretty much seen it all.

However, common sense dictated that he could be on the force for fifty years and still meet new dangers.

Which seemed about right because he didn't have the foggiest notion what was going on tonight.

He'd been stretched out on the couch, contemplating either another half hour of HBO or calling it a night, when the call had come in to mount up. He'd made it to headquarters in twenty minutes. Five minutes later, he and the other guys were on their way down to the Zone.

Jameson had stayed silent during the trip, refusing to give any info as to their mission, which had worried Dolson.

Usually, their CO gave them everything he knew up front, the better to accomplish the mission. But this time, the lieutenant stayed mute, although Dolson, sitting right next to him in the command van, noticed him clenching his weapon a little tighter than he normally did.

If Sgt. Dolson didn't know better, he'd have thought that his commander was pissed-pants scared.

When they got to the heart of the Zone, the corner of Twenty-Seventh and Woodbridge, Jameson got out of the van and spent a few minutes conferring with a couple of uniforms out on the street. The men left behind looked at each other, not saying anything while communicating volumes with their stares.

It didn't exactly surprise them that they'd ended up here. Hell, when they'd saddled up, Dolson had half suspected they were heading to the Zone. But now that they'd arrived he had no doubt that the minds of the other men, just like his, were playing through the various stories they'd heard coming out of this hellspot over the last few weeks.

Rumors about people disappearing. Word of dead bodies. Not just wounded but savaged. Tales of winos and other dead-enders with the flesh torn off of them in chunks, like some giant monster had taken bites out of them. Whispers about packs of wild animals roaming the streets, jumping on and devouring anyone who strayed from the safety of lights and numbers.

Dolson shook his head, struggling to bring his thoughts back to reality. He could think of any number of reasons why the squad had been called out here in the early evening. Hell, they went through this same drill at least a couple times each month to bust drug labs. The newest generation of meth heads seemed to feel it mandatory to locate their kitchens in decrepit, desolated buildings.

One of the younger guys on the squad, a rookie, started to speak, but before he could get anything coherent out of his mouth the back doors unlatched and swung open.

Jameson stood there, his posture even tighter, more strained, than it had been on the ride over.

He began giving orders.

****

All of that had transpired nearly a half hour ago, and now Dolson lay prone on the roof of the building in question, his sniper rifle by his side and a pair of night vision goggles dangling from his neck.

Posting a man on the roof of a target building was standard routine. The idea being that, if an assault came about, the rats would flee the sinking ship, to be picked off or apprehended, depending on their danger quotient, by the men stationed at the strategic points around the neighborhood. But you needed someone as kind of an overhead backup, able to provide intel on any aberrant movements so that none of the fish escaped the net.

So while a civilian might see being positioned at the top of the target building as the most dangerous slot, it was usually the safest. Because, again, most ordinary malefactors would be fleeing the site, and thus away from you.

True enough for most malefactors. But there'd been those stories coming out of this neighborhood lately, not to mention the shadowy whispers between the guys, made over a third or fourth drink of the night, of something going on with the higher ups. Talk of something they didn't want the troops, let alone the civilian population, to know about.

All of which added up to Dolson not feeling as complacent in the top slot as he would have. Not knowing what they were up against made him feel off balance, and it didn't help any that before they broke off to their positions Jameson had cautioned them to be ready for a long wait.

Dolson had found a position on the roof from which he could see nearly 360 degrees, leaving one small slice of terrain out of sight. He'd set up a plan to alternate his position every ten minutes or so, thus making up for the deficit. It was now almost time for his next rotation. As he came to his feet, rifle in hand, he heard slight scraping behind him.

Conditioned by long and arduous training, Dolson managed to whirl around without making any sound, no small feat on the cinder and trash littered rooftop. At the end of his move, he faced a small door, set into the roof at an incline, which he'd determined earlier led to a tiny attic space. He figured that back in the days when this building had been occupied, the space had served as an extra storage attic for maintenance supplies.

When he'd looked into the cubbyhole earlier, a few stepladders remained, along with a half a dozen empty paint buckets, their lids gone and assorted ribbons of dried and flaked off paint staining the sides. A rat had run across Dolson's foot with the opening of the doorway, only to be expected in buildings like this.

After that initial inspection, he'd closed the door and hadn't thought more about it. This building, due to the turmoil and vicissitudes of existence in the slums, had long ago lost any viable neighbors. The closest building of any comparable height stood nearly a hundred feet away, so if anyone planned on leaving, they sure wouldn't do it by going up to the roof.

But now, as he whirled around and faced that long-abandoned door, it stood open, rocking back and forth on its hinges.

Dolson took in a shallow breath. Without moving his head, he cast his gaze as far as he could to both sides. The rooftop, at least what he could see of it, appeared still, deserted. He wanted to tell himself that earlier he hadn't shut the door firmly enough, though he knew he had. Or that a stray gust of wind had kicked it open, even though there had been no breeze to speak of since he'd assumed his post.

He narrowed his breathing even more, straining his ears as hard as he could.

Nothing. No sound, no motions, no expanding or contracting of shadows. As far as he could tell, he stood alone on the rooftop.

Yet that little door continued to swing, slower and slower with each rotation.

He tightened his finger, just the slightest bit, on the rifle's trigger as he lowered himself into a barely perceptible crouch. Not enough to make it obvious that he was preparing for action, but enough to at least begin the gradual lessening of himself as a target.

He wondered if any of his comrades, stationed on other roofs and ground locations around the neighborhood, had eyes on him. If so, he had a chance. While a civilian would merely see him standing still, someone with training would notice him getting ready for action.

The door stopped swinging midway through another rotation and hung ajar.

Dolson shifted his left foot about a degree, prepping himself for a pivot. But just as he tensed his core to make his move, behind him sounded a low, liquidy growl.

Dolson had grown up on a farm, spent his youth hunting with his dad. And while encounters with such creatures weren't an everyday occurrence, he knew a wolf when he heard one.

Not wasting any more time, Dolson pivoted all the way around, bringing up his rifle. His sidearm would have been better at short range, but he didn't have time enough to pull the holstered weapon.

As it was, he didn't have any time – period.

As he completed his turn, a weight struck him in the middle of his chest. At least a hundred pounds, moving at speed, it rocked him backwards onto the roof. The snarling thing landed on top of him, and hot saliva gushed onto his face. A pair of jaws above him loomed open, as small, but sharp teeth edged toward his throat.

Dolson tried to throw his forearm up in defense, but he didn't have the time as what felt like a hundred small razors sliced into his neck. He could only attempt to scream, or shout, but the time for any action had long passed.

His eyes fluttered as he felt blood gushing from his throat and onto his chest. The beast above him continued gobbling bites out of his neck, growling and snarling as it did so.

Dolson felt his arms and legs getting cold and, just as he lost consciousness for good, the thing on top of him reared up and glared down into his eyes.

With his last flicker of awareness, the cop thought he must be hallucinating because the thing devouring him looked like a ten-year old boy.

The tendons in the thing's neck stretched to their limit as it released a low, mournful howl. Then its open mouth dived once more towards Dolson.

And that was the last the young sergeant knew.

****

Several moments later, the swinging door that led to the small attic shifted all the way open. Following a soft bark that came from the edge of the roof, a line of half a dozen small shapes exited the attic, traipsed across the roof, and dropped over the side.

Most of them looked longingly at the fresh meat in the form of the shredded police officer, but none dared break the commands given them earlier, so they continued past Dolson's body without pausing.

Except for the last one in line. At only six years old, the youngest and smallest of this small pack, he couldn't resist the temptation and, as he passed by the body, dropped to his knees and lapped up some of the cooling blood.

Then scrambled to catch up to his fellows as they left the building and entered the city at large.

Chapter Forty-four

They walked out of the hospital together about an hour after her father left. Karen had had time to get dressed after her exam and talk with the doctor for a few minutes, who reported that he couldn't find more than superficial damage, which he treated. Karen nodded and thanked him, all the while knowing that his report was only half correct. No physical damage, of course. Other than the bruises and scrapes she'd sustained upon her initial capture.

But the doctor couldn't see the mental harm she'd experienced. Or maybe, she considered as she sat in the coffee shop waiting for Woodson to show up, the term "damage" wasn't specific enough.

What did you call it, after all, when you'd managed to peek around the wall and seen an entire new reality? When you're a grown woman, mature and worldly-wise, and in one night you discover that the boogeyman does exist after all?

What would one call such a fundamental change to the psyche?

Like most people with any awareness at all, Karen had over the years picked up the inane chatter people made about UFO's, contact with aliens, and what not. And as she sipped her rancid hospital cafeteria coffee, she recalled several times when she'd heard the proposition that, if scientists could prove that extraterrestrials existed, the way humanity looked at the universe would forever alter.

Overblown hokum, most likely. And yet, as she sat at a small Formica table sipping on a cup full of lukewarm coffee, that's how she felt.

Despite the horror of this night, she felt more aware and alert than she had in the last year. Not aware of it at the time, she could look back now and realize that ever since David's killing she'd lived in a fugue state, sleepwalking through life rather than living it. But something had happened down in that basement, something that had flipped a switch inside of her. Now, for the first time in nearly twelve months, Karen Bannister wanted to see what the next day held.

She even felt, though she hadn't shown it earlier, ready to try mending with her dad. It wasn't as if she had regained her faith and trust in the police, or that she wouldn't have trouble dealing every time she saw and encountered an officer. David Parsons was still dead; nothing had changed on that level. But the process of change had begun within her and, though anxious, she wanted to see where it would take her.

First, though, she had to get through the rest of this night.

As she looked up to see Jared Woodson coming through the swinging doors that separated the cashier's area from the coffee shop proper, she knew that it was time to show someone else a glimpse behind the wall.

Getting through the next five minutes or so would be the most difficult item on her agenda.

****

"Come again?" Woodson asked, his frown showing that he worried something had happened to unhinge her.

"I told you you'd find it hard to believe," she said.

They were sitting in his car, parked outside the hospital. "You serious? Hard to believe is a white slavery ring operating in the heart of the city. Or Russian gangsters trying to make the Zone their own turf, for whatever reason. Those things are hard to believe. But you're talking about a freakin' werewolf."

"Not a werewolf," Karen said, wondering if she'd made a mistake. "I didn't say that."

"You said he was part human, part wolf. What else could that be?"

"He said he was a hybrid, some kind of mutation from way back. Hell, for all he knows he may be from a completely different evolutionary line. Regardless, his kind is why all those old ghost stories came about."

"Are we talking the whole nine yards here? Full moon, clothes ripping off as he changes? That kind of thing?"

The blatant sarcasm in his tone, plus a brief shake of his head, pretty much let Karen know that he didn't believe a word she was saying, and she couldn't see any reason to blame him.

"No," she said. "It's not like that at all."

"Then what is it like? And make it good, Karen, because otherwise I'm out of here."

She paused, taking her time to get it all straight in her head, before plunging in.

"He looks like us, except for a lot more hair. His ears are kind of pointed, though I've seen one or two people in the past with pointier ears. And his face ..."

"Yeah?"

"His face and head look kind of bestial, especially straight on. His jaw's longer than most, with definitely pointed teeth."

She stopped, giving Woodson a minute to soak all that in.

"So what you're saying is that, with a lot of clothes and maybe a hat or scarf ..."

"Right. He could walk down the street and pass for just a really ugly man."

"But he's not just a man, right?"

"No." Karen averted her eyes from Woodson's face. She'd intended to tell him everything, at least everything as far as she knew it, but found herself vacillating.

She couldn't quite figure out why. After all, it wasn't like she owed the sire anything.

242

"He attacks people, right?" Jared continued. "He eats people to stay alive."

"Not ... not much anymore. He and his kind are – I guess you'd say they're omnivores. They can eat just about anything, like us. It's just that in the past ..."

"They're animals, right?"

"Yes, but not ..." Karen started flushing and stammering. She hadn't expected this to be easy, but even so ...

"Alright," Woodson jumped in, "let's say for a minute that I believe you. You're describing a predator, an animal. An entirely new species, right?"

"Exactly. But not new. They've been around for as long as we have."

"Except you said he's the last?"

Karen didn't respond at first. She turned away from Woodson and looked out over the hospital parking lot.

Cars. Buildings. Asphalt. People. All of it looked so normal, so prosaic.

She saw it now as a thin surface veneer for everything that resided beneath it.

"They live a long time," she finally said, "how long, he wasn't too sure. He doesn't remember much about his youth. But he does remember being around during the time of the French and Indian Wars."

Even without looking his direction, she could feel Woodson's stare.

"Seriously," she said. "That was the first time he remembers having to retreat from humans. When the colonists began to probe deeper into the forests, he had to move back."

"The Indians?" Woodson asked.

"Never bothered him much. He's such a creature of the wild that he fit in rather well with their world view. They just accepted him and his kind as part of the natural world."

"Like the stories of the Sasquatch up in the northwest."

"Exactly."

"His kind? How many are there?"

"None, now. At least none that he knows of. Once they were so numerous that he guesses they must have numbered in the thousands, according to him both here and in Europe. At least until the Industrial Revolution began and land started being gobbled up."

"So they can live in the wild?" Woodson asked.

"So he says. And while they can adapt if they need to, living in civilization doesn't really suit them."

"Like an animal living in captivity?"

"I guess. Actually, with their intelligence, maybe harder than on an actual wild animal."

"So what happened to them?" Woodson asked.

Karen shrugged.

"As they got more and more encroached on, people naturally mistook them for wolves. An easy mistake to make, especially at night."

"You mean they were shot? Hunted down?"

"The same old story," Karen said. "How many times has it happened throughout history?"

Woodson shook his head and leaned his head back against the seat's headrest.

"Miss Bannister, do you have any idea how insane this all sounds?"

"Probably about as nuts as it sounded to me a few hours ago. But I was in there. I saw him, spoke with him. And I saw the others, all those kids."

Woodson sat up again and turned to face her, the first time he'd looked at her since they'd entered the car.

"Long as we're at it," he said, "how about you explain that part to me. Let's say there's this animal, or mutant, or whatever the hell he is. Okay, if I really stretch it, I can buy that. By the way, do silver bullets kill him?"

"Of course," Karen said.

Woodson looked at her.

"The same as they would anyone else," she clarified. "The same as regular bullets would."

Woodson laughed at that one and leaned back in his seat again.

"Supposing," he said, "just supposing, mind you, that all this is true. What's the deal with the kids? Some kind of psycho/pervo thing?"

"Quite the opposite," Karen said. "He's trying to save them."

"Save them? By turning them into killers?"

"It's not like that."

"Really? You saying we've been wrong all along and that pack of brats aren't the ones who've gone around slaughtering people, trying to eat them? That's some other pack of wild kids?"

"No, that's not what I'm saying. What I mean is ... oh, dammit, this is too much to try to explain all at once. I need a favor."

"Sure? Why not? This night's already gotten about as crazy as it can get. What do you need?"

Karen took in a deep breath, unable to keep her hands and arms from trembling.

"I need you to come with me. To meet with him. He needs our help."

And that, she figured, was probably the last thing he'd expected.

Chapter Forty-five

A handful of them huddled on a rooftop a few blocks from the lair. Six, to be precise. A couple larger and heavier than Simon, but because he had been first with the sire they deferred to him. All of them, like Simon, beginning to chafe under the sire's rule.

Fortunately, at the time that Simon and the sire had squared off, these six brothers of his were off in other parts of the building, searching for stray vermin. So when he'd left after facing down the old man, Simon had managed to round them up and take them away.

But now they had work to do.

"The woman got away from the old man," Simon said. "Do any of you know who she is?"

Three or four heads nodded.

"She works at that charity place," one said. "She's the one who's always coming down here poking around."

A few soft barks of assent came from the others.

"So okay," Simon said. "But the question is, what did the old dude want with her? Why did he let her go? And how do we take her out of the picture?"

The smallest one whimpered.

Simon turned a baleful eye on him.

"You got a problem?" he asked the little cub.

The smaller kid shook his head and crouched farther into himself.

"She's been around for a while," said Peter, a blond kid slightly larger than Simon. "I stayed at that shelter place for a while a few years back. Heard a lot about her."

"Such as?" Simon asked.

"Such as her dad's some kind of cop. A big shot. He came in once to talk to her."

"Anybody know her name?" Simon asked.

Another cub about the same size as Peter spoke up.

"I think so. I was out on the street the other day when she was snooping around, asking questions. Heard her introduce herself to some dudes."

"Well, if we know her name," Simon said, "we can track down her old man."

"Unless she's married," piped up one of the younger ones.

"Fifty/fifty shot either way. And just think. If we can knock off a cop in their main building, imagine how scared everyone will be of us then."

"You sure about that?" Peter asked. "The sire wants us to stay low for as long as we can."

Simon turned to him.

"Aren't you getting a little sick and tired of doing what that old bastard says?"

A chorus of high pitched barks answered him.

"So let's do it. Head downtown and do the old man in. Scare the piss out of the girl, get her so messed up she leaves the sire all to us."

More happy barks this time, and Simon figured that they thought it was all just a big adventure. Especially the younger ones. But he looked towards Peter and the other big kid, and both of them gave him a quick, subtle nod.

Sure, they knew the score. And they couldn't wait to be one of the ones calling the shots.

"How we going to get there?" Peter asked. "The main cop shop's downtown, and that's a hell of a long ways from here."

Simon grinned at him and turned to look out over the roof's edge at the city beyond.

"Hell, man. About time you guys learned to hitch on subways."

Chapter Forty-six

"Dolson, goddamnit, respond!"

Roy Jameson released the communication button and waited for his sergeant to call in. He'd made three attempts and, as about ten ticks of the clock went by, he knew the man wasn't going to answer.

He looked at his grid sheet, double-checking to make sure who was closest to Dolson's position, when his cell buzzed.

Shit, he thought, *pouring when it should ...*

His communication link buzzed on a separate channel.

"Yello?"

"Everything still tight?" Leo Bannister's voice said in his ear.

Jameson grimaced, not sure how much to say. Even forgetting their difference in rank, the old man had been around the department a good twenty years longer and knew how to cause a lot of trouble if you crossed him.

More than that, though, Jameson suspected that Bannister knew a hell of a lot more about what was going on around here than he'd shared.

So what the hell? Give it to him straight out.

"No, Leo, things are most definitely not still tight out here. In the last five minutes I've lost contact with two of my guys. I think it's time to hit that place before this gets completely out of hand."

"Not sure I'd recommend that, Roy. You've got an unknown contingent in there and ..."

"An unknown contingent of what? It's time that either you or the chief give it to me straight, Leo. Who the hell's hiding out in that building?"

"If you go in there," Bannister said, his voice lower than normal, "it may be a public relations disaster like we've never had before."

Jameson's throat tightened up and he paused to wipe his sweaty palm across his pants leg.

"You're saying that we have something different here than a bunch of doped-up gangbangers?"

"I'm saying we have something a lot more different."

"Then, dammit, tell me what! I can't conduct an operation if I don't know what I'm looking for."

"You're not needing to conduct an op, Roy. Just keep the area secured until I figure out what to do with ..."

"With what? Here's how it's going down. I'm the officer on scene here, not you and not Chief Allen, provided that he's even in the loop at all. So either you give it all to me or we're going in full out. What's it going to be?"

Bannister sighed, and Jameson could almost hear his resignation.

"Okay, Roy, but tell me one thing first. Is anyone else next to you right now?"

"Just my driver, and he's up front. But I'm running out of time, so if you're going to lay it out for me, do it now."

"Alright, then. But you'd better be sitting down for this one."

"Whatever, Leo. Just make it quick. If you count your two guys from the other day, these punks have taken out at least four cops. So whatever you have to say, say it quick."

Chapter Forty-seven

"He didn't like it," Lewis Preston said.

Leo turned and looked at his old friend, wondering if either of them had ever looked so worn down.

"That's one way of putting it," he said.

"So? I noticed you still didn't quite give it all to him."

"I gave him enough to get the job done. Any more and there's a trace of leakage."

"And of course," the ME said as he tipped the last few drops from the bottle into his glass, "we couldn't have that."

"You know damned well we couldn't. If word got out ..."

"Leo, old pal. You're starting to sound like a broken record. Who are you kidding? Word's already gotten out. You think all those people in those streets don't know that they're in danger? Who the hell are you protecting? The public? Chief Allen? Yourself?"

Seated across from the coroner's desk, where it seemed he'd been camped out for an eternity, Bannister stared into his own drink.

"Won't find the answers looking in there, buddy," Lewis said.

"I know," Bannister replied, "but at the moment I don't know where the hell else to look."

"Maybe so, but if you don't at least try to ..."

He stopped, tilted his head. Bannister, alerted by the cessation of his friend's speech, looked up as well.

"What is it?" he said.

"Shhh." The ME frowned. At sixty-four, his hearing wasn't what it used to be, but he could still get around without any kind of mechanical aid.

"Thought I heard something. Over in the corner."

Bannister glanced toward the far corner. He saw only the same sterile, shiny surfaces that the morgue had always held. In some ways, it had always appeared to him as some sort of futuristic environment. As if dirt or anything foreign could never touch down here.

"I don't see anything," he said.

"I know," the ME replied, "but ..."

He got up and headed over to the far corner of the room. Although bright overhead lights lit up the morgue, the illumination didn't extend into the corners. Not usually a problem, as the areas of shadow were small and oddly-spaced.

The ME made it about halfway to that corner, stopped for a moment, then came back and sat behind his desk. Bannister looked at him, waiting.

"I think there's something in here," he whispered.

The police captain looked at his old friend with more than a shade of doubt but was wise enough to keep silent.

"Something's moving over there," the ME continued, still in that sibilant tone. "Between the supply cabinets and those shelves."

Leo's hand drifted towards his hip. Higher ranks didn't ordinarily carry sidearms, but he'd made a habit of having his for the last few days. He didn't draw, though, because he still didn't see an actual danger.

"Are you sure?" he whispered to his friend. "I don't see anything."

"It wasn't an actual shape or anything, more like a shifting of the shadows."

"Let's stand up, then, and head out the door."

The two men got to their feet, but just as they turned towards the outer door they both heard a distinct clacking noise.

The sound of a bolt being thrown.

"That's the outer door bolt," Preston said, in his unease forgetting to lower his voice. "What's ..."

Leo had drawn his gun now, but before he could complete his turn towards the door, a small click echoed back and forth off the stainless steel objects and implements in the lab, and the lights went out.

"What the ..." Leo said as he heard a thump next to him and felt, without seeing, the ME fall to the floor.

In the same instant that his friend's body hit the floor, Leo heard the most agonizing scream ever. Before he could react, something heavy slammed into his back, knocking him to the floor.

His breath left him as, lungs struggling for whatever wisp of air they could find, he hit the floor headfirst. A tiny part of his brain wondered why hitting the hard tile didn't hurt more than it did; then he realized two things.

One, his friend had stopped screaming.

And he himself was lying in a puddle of warm, viscous liquid.

Leo Bannister had been a tough cop for most of his life, with little that he hadn't seen or experienced. But this savage attack out of the darkness, in what should have been a secure environment, brought the gorge up into his throat.

Even so, he pressed his palms down to the floor, slipping and sliding in his old friend's blood, and pushed himself to his knees. Gun still in hand, he didn't dare shoot because of his lack of vision. If he could get to his feet he had a chance of backing himself up against a wall.

His mind, in these few seconds, focused on survival and escape. The amount of blood on the floor, soaking into his clothes, plus the total silence from Preston, told Bannister there was no help for his friend.

All of this went through his mind in the flash of a synapse. Just as he felt a slight pang of victory by getting to his knees, low, savage growls sounded behind him and on all sides. The half second he had to get his arms in front of his face wasn't nearly enough.

Sharpened, strengthened teeth sliced into his jugular. As blood gushed out of his neck and cascaded down his chest, Captain Leo Bannister felt the sharp gouges of similar teeth attacking him from every direction.

And then it all went black.

Chapter Forty-eight

Karen and Woodson spotted the black command van almost immediately. Hard not to, seeing as how the thing stuck out in a neighborhood that rarely saw a parked vehicle, let alone an intact one.

"Should we just go on up to them?" Woodson asked.

They had pressed themselves up against a brick front two blocks away. The whole area appeared deserted, which impressed Karen as otherworldly. On any regular night, even a weeknight getting on to one in the morning, this area should have been teeming with people of all sorts, victims and victimizers, old and young, indigenous and visiting, as the Zone continued with its own individual way of life.

Now, only a few people loitered, fading in and out of doorways. Those Karen could see seemed to be surveying the neighborhood, maybe to report back to others.

"Think the cops in that van realize how surreal this all looks?" she asked her companion.

"I would think so. Anyone with any basic knowledge of the city would realize this scene isn't exactly normal."

"They're all probably afraid."

"Or just waiting to see who comes out on top."

Woodson looked around and rubbed the back of his head.

"This isn't cool at all," he said. "I should be down here with a camera crew, maybe two. Barb should know all about this. Hell, it's obviously hot enough to be a national story, and I'm just sitting on the damned thing."

Karen looked at him, trying to drum up empathy for his point of view. But the idea of what would happen to those kids when this came out overrode everything for her.

"I made a deal with their leader, Jared. Told him I would do my best to get him to some sort of safety. I need to honor that deal."

He turned to her now, impatience blanketing his face.

"That's just my point," he said. "You made a deal with a monster who ..."

"I told you he's not a real ..."

"I'm not talking that kind of monster! How long has that guy been living in that damned bombed out building with a bunch of young kids? Kids he scraped off the streets in order to do God knows what with."

Karen hissed. She wasn't proud of her reaction, but at the moment couldn't control herself.

"Where's this coming from? I already explained to you, he didn't 'scrape' them off the streets. He rescued them. Took them in and gave them protection. Just like we do down at the shelter only, for my money, a hell of a lot more effectively."

Woodson glared at her, one of the hardest looks she'd seen on him yet.

"You can't possibly buy that. He was rescuing them? By turning them into killers?"

Karen started to reply, then hesitated.

"You have kids?" she asked Woodson.

"Two," he said. "And yes, both boys. Not much older than the ones you're talking about."

"Married?" she asked even as she automatically glanced down at his left hand.

He shook his head.

"I get them every other weekend, and whenever else Maggie and I can work it out. So I hope you'll pardon me if I find all this kind of hard to take."

Karen considered the argument, but didn't really see the point. She'd explained it once, and if he hadn't gotten it then, why bother trying again?

"You with me or not?" she asked instead.

"I'm with you, but only because when this does break it's going to be one hell of a story. And I'm going to be on the inside track."

"Speaking of inside," Karen said, "do we stop by the van there, or are you game to go in on our own?"

Woodson hesitated, glancing both ways up and down the street.

"You're assuming we can get past them without being seen. It's fairly obvious that they've got the whole neighborhood staked out. Far as that goes, how do we know they aren't about to move on the place right now?"

"Why would they?" she asked.

"Think like a cop, Karen. Hell, you were raised by one. They're not just hanging around for the hell of it. It's obvious there's a raid about to go down. So what say we start acting like adults and call your dad?"

Now it was Karen's turn to pause.

"Jared," she said, "if I can get those kids out of there, and into some type of official custody without anyone coming to harm, I'll take whatever lumps come my way. It's not like Dad and I have been on the best of terms anyway."

"That's a pretty big if."

"Then look at it this way. If we could ..."

She stopped talking then, her face tensing up. Next to her, Woodson made half a turn as she saw the doors of the police command van opening and a black-clad man step out. A youngish guy, no more than forty, but even from the distance and at night, Karen could see the lines etched into his face.

"I'd suggest you two get in here," the black-clad man said, "before you blow things all to hell."

257

Chapter Forty-nine

"You realize I should have you two escorted home?"

The three of them sat in the back of the command van. Jameson in a swivel chair up towards the driver's section that constituted the point of honor, with Jared and Karen squatting on a bench that ran the length of the van. The two of them sat side by side, and Jared wondered if he was the only one who felt like a recalcitrant third-grader called into the principal's office.

"Lieutenant Jameson, let me explain ..."

"Not now, Miss Bannister. When I want an explanation I'll ask for one. Right now I'm going to be the one talking."

Jared looked closer at the cop. The words were the right ones. Irritated authority figure having to deal with smart-ass civilians. But the tone didn't match the rhetoric. Hulking there in his combat blacks, some sort of assault weapon by his knee, the man should have carried the tone and tenor of John Wayne or Clint Eastwood. Instead, he sounded sympathetic.

That didn't track at all. Besides, the man looked more than worried. Those lines in his face looked new, and he kept clenching and unclenching his hands.

A cold ball formed in Jared's gut as he wondered what Jameson knew that they didn't.

"Okay," Karen said, "so talk."

"Here's what I know. I'm in the middle of some kind of screwed-up mess. I was ordered out here to put a cordon around the building over on that corner and make sure nobody left. I was told it had to do with some kind of aberrant gang activity of the last few weeks. But the building is completely dark, no sign of life whatsoever, and I've recently lost two of my men."

"Lost?"

"Lost, Mr. Woodson. As in not at their assigned posts. Not responding to their call-ins."

"When did this happen?" Jared asked.

"More than an hour ago. And when I called in to the chief's office, I was reminded, somewhat harshly, that the op was being run through your father and that I had to take my orders from him."

Karen and Jared looked at each other, but stayed silent.

"But that's not the worst of it," Jameson continued, "not by a long shot. And this is the point where you need to keep it together, Miss Bannister."

A pang of fearful anticipation crossed Karen's face as she reached out and grasped Jared's bandaged wrist.

Before he could stop himself, he let out a small groan.

"Sorry," she whispered as she let go. She glanced at him and, for an instant there, Jared thought he saw more than just ordinary sympathy in her eyes.

"What is it?" she said, turning back to Jameson.

"I just got a call from downtown, and I'm afraid I've got some bad news for you."

Jameson didn't have to say anymore; the message was obvious. And Jared wondered whether this would be the breaking point for Karen Bannister. If he was reading Jameson's veiled words correctly, this made two deaths of family, or almost family, within a year, which would be enough to put anyone down, at least for a while.

But there was more to it, and an instant later Jared began to comprehend the true depth of her loss.

Looking at Karen, Jared could see her shoulders hunched and her head downcast.

She didn't cry, at least not yet. A fact that he found remarkable.

"I'm sorry, Miss Bannister," Jameson said from what seemed like a thousand miles away. "But we need to talk about this."

"Never a chance," Karen mumbled, and the two men had to strain to hear her. "Never a chance."

Jared understood, and as he looked at Lieutenant Jameson he figured the cop got it as well.

It's tough when a parent dies.

Even tougher when they die with unfinished business between them and their children.

"Never the chance to tell him," she said.

"Miss Bannister," Jameson said, "I really do need to talk to you."

"Why?" Jared asked in the most neutral tone he could muster. "Can't you give her a while?"

"I'm afraid I can't. And neither can anyone else. Her father and another man were found dead a while back. In the morgue downtown. And their wounds look exactly like those of the victims of this 'gang' I'm supposed to be surveying."

Karen looked up at that.

"So you see," Jameson continued, "I really do need to know everything you two can tell me."

****

They exited the van about half an hour later, leaving behind a bewildered policeman, who himself left them with a stern warning to go home. Mindful of Karen's loss, Jameson offered to call a patrol car to take them home.

"That's okay," Jared intervened. "We can make our own way."

"Suit yourself," Jameson replied. "Hopefully by tomorrow I can call you and let you know this is all wrapped up. And ma'am," he turned to look directly at Karen," I really am sorry for your loss."

Karen nodded and gave him a brief smile, then the two of them turned away. Without speaking, they began walking down the sidewalk away from the police van.

They turned a corner and stopped, glancing around to make sure no one was near them.

"We have to try," Karen said. "I gave him my word."

"I don't even come close to agreeing with you there," Jared said, "but if you're bound and determined, you can't go it alone. But how do we get past Jameson's men?"

"Easy," she said. "We don't. But once two civilians are inside, they'll be that much more hesitant to storm the ramparts. Which should give us the time we need."

A sharp, jangly fear ran up and down Jared's spine, but he could tell that nothing short of knocking Karen out and tying her up would change her mind. He'd have worried that this wildass play was an extreme reaction to the news she'd just received, if not for the fact that it had more or less been the plan all along.

He just hoped that her instincts were right, and that there wasn't anything to be really afraid of inside that building.

Just kids, he tried to reassure himself. According to her descriptions, not that much older than his own two boys.

But oh, what a difference between their lives.

"Okay," he said, "let's go."

Chapter Fifty

They paused in front of the main outer door, and looked at each other. Both hoping for a sign of strength or confidence in the other's face and both disappointed, seeing only fear and trepidation.

And Jared was pretty sure that she saw his weakness. He had to lean his relatively uninjured side against the door jamb, fearing his legs would buckle at any moment. The pain killers he'd received earlier had worn off, and his arm was throbbing again.

"You ready for this?" he asked her.

"Not even close. But I've got to get it over with, so ..."

Jared wondered about her. Less than an hour ago, she'd gotten the news of her father's savage murder. Yet her set face and clear eyes showed no sign of trauma. True, the two of them had been on the outs for the last year, but she still should be showing something.

So either she was cold as ice and wouldn't allow herself to break down until the time was clear, or she was in shock. If the former, that was her deal, but if the latter, it involved him, too.

"So," Jared said, "do we knock or just go in?"

It surprised him that the question came out sounding like a joke, and it startled him even more when she responded with the slightest of grins.

It wasn't much, but it was something.

"Do you really think they'd answer if we knocked?" she asked.

Jared shook his head.

"And besides," she said as she reached out to open the door, "it'd be really surprising if they didn't already know we were here."

****

There had been few times in his career when Jared had wished more that he had a video and sound crew with him. This long, meticulous walk down the main hallway of a tottering old building, lit only by glimpses of illumination from streetlights that struggled past the tears, rents, and gaps in the walls, begged for some videotape.

Although the hall had a tile floor, so many decades of dust, dirt, and droppings had accumulated that their steps made hardly any sound. As they progressed, Jared realized that the only noise in the place came from his own half shuffling, half limping gait. At one point, he tried to stand up straighter and walk normal, but the sharp twinges in his leg and back wouldn't allow it. But even if they'd both moved as silently as possible, it probably wouldn't matter.

If the old man hadn't exaggerated to Karen, he'd trained those young kids in such a way that their hearing, while not as sharp as a wild animal's, rated far above those of ordinary people.

With such feeble illumination, they had to walk cautiously. So much trash littered the floor that walking at a normal pace, even had Jared been able to do so, would have had them tripping and falling in no time.

They passed an assortment of rooms, most with doors shut but some with them open. And more than a few that at some point had had the doors torn off the hinges, leaving gloomy rooms staring out at the interlopers. Jared found his heart quickening as he contemplated what might lurk in those darkened spaces.

He wasn't the only one with such concerns because a few seconds later Karen's fingers entwined his.

"Where exactly are we headed?" he asked, mainly from a desire to hear some normal noise.

"See that 'exit' door at the far end? Just to the right of it is a set of stairs that leads down to the basement. They should be waiting for us there."

Not for the first time, Jared considered how illogical this entire move was. Karen could be leading him into a trap. He didn't bother pointing this out because back in the command van Lieutenant Jameson had made clear just how dangerous this building was.

But the two of them had come on in anyway.

"Don't worry," she said, and Jared had the wild thought that she'd been reading his mind. "Like I said before, if he wanted to hurt me, wouldn't he have done it before?"

"Maybe he has a larger plan. Considering that he's not exactly normal, how can we tell what ..."

He stopped. Without his realizing it, they'd arrived at the end of the hallway. Karen continued walking forward, but Jared tightened his grip on her hand and yanked her back.

She stumbled over a chunk of bricks on the floor, but managed to stay upright.

"Miss Bannister, before we go any farther, I need to know something."

Around them, the building seemed nearly silent. It bothered Jared more than a little to think that, if Karen had been telling the truth, an entire pack of, for all intents and purposes, wild animals lurked just feet away from where they stood.

"What?" she asked. "What do you want to know?"

"Not want to know. Need to. Tell me straight out. What are your plans for this man and those kids? You realize that, if what they've told you is true, they're a bunch of killers."

"Survivors," Karen said. "There's a difference."

And there it was. The thing he had feared.

"So what is it you want to do with them? Truth."

Karen hesitated, and even in the gloom of the hallway he could see her indecision.

"The cops won't let them go," he said. "You know that, don't you?"

For a moment there, Karen hunched her shoulders, as if the strain had become too much for her frame to bear.

"You've got to trust me," she said. "For just a little bit longer. Please."

He tried to stare her down, but it didn't work. Maybe she was in shock from learning about the captain's death, but even so Jared sensed that her instincts were headed in the right direction.

Shrugging, he straightened up as much as he could.

"So show me the way," he said, "for just a little longer."

****

The basement looked, sounded, and smelled almost exactly as she had described. As they passed through the doorway into the one large room, Jared couldn't help but wonder if he would ever see the outside again.

This place felt more than just dangerous.

Life-threatening.

The rustling of small bodies in the shadows, the smell of unwashed and, in some cases, decaying flesh, and the various pairs of eyes gleaming in the moonlight slanting in through the windows.

It didn't help any that, as soon as they walked through the door a little boy, no more than three or four, came scuttling up to them on all fours.

Actually scuttling, on his hands and knees.

The kid shied away from Jared, but he rubbed up against Karen's leg, sniffing her up and down and making something that sounded almost like a purr. As an experiment, Jared bent down to pat him on the shoulder.

He never made contact. With his hand about a quarter-inch from the boy's flesh, the kid jerked his shoulder away. He then gave a little half leap and twisted in the air, landing on all fours again but this time facing Jared. The little mouth, still half-filled with baby teeth, growled and, although the child couldn't weigh more than forty pounds, Jared took a step back, his blood running cold.

From one of the far corners a sharp bark sounded out, and the child, taking time to gesture defiance by snapping his teeth in Jared's direction, scurried off to join his fellows in the shadows.

"My God!" Jared said. "The kid thinks he's an animal."

"He's been trained that way," said a sharp, scratchy voice from the corner where the bark had sounded. "Had you continued to instigate, you would have found yourself, at the very least, mauled pretty badly."

Jared glanced at Karen, who nodded.

"Why train a little kid to kill?" he directed his question at the corner.

"Not to kill, to live," the scratchy voice said.

Then came a rustling, a shifting around in that corner. A moment later the old man walked out from the shadows.

Even having been prepared by Karen's story, Jared lurched back a step when he saw the figure.

He looked almost exactly as Karen had described. A form that, with full clothing and in dim light, could pass for a deformed, ugly human, but one that in clear light and up close, appeared distinctly lupine.

Despite the tension and uncertainty of the situation, Jared quivered at the thought that he stood before an entirely unknown species.

Even more, if the being had been truthful with Karen, the last of his kind.

As a newsman, Jared struggled to keep his mind open and objective, soaking in as much information as possible. As a regular person, he felt his reason tottering.

"To live," the creature repeated. "Look around you, man. These are the rejects, the castoffs, the children no one wanted. They were thrown out into the world, with most of those doing the throwing no doubt hoping they would die off. I'm sheltering them while teaching them to defend themselves."

In his peripheral vision, Jared noticed Karen standing stock still, her gaze fixed on the sire.

"But in the process of surviving, they've been killing," Jared pointed out.

The being sighed, and as his face softened he looked, for just a moment, a little more human.

"I know," he said, "and that wasn't my intention. For a few years things were fine, but as the first ones grew older, their – appetites – grew as well."

Jared, taking what Karen had told him earlier and adding it to this revelation, thought he got it.

"You found them lost and alone," he said.

The old one nodded his wolf-shaped head.

"Not all at once, but over a period of time," Jared continued. "One or two at a time."

"Yes. It makes sense to you now?"

"I think so." He looked at Karen, who nodded to him. "Karen said you were the last of your kind?"

The wolfman shrugged.

"As far as I know. In the last century or so, I've traveled all of the wooded areas of the continent, as well as much of Europe as I could get to. I know what to look for, in terms of spoor, shelter, and remains."

At the last word, his tone dropped a few levels, and a distinct hint of sadness entered his speech.

"And I haven't found any others."

Woodson nodded again, excitement causing his breath to come a little quicker.

For a moment there, he almost forgot about his wounds.

"So as a castoff yourself ..."

"Yes, I wanted to help others like myself."

"But you couldn't teach them how to survive in civilization, right? Because it wasn't your natural environment."

The beast in front of him nodded, and Woodson caught the pang of sorrow again.

"I did the best I could, the only way I could," he said.

Noticing the intense silence in the room, Jared glanced around. All of the little kids were sitting on their haunches, heads cocked forward as if in intense concentration. Whether out of respect, fear, or simple confusion, they crouched motionless, as if they knew their future was about to be decided.

Jared couldn't help but wonder about the effect they would have had on an elderly homeless person scraping his life by in the alleys of the Zone.

"What do you think?" Karen asked.

Jared glanced at her, uncertain of what to say.

"We need to leave here," the sire said. "Obviously, it's too dangerous for my litter to stay here in your city."

"Dangerous for them?" Jared asked.

"Partially, but primarily dangerous for all of you. What's happened the last few weeks clearly shows that."

Jared nodded.

"So are you saying you want us to help you somehow? Help you relocate to ... where?"

The beast man slumped a bit more, confusion mixing with the mournfulness of his expression.

"I'm not sure," he said, "that's why I first reached out to the female here. To see if by chance she could help me out."

"Well, you see," Jared said, "there's a problem there."

The creature cocked his eyebrow up in question.

Jared looked at Karen, but the stoicism of her manner showed that she didn't intend to enter the conversation. Jared didn't feel it his place, but the thing had to come out in the open.

"An hour or so ago," he said, "there's a good chance that someone in your – pack – here attacked and killed her father, along with another man."

A low, mournful wail issued from the creature, and it slumped to his knees. It clasped its head in its hands and rocked back and forth.

Around and behind them, the cubs began to wail as well, a low yet sharp sound that set Jared's teeth on edge.

The wolfman then went quiet before slumping all the way to the floor.

Woodson and Karen glanced at each other, not sure what to do next.

"I had such hopes for him," the creature said, more to himself than to them. "Such hopes and he's gone so far. Oh, God."

The feeling of unreality that Jared had had since entering the basement, indeed since Karen had told him the sire's story, only intensified now. A news reporter his entire working life, he now found it impossible to put into words, even in his mind, what it felt like to see this oddly-shaped, inhuman creature kneeling on the floor, sobbing for something he'd lost some-where along the way.

And pleading to a God he couldn't have ever worshiped.

"Excuse me," Jared said, stumbling for a moment when he realized he didn't even know how to address this creature. It seemed so human, yet it wasn't. "Who's 'he'?"

The wolfman shuddered, seemed to pull himself togeth-er, then managed to stand up.

"His name isn't important. What matters is that he was my first."

"Your first?" Jared asked, then in the next instant nodded.

"You mean the first one you saved. The first one you started – training?"

The creature nodded, still looking mournful.

If a human emotion could be ascribed to something so inhuman.

"I didn't plan it that way. I had left the forests and begun blending into civilization. As long as I wore enough clothing and kept to the shadows and darkened areas, I could get by."

"How did you live?"

"By theft, of course. I couldn't hold a job or rent a home. I'd spent decades scouring the world, looking for any others like myself. I knew some had once existed, having crossed paths with them from time to time in the distant past. But for long stretches I hadn't come across any others. So I came into the cities to continue my search."

Jared looked at Karen, still standing motionless. She had told him part of this, but the creature was filling in some of the gaps, and his common sense could fill in others.

"And you found your first abandoned child?" he asked.

"Infant," the creature corrected him. "Little more than one month old, left behind in a garbage-strewn alley to die. It was just lying there, crying and thrashing. It smelled – irresistible."

Jared's stomach clenched.

"You didn't intend to save it, did you?"

The creature shook its head.

"Not at first. After all, we're of different species, and when I saw it lying there, squirming in its own waste, I first saw nothing but a warm meal."

Karen finally reacted. Standing next to her, the two of them almost touching, Jared saw her flinch.

"But?" he prodded.

"But as I approached it, silently and in the shadows, I noticed at least a half a dozen people walk past, stop and notice it, then move on. I waited till enough time had ticked by without any new passersby, and moved for the bundle. By that time, something had happened."

"Happened?"

"For some reason, I no longer saw it as food. It was crying, squalling really, and all those people kept ignoring it. It made me feel – something."

Jared nodded and saw Karen's face return to its normal calm. He knew that in the days to come he would look back at this encounter and have trouble believing it had ever happened.

But for now, it all seemed to make perfect sense.

"So you took care of the baby," he said, not as question.

The creature nodded.

"I found an abandoned place, not this one, as a sanctuary to keep it safe. But I had no way of knowing if anything would happen to me, or how long I'd survive."

The last few pieces clicked into place in Jared's head as Karen reached out and grasped his hand.

This time, she took hold of the uninjured one.

"So you taught it to survive," he said to the creature, "just in case you weren't around to protect it."

The beast's head slumped, as if too tired to support himself.

"Yes," he said, his voice lower, almost, but not quite, a whisper. "I wanted to give him every possible tool to survive, but all I knew was what I'd learned as a 'wolf' as you'd call it. So I followed that path."

For the first time in several minutes, Karen spoke up.

"And you succeeded."

The head lifted, the eyes flashed. *Almost in pride,* Jared thought.

"Yes I succeeded. With him and," he paused and lifted up his hand in a gesture that encompassed the room, "with all of them."

"But why the killings?" Jared asked. "If you've been collecting and guarding these kids for all this time, why was it necessary to suddenly begin murdering people?"

The creature sighed.

"Not my intention," it said. "What happened was ..."

With a crash, the heavy iron door that sealed off the basement slammed open, causing the three adults to spin around and the boys to scamper. With the outburst they began howling and whining, raising a cacophony such as Jared didn't think he'd ever heard before.

As he whirled towards the door, he saw a teenage boy bounding through, snarling and growling as he crossed the room. Behind him came five or six others, similar to the ones already in the basement though a few larger, older, and despite the tumult in the basement, all of these new arrivals kept in a compact group.

Headed straight for the creature.

The wolfman surged forward, one of his long, hairy arms, coming up to sweep Jared and Karen aside. The two of them smashed into the wall as he leaped past them, arms outstretched to bar the way of the small pack loping towards him.

The one in front, the oldest, snarled, lips pulling back to show teeth artificially sharpened and strengthened by years of raw diet.

When his sire barked at him, the younger man paused, a moment of indecision showing on his face. Then his features composed, and with a low, throaty growl he rushed towards the creature that had saved and nurtured him for years.

And so it began.

Chapter Fifty-one

Jared and Karen smashed into the wall, their breath knocked from their bodies. Jared reached out with his good arm to grab Karen so she didn't fall to the floor, but as he did so his wounded leg gave out, and they both ended up on the ground. She clambered up and reached down to help him get to his feet. Nearly biting his tongue to keep from crying out, Jared took an instant to make sure she wasn't hurt, then turned his attention back to the hell unfolding before them.

The basement had become one swirling mass of bodies. All the savages flashed back and forth, biting, clawing and snarling at each other. At first, Jared had assumed the new arrivals, outnumbered nearly three to one, would go down quickly. But as the lines of battle began to solidify, more young ones entered the basement, and he realized that the young renegade had recruited more than just a few of the original pack.

Two young boys rolled past, growling and snapping at each other. They stopped at Karen's feet just as one of them found, with his teeth, the jugular of the other. Karen and Jared stepped back to avoid the spray of warm blood that flashed across the area.

With a whimper, the loser collapsed onto the floor. The victor took a moment to savor the taste and thrill of the blood before rising up, shaking his head, and turning back into the battle.

He made it all of two feet before another child, a blond-haired boy, tackled him around the knees, crashing him head-first to the dirty cement floor. Despite the roaring and growling that filled the basement, like lurking in the midst of a pack of wolves, Karen and Jared heard the crack his head made as it smashed into the floor.

A small pool of blood seeped from his flattened head, and the blond boy who'd tackled him paused to raise his head and howl at the ceiling before he crouched and began lapping up the blood.

Karen's hand tightened around Jared's elbow, but she didn't look away.

"We have to get out of here," she said, her tone almost apologetic at stating something so obvious.

Glancing at her, Jared saw her eyes had brightened and she wore a look of concentration, as if the blow of her father's death had receded, replaced by the practicalities of survival.

"That way," he said, nodding towards her left.

He hoped that, if they stayed close to the wall and called as little attention to themselves as possible, the pack of wild animals would ignore them and continue to rend itself apart.

But they'd made it only a few steps when a new sound, or rather a familiar sound with a deeper, more resonant pitch, caught their attention, and both of them turned to look back to the far side of the room.

At the sight, Jared felt his breath stop, Karen stiffening up next to him.

Upon entering the basement, the older teen--the wolf-man's first save--had made a beeline for the creature. At this point, the two of them were locked into a fierce struggle. And although the wolfman was old, he was putting up one hell of a battle against the younger pup.

The kid had pinioned the old guy's shoulders and was straining to connect his teeth with the other's jugular. The wolfman jerked and pulled his neck out of range while at the same time trying to get his own teeth within range of the young,

274

flushed neck.

At the same time, the two of them uttered a chorus of growls and snarls, an unending dirge of hatred.

"Let's go," Jared said, "no one's paying any attention to us."

"Wait!" Karen halted in place. "We've got to save him."

Looking back, Jared saw that the action hadn't changed a whole lot in the last few seconds. Except that, if anything, the elderly combatant was starting to sag a bit towards the ground.

Then, with a horrid snarl and surge of strength, the old one reared up and made a snapping lunge for his tormentor's throat.

And missed.

In the time it took Jared to take a breath, the young kid fastened his jaws on his antagonist's throat. With a roar muffled by flesh and blood, he began shaking his victim back and forth, like a dog with a dead possum.

"Oh God," Karen moaned, and Jared worried she would fall back into shock again. Grabbing her by the arm, he resumed steering her along the wall and towards the door that would get them out of this hellhole. But they only made it a few paces before he had to stop, squeezing his eyes shut. His leg, arm and back had now become a single throbbing mass, and his stomach clenched at the agony.

Jared trembled, worried that he didn't have the strength to get the two of them to safety, when he felt her hand brush his arm.

As he opened his eyes Karen stepped in front of him, took his hand and began leading them out.

Behind them cascaded a mixture of rage, fear and savagery that could not have been made by mere human beings. They'd moved about two feet when one of the children, greasy hair matted to his head and dirty arms uplifted, charged at them. Karen jerked backwards, but before she could get far, Jared lashed out with the heel of his good hand and snapped the kid under the chin as hard as he could.

Even with all the tumult around them, Jared made out the snap of the boy's neck as his body flopped to the side. He figured somewhere down the line he'd have problems with what he'd just done, but for now they needed to get out of there.

Karen kept glancing over her shoulder, no doubt hoping for some sign that the beast man had survived his encounter with his deadly pupil, but to no avail.

"Where's the police?" she yelled at him.

"Damned if I know." Jared had been wondering the same thing himself. Where were all of Jameson's people, who supposedly had this damned building staked out? Surely, they'd noticed that something bad was going down.

They'd made it about halfway out of the basement when the central metal door flew open, propelled inward by some kind of blast. Flickers of flame licked around the door jamb as a new tenor of sound erupted.

These may have been human children, but almost from birth most of them had been indoctrinated in the way of the beast, the only way that the wolfman knew. And whether through intent or accident, Jared couldn't begin to guess which, he'd instilled in them one of the most primal fears a wild thing possesses.

The fear of fire.

Almost instantaneous with the exploding inward of the door and the flash of fire in the room, the assorted growls, snarls, and barks became whimpers and whines. Nearly all of the small, individual scuffles among the children stopped as the ones still on their feet scampered towards the shadowy corners.

Allowing Jared and Karen to see that nearly half of the original pack of children now lay dead on the floor.

Nearly a dozen heavily armed and armored figures came rushing through the doorway, causing Jared to realize that the cops hadn't been lagging outside. His perception of time had accelerated, and they'd come as quickly as the commotion started.

But it became apparent within a few seconds that no matter how much weaponry and training Jameson's officers had, nothing could have prepared them for this.

The scrawny cubs, all short-statured and thin of frame, cowered in the corners, whimpering at the sight of these strange, fearsome creatures entering their domain.

All of them, except one.

Standing erect in the middle of the room, the young man who'd led the attack, his face and neck still stained with the blood of his mentor, threw back his head and howled the most fearsome noise that Jared had yet heard. Then he snapped his head to both sides, snarls coming from his throat, and fixed his gaze on the doorway that marked the only path to freedom and charged.

The cops in his line of flight hesitated, probably not wishing to fire on an unarmed youth.

That bit of hesitation proved deadly.

When still about five feet out from the nearest officer, who held his rifle half down at his side, the youth jumped into the air and dove towards the doorway. His acolytes, those still alive, followed his lead, while the ones loyal to their sire held back.

The cops' training overcame their instinctive reluctance to fire, but not before the leader and a couple of the cubs nearest to him made it through the first line of fire.

The others were not so fortunate as, wild and fearsome as they may have appeared, they couldn't prevail against nearly a score of Jameson's heavily armed and trained men.

The cops would almost certainly face questioning and recriminations in the days to follow, but to a man they did the only thing they could do.

They began firing at the children.

Along with the howls, barks, and snarls that had filled this basement for longer than Jared could remember, came the new sounds of yelps and whimpers, the sounds they'd learned from their father figure, as bullets hammered into arms, legs, and the occasional abdomen. Karen gasped, and Jared couldn't blame her as he closed his own eyes rather than watch the slaughter.

Despite the continual, deafening firing within that enclosed space, both Karen and Jared thought they heard, over all that tumult, two or three isolated snapping sounds.

Finally, those still alive ceased moving forward for a second before falling to the floor in supine gestures of submission.

And damned if a couple of them, Jared noticed, didn't roll on their backs and expose their stomachs to the invaders.

The cops spread out and began looping plastic handcuffs around the wrists of those children still alive. Other than a few whimpers, the pack stayed quiet. With nothing else to do, Jared and Karen clasped hands and took themselves out of that abattoir.

Not smoothly, Jared knew, as the two of them, panting and covered with sweat, clung together and lurched across the threshold.

But at least alive. Exiting the basement, Jared had barely taken a breath before realizing that their night of horror had not yet ended.

Lieutenant Jameson stood about ten feet down the hall, gripping what looked to Jared like some kind of nine millimeter.

As they came within sight, he glanced at them for a moment, then turned his gaze back to the floor.

The older kid, who the wolf creature had referred to as his first save, lay on the dirty concrete, blood pooling out from his back.

The other two cubs who'd managed to breach the SWAT force were just as dead.

Karen gripped Jared's hand harder and swayed back and forth.

"Steady, there," Jared said in a low voice. "Don't buckle on me yet."

Jameson looked up at them again as the two came closer.

At that moment, had he cudgeled his brain for every single memory of his journalistic career, Jared could not have thought of an instance where a person looked so completely empty and defeated as the tough SWAT cop did at this moment.

"I had to," Jameson said, for some reason looking at Karen. "I didn't want to, but I had to. They were coming at me. They were ..."

He paused, fumbling for words, and before Jared could do anything Karen placed her hand on his arm. Jared hobbled over and draped his good arm around the cop.

"It's okay, man. It's okay."

But it wasn't okay, and all three of them standing in that hallway knew so. Even if the department cleared it as a good shoot, even if by some unbelievable stretch public opinion came out on Jameson's side, the lieutenant would never forget that he had gunned down three unarmed, at least technically, children.

Standing on either side of the cop, Jared and Karen glanced at each other.

All of them, that glance said, were going to come away from this with scars on their souls.

But none more so than the man standing between them.

Chapter Fifty-two

They released her from the hospital the next day, shortly before noon. As Karen stood at the reception counter and signed the necessary papers, she inquired as to Jared's condition.

"We're not supposed to reveal information to anyone other than next of kin," the young brunette nurse said. "But considering the circumstances ..." She reached over and grabbed a sticky note from the side of her desk and scrawled something on it, then handed it to Karen.

She glanced down and saw the number 810.

"North wing," the nurse said, "second doorway to your right."

Karen nodded at her and headed off in the direction indicated.

When the elevator let her out onto the eighth floor of the north wing, she saw a man standing in the corridor conversing with two doctors. As she came closer, Karen recognized Police Chief Paul Allen.

She thought about ducking back into the elevator, or at least into a room to the side, but as she did so, the chief looked up and waved her over.

Allen began walking her way, and the two of them met about five doors down from room 810.

"Karen, hello. Please accept my condolences."

"Chief," she said, keeping her tone as neutral as possible.

"I assume you're heading in to see Mr. Woodson?"

"That's the idea."

Karen felt herself tensing a bit, almost expecting to be officially rebuffed.

"I wonder if I could speak to you a moment before you do so." As he spoke, the head cop turned to the two doctors and inclined his head in a subtle command to depart.

After the two walked off and around a bend in the corridor, Chief Allen turned his full attention back to her.

"You're not going to stop me from seeing him, are you?" Karen asked.

"Of course not. As I said, I just want a few minutes conversation."

"Okay."

"And I'd like it to be just between the two of us."

Tiny points of light danced in front of Karen's eyes.

"I don't know if I should agree to that."

The police official frowned and looked as if he wanted to harumpph. Instead, he held up a placating hand.

"Tell you what. Give me five minutes off the record. At the end of that, we can either continue our talk or stop it completely. Your call."

Karen thought for a minute.

"Counteroffer," she finally said. "You answer a question for me, then I'll give you three minutes."

Chief Allen, who in his position probably found it rare to negotiate, smiled.

"Fair enough. Ask away."

"How's Jared doing?"

The smiled flickered, then faded away.

"Physically, he seems to be okay, but as you may have noticed, in all the turmoil last night, he got quite a bit more banged up than you did."

"Okay, three minutes off the record."

The chief crooked a thumb towards a couple of chairs that sat outside a room about three doors away, and Karen followed him to take a seat.

Sitting down, Allen tugged at his jacket to straighten it, then began.

"Lieutenant Jameson has informed me of the role you two played in the – incident – last night."

"By role you mean blundering in and damned near getting ourselves killed?"

"Regardless," said the chief, "you're a smart enough person that I'm sure you realize the kind of dilemma we're in."

"Sorry, sir. I wasn't aware that we were in any sort of dilemma."

Allen's composure slipped a bit at that. A bit, but not much.

"Okay, since we're off the record for another minute or so, the dilemma I have."

"Which is?"

Allen paused a moment to smooth the creases in his pant legs.

"Please don't toy with me, Karen. Besides your father, I have a dead coroner, a series of murders and, at the latest count, nearly thirty dead children lying in an abandoned building downtown, some of them gunned down by this city's police officers. Not to mention a SWAT commander who himself shot three unarmed kids."

"When you put it that way," Karen said with not a trace of sarcasm, "I guess you are in a bind. If it helps, all those kids weren't exactly unarmed. Your guys did what they had to do. Trust me, nightsticks, Mace, or hand to hand combat wouldn't have worked."

"So I've been told," Allen replied, "but to be honest, I'm still trying to assimilate the information from the various reports I got. Truthfully, it all seems unbelievable."

"I wish it were, sir. But I was there; Mr. Woodson was there; and all your men were there. And we all saw the same thing."

The chief looked both ways down the empty corridor.

"Are you suggesting that there actually was something like a werewolf involved in this mess?"

Karen took a moment to gather her thoughts.

"There was something unique at the heart of it. I wouldn't call him a werewolf, but he definitely was – something different."

"That would be the strange-looking, hairy creature that they found in the basement?"

"Right. The sire."

The chief went silent for a moment, concentration showing on his face.

"Your three minutes are about up."

The older man rubbed his face with his hands, then sat up a little straighter.

"I need your help, Karen. In a big way."

"I'm not sure what I can do for you. After all ..."

"Some of them got away."

Karen felt her breath catch.

"Excuse me?"

"Some of those kids got away. We're trying to determine how many. But at least a handful of those vicious little bastards got loose from the basement."

"And you know this how?"

"Despite what the press will probably do to him, Jameson knows his work. He had observers stationed a couple of blocks away, kind of a fallback option. And while they weren't in the right position to intervene, they saw enough to convince us that at least four or five of those kids got out and are on the loose."

She mentally commanded herself to resume breathing.

"So what do you want from me?" she asked.

"The way I see it, I have two problems. Well, I actually have several, but two that you may be able to help me with. First, we have this circumstance of a handful of those children loose and running around this city. Including my own department, you have the most extensive experience with them. And I think you could be useful in helping to track them down."

He stopped, as if waiting for an answer.

"The other?" Karen said

"Excuse me?"

"You mentioned two problems. What's the other?"

"The other is that we have a dozen or so of those little ones who made it through last night, and quite frankly we don't know what to do with them. It's not like we can run them through the system and farm them out to foster homes."

"No one actually suggested that, did they?"

The chief produced a small grin at that.

"No, but that's my point. I've had a couple of social services people brainstorming all night, and they just don't know what to do."

"And you think I have an answer?" Karen asked.

"No. But I assume if anyone could come up with one, it would be you. I need you, Karen. Those kids need you. From what I gather of the situation, I doubt that they can ever be matriculated back into normal society, but if there's even a chance ..."

Karen turned away from him and, knotting her hands, peered down at the floor.

"I have to bury my dad," she whispered after a few seconds.

"I know, and naturally ..."

"Mr. Woodson and his sons may need some help, at least until he's got it all together again."

"I'm sure his station will do what they can for him."

"Probably."

She continued to stare down at the floor.

"Karen, I can understand if you need some time to sort through this. After what you just went through ..."

"I'll need to clear it with the shelter," she said, still without looking up. "But since my position is grant funded, I think we should be able to work it out."

"Thank you."

"Don't thank me yet, Mr. Allen. I'm not a psychological expert, and I really have no idea how to go about what you want."

"We can place other people at your disposal, if you need them. I just want someone who has a vested interest spearheading this."

Before Karen could respond, the door to room 810 opened and a nurse stepped out. Karen stood and walked over to her.

"Is he conscious?" she asked.

"Yes. And you are?"

"Just – just a friend."

The nurse looked closer at Karen and, no doubt understanding the significance of the cuts, scratches, and bruises all over her, nodded.

"He woke up a few minutes ago, but he's not very responsive."

"Can I ..."

The nurse seemed about to say no, but at a nod from Allen, badge prominent on his coat, she acceded and stepped away from the door.

Karen tiptoed inside.

"Miss Bannister?" Allen called out behind her.

She stopped, half across the threshold, and looked back at him.

"I'll call you this evening," she said. "We should probably get the details firmed up before Dad's funeral."

"Of course," he said. "I'll wait to hear from you."

"Chief," she called out as he began walking away. "If your people come across any of the ones that got away, please ask them to be as careful as they can. Those kids aren't responsible for what they've become, and the one who was responsible did the best he knew how."

He nodded and moved off down the corridor, leaving her to step inside to see Jared.

As she entered the room, Karen didn't even think it ironic that, at least for some time to come, she would be working for the police force.

In fact, at the moment it seemed the most natural thing in the world.

"Good morning," a voice croaked from the bed, "you look like hell."

Maybe I do, Karen thought, *though my few scratches don't begin to compare with how torn up you are.*

But they were alive, both of them, and at least for now the horror had ended.

And that, too, seemed as it should. Without answering, she sat next to him. They stared at each other for a minute before Karen reached out and clasped his good hand in hers.

The last time they'd held hands, only a few hours before, she'd been terrified that she would die. Now, feeling his fingers grip hers, she wondered if she had what it took to begin living again.

"So," he said, his voice a bit firmer than a moment ago, "what're you doing Saturday night?"

Karen laughed, her self-doubt starting to fade.

But she couldn't help but feel a bit contrite at the knowledge that it was her first laugh, probably her first smile, in nearly a year.

She only wished that her dad were here to see it.

About the Contributors

Kevin R. Doyle:

A high school teacher, college instructor and fiction writer living in central Missouri, Kevin R. Doyle has seen his short stories, mainly in the horror and suspense fields, published in over twenty-five small press magazines, both print and online. In 2012 he began venturing into the book publication field. First with a mainstream novelette and then, in 2014, with the release of his first full-length mystery novel.

A native of Kansas and graduate of Wichita State University, Doyle teaches English and public speaking at a high school in rural Missouri and has taught English, journalism and Spanish at a number of community colleges in both Kansas and Missouri. In the summertime, he can be found either toiling away at the computer or vacationing along the Gulf Coast.

You can find out more information at his website, www.kevindoylefiction.com, or contact him on Facebook at www.facebook.com/kevindoylefiction.

Teresa Tunaley:

Originating from the UK but residing in the Canary Islands for the last 10 years, freelance artist Teresa Tunaley devotes time to her love of art and painting. For more than 30 years she has been doodling with pencils and dabbling with watercolors. More recently she has been painting traditionally in oil and creating large canvasses full of color and life. Sometimes she uses a more modern technique using software such as Photoshop, Corel Draw and Paint Shop Pro to produce her creations for online publications.

During her art career, she has produced countless illustrations, book covers and paintings. Along with published stories and poetry, she can be credited with award winning cover art and illustrations for author stories. Her work can be seen online and in print across the UK, US, Canada and Europe.

In May 2011, she opened a new Exhibition in Puerto del Santiago (Tenerife, Spain) entitled Tutto per la vita (All for the life). She has over 30 works on show and is hoping to be selected to participate in the Capitals annual Art Festival. Should she win, there will be invitations to exhibit her work in a whirlwind trip across Spain and Italy.

Touching and spectacular "has been the inauguration; Tutto Per la vita" Some thirty of their works appeared, giving you a journey to Spain, Africa, America, Japan and Thailandia. The work was intense with feeling, in full color and textures, where figures, landscapes and moments will leave the visitor with a memory of a magical trip."

Jose Francisco Morales
Comisario de la Exposicion (Tenerife)
http://www.artesigloxxi.org

"I like to think that I am very versatile in my choice of subject matter," says Teresa. "My new surroundings provide the inspiration for me to paint on a daily basis and the fact that others may enjoy my work gives me the confidence to continue."

Website: www.artstopper.com

Printed in Great Britain
by Amazon

82749942R10171